The Battle for France

Book 7 in the Struggle f

Gri

The Battle for France

Published by Sword Books Ltd 2021

Copyright ©Griff Hosker First Edition

The author has asserted their moral right under the Copyright, Designs and Patents Act, 1988, to be identified as the author of this work.
All Rights Reserved. No part of this publication may be reproduced, copied, stored in a retrieval system, or transmitted, in any form or by any means, without the prior written consent of the copyright holder, nor be otherwise circulated in any form of binding or cover other than that in which it is published and without a similar condition being imposed on the subsequent purchaser.
A CIP catalogue record for this title is available from the British Library.

Cover by Design for Writers

Dedication

To my four grandchildren, Thomas, Samuel, Isabelle, and Michael. You bring joy to an old man!

Contents

The Battle for France i
Dedication iii
List of important characters in the novel 2
Royal Family Tree of England 3
Map of France 1417 4
Prologue 5
Chapter 1 9
Chapter 2 19
Chapter 3 30
Chapter 4 41
Chapter 5 50
Chapter 6 59
Map of Paris and its environs 68
Chapter 7 69
Chapter 8 80
Chapter 9 88
Chapter 10 97
Chapter 11 106
Chapter 12 120
Chapter 13 129
Chapter 14 142
Chapter 15 154
Chapter 16 164
The Battle of Verneuil 1424 174
Chapter 17 175
Chapter 18 180
Epilogue 192
Glossary 197
Maps 199
Historical Notes 201
Other books by Griff Hosker 204

List of important characters in the novel

(Fictional characters are italicized)

- *Sir William Strongstaff*
- King Henry V
- Katherine of Valois- Daughter of King Charles of France
- King Charles VI, the Beloved and later the Mad of France
- Humphrey, Duke of Gloucester (the King's brother)
- Thomas, Duke of Clarence (the King's brother)
- John, Duke of Bedford (the King's brother)
- Edmund Mortimer, Earl of March
- Ralph Neville, 4th Baron Neville of Raby, and 1st Earl of Westmorland
- Sir Thomas Fitzalan, Earl of Arundel
- Thomas Arundel-Archbishop of Canterbury
- Bishop Henry Beaufort
- Richard Beauchamp, 13th Earl of Warwick
- John de Mowbray, 2nd Duke of Norfolk, the Earl Marshal
- Thomas Montague, 4th Earl of Salisbury
- Nicholas Merbury- Master of the Ordnance
- Gilbert Talbot, 5th Baron Talbot
- John Cornwaille, 1st Baron Fanhope
- John Holland, 2nd Duke of Exeter (The King's uncle)
- Charles, Dauphin of France (King Charles' heir)
- Duke John, 'the Fearless', of Burgundy
- Duke Philippe, the son of Duke John
- Tanneguy du Châtel- leader of the Armagnac armies
- John Stewart, Earl of Buchan
- Archibald Douglas, 4th Earl of Douglas

The Battle for France

Royal Family Tree of England

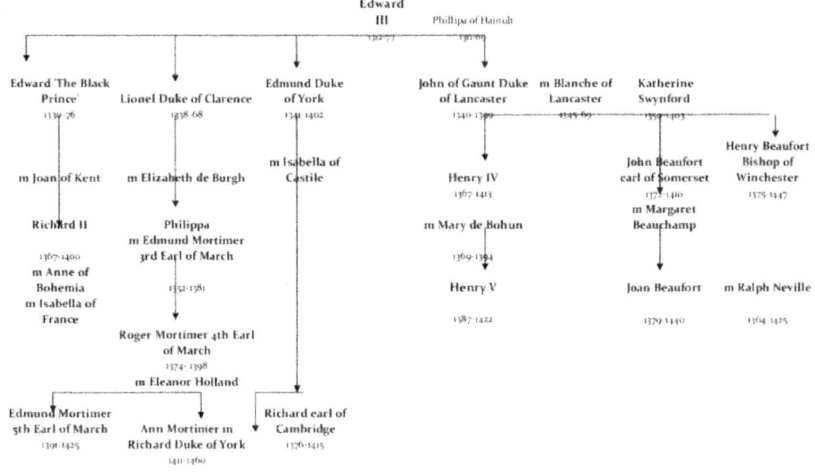

The Battle for France

Map of France 1417

Prologue

I had been almost killed when we had raided Agincourt to avenge the murder of the squires. My left knee was so badly hurt that the doctors, the 'leeches' Rafe called them, had wanted to take my leg. The slow and almost stately journey home meant that I did not reach my home until more than a month after we fled France. We simply slipped into the country. The King had been lauded in London but the men who had fought, because they came back in a trickle, received no accolade. The whole victory was ascribed to King Henry. I suppose that is as it should have been. Harfleur had been besieged but a victory at sea meant that the Earl of Dorset was now safe. We had won the battles, but France was still to be recovered. That was far from my mind as we headed home. Sir Ralph and I had both suffered life-threatening injuries and the men who returned with us forced us to go slowly. They did not wish to risk the work of Rafe and the Calais doctor to be undone. Rafe Red Beard and James Jameson were the old, wounded soldiers who had come to France almost as servants and yet were now the masters of our journey home. Unlike many of my wounded and lamed men at arms, they still wished to be warriors and as my armed servants I could not have done what I had done without them. My other rock was my new squire, Michael of Kildale. He had been the only survivor of a bandit attack on warriors returning from Agincourt and although he had only been with us a short time, I now knew he had been sent to us for a purpose. He completed my retinue. My wife had seen our taking him as the supreme act of a Christian. '*It is like the parable of the Good Samaritan and God will reward us for it*' she had said.

It was when we neared my home at Weedon and as I allowed myself the luxury of anticipating a time of peace with my family that a feeling of dread descended upon me. My men had chosen good roads but they had avoided congested ones and so we had not come through Northampton where one of my sons lived. We approached Weedon along a little-used but flat road which was not cobbled and yet was not rutted. They wished me to have as smooth a journey as possible. I saw that there were many horses in the courtyard of my walled manor, and I recognised men from the retinues of my sons and son in law. I wondered how they could have known of our return. We had not sent men ahead for I did not wish a great deal of fuss to be made.

Old Peter acted as a doorman for me. He had fought for me many years ago but old age had caught up with him. He seemed to be part of the manor and I could not imagine the hall without him. He hobbled from the door as the wagon drew close and his face was as black as night. He shook his head, "My lord, you have barely made it in time. The priests are with Lady Eleanor, come quickly while there is time!"

He could not possibly know that I was unable to climb down from the wagon. Rafe, James and Michael helped me to gingerly step from the wagon. They had cut me a blackthorn stick when we had travelled from Dover to Canterbury and I used that to support me as I headed into my hall. I would not be carried! My family were gathered in the Great Hall and Henry, my youngest son said, simply, "It is our mother, father, she is dying."

I went to the staircase and began to climb. I cursed the treacherous French knights. Each moment it took me to struggle up the stairs was time I would never have with my wife. I cursed the kings I had served who had used me for my whole life and taken me from my wife and my family. When I reached the bedchamber, I was sweating, and my leg was in agony but that was as nothing as I peered through the door of our bedchamber. I looked at my wife and saw someone I barely recognised. She was thin and emaciated; her face was grey. I saw doctors and priests.

A doctor I did not know said, simply, "Lady Eleanor contracted the flux, and we were unable to save her, lord."

I gritted my teeth. Doctors used the term *'flux'* when they had no idea what the illness was that they were treating. The leeches who had almost killed Prince Henry at Shrewsbury had been the same as the ones at Agincourt who had almost cost me my leg.

My wife opened her eyes and when they lighted upon me she smiled, "You leeches may go for my husband is here."

I could not help smiling for this was the Eleanor I would always remember. She ruled the hall with a rod of iron. One of the priests said, "The doctors mean well, Lady Eleanor, and they have done their best!"

She nodded, "And I am now shriven, you may leave me as well for I would be alone with my husband."

No one argued with my wife and they left. I sat on the bed and, holding her right hand in my two, kissed her. "I am sorry I was not here."

She smiled and tried to squeeze my hand. There was no strength left in this woman who had been my wife for more than thirty years. She

The Battle for France

had been my rock through all that time and whatever success I had enjoyed much of it was down to her holding my family together for me. I knew that few couples enjoyed such a long marriage, but it was still not long enough. "You avenged Walter and the others?" I nodded. "Good, for that was the cruellest act that I ever heard. You were doing God's work when you slew them. It is true that we have not had time enough together, Will, but I always understood that for you were appointed guardian of kings by kings. You were, you are, the protector of the kings and crown of England. They have not always deserved you but now, I think we might have a good king and I go to my grave content that I, too, paid a part in saving this country that I love." She tried to smile, "When he was Hal he was as dear to me as Thomas or Henry and a lovely youth. Between us we made a fine king."

"Do not go, my love." I felt the tears welling in my eyes. "If we pray hard enough then God may spare you."

She shook her head, "Would that I could stay but I cannot. I am just pleased that God allowed you to return so that we could have this moment. I know that you will look after the children and the people for that is your way but look after yourself also. You are now too old to fight. You have been skilled but not without luck. That luck may run out and I would hate to think of you crippled." She would die thinking me whole and I did not disillusion her. She smiled and closed her eyes. I thought her dead until she tried to squeeze my hand again. "You should be a counsellor to the king. You need fight no more. I beg you to serve him still for King Richard, for all his mistakes, was a better king than he might have been and that was down to you. You should have received more honours, but I am content that I have been privileged to be your wife for all these years. Promise me that you will help King Henry with advice." I nodded. She smiled and, in her eyes, I saw the young girl I had married. "You remember that first day, at the farm? We have come far, my love, from that plague ridden hovel and I have loved every moment of the journey with you." I kissed her again and she closed her eyes. I just held her hand and, after a short while they jerked open, "Michael, he is unhurt?"

"He is, my love, and waits with the others."

"I like him and know that he was sent for a purpose. I would have enjoyed watching him grow for we could have done as we did with Hal. That was a Christian thing you did my love and God sent him to us. We should have adopted him; perhaps you could do so now. I will not be here, and our children have their families. I would like him to have Weedon. Thomas and Henry have grander homes. I know that they look upon this as a yeoman's home, but I love it here and always have. You have Michael and he will be a comfort to you. I pray you to adopt him. He deserves a family, and you are a good man." She winced in pain. "Darkness grows and I fear I am slipping. I will wait for you in heaven but do not rush to come to me." There was a twinkle in her eye. Know that I will watch over you from heaven and that I love you."

"As I love you and will always love you."

Her fingers lost their grip and her head lolled on the side; my wife died, and I wept. I know not how long I held her in my arms for I was in darkness and despair too.

Chapter 1

The doctor in Calais and Rafe had saved my leg. It ached and I could not climb stairs easily, but I could ride and, if it was not too far, I could walk. After my wife was buried and laid in the village church with the stone effigy, carved by the King's masons, on it, I threw myself into the running of the manor. My sons tried to persuade me to rest more but that was not my way. I had made a promise to my dying wife and such an oath is binding. When I was not working, I could often be found in the small chapel we had built in my manor. I prayed to God for my wife and I hoped that she would speak to me. She did not. It was Michael who saved me. I had saved him, but he had repaid me many times over and he, I think, understood my pain better than any. When I was tetchy and irritable, he knew the right thing to say. When I needed humouring, he had the skill to do that too. I might have lost my ability to move easily but I still had my skills as a warrior, and I came from my dark place by teaching Michael to become as good a knight as me. I had more than forty years of experience to pass on. I had done some of that with my sons but not as much as I did with Michael and I saw, in him, the young Will Strongstaff. Rafe and James also helped and the four of us often spent many hours practising.

Rafe and James were as good for me as they were for Michael. They kept me rooted to what I was, a camp follower and a soldier. The two of them were like an old married couple and I have never seen two as close that were not brothers. Between the two of them they had saved Michael and he was the son they would never have. I think that when I was drawn closer to Michael I was pulled away from my sons and my daughter. I had thought that we were close but the three of them rarely visited Weedon. I knew, as my wife had known, that they thought of it as a small mean home. That hurt and saddened me but I knew that any chasm that grew between us was my fault. I had always put the crown first and they had been secondary. Of course, I had made them lords and given them land and power and that, too changed them. We drifted apart. There was no huge row or falling out it was just that we rarely saw each other, and I threw myself into training Michael and doing my wife's work running the manor.

The Battle for France

I was not the only one who had been wounded Many would not go to war again. We had taken a great number of coins and treasure. As was my practice it was equitably shared and it meant that many of my archers and men at arms chose that moment to become farmers or, in some cases, bowyers and fletchers. In times of need and if England was threatened, they would take up arms but the days of serving English kings abroad was gone. It was a young man's game. My wife was right. I could serve King Henry best, if he needed me, as a counsellor. The Black Prince had made me his son's bodyguard and weapon trainer. I could no longer do that. The last battles had shown me that my reactions were slowing and with a damaged knee then my mobility would be gone. It was why the three of us threw so much of our efforts into making Michael as good a warrior as possible. When he was ready, I would knight him. I was rich beyond my wildest dreams. We had never been profligate as a couple and my wife had carefully managed our money. I began to think how I could divide my money when I died. I began to make notes on parchment. It was neither morbid not maudlin, the death of my wife had made me realise that my time on this earth was limited.

We had a good year of peace. On the odd occasion that I visited them my children fretted and fussed that I was now alone but I was not. My wife had made the farm so efficient that my steward could run it and the only requirement of me was that I administered the law. The knights from Dauentre, Stockton and Middleham who had served me wrote to me regularly and I knew, from their letters, that Agincourt and the vengeance trail we had taken would be their last foreign foray. So, when I received a message, delivered by a pursuivant to attend a meeting at Windsor I was dismayed. Was my peaceful life about to be shattered?

It was a command from the King and so I took Rafe and James to act as my servants along with Michael. We took pack animals for I was going to court. I was a Knight of the Garter and that had certain responsibilities. I was probably as familiar with the King's great castle at Windsor as he was himself. I had spent time there with his father, King Henry and his cousin, King Richard. My surcoat was well known, and I had a reputation which ensured that I was promptly admitted.

The official who greeted me said, "Welcome, Sir William. The King asked us to provide a room large enough for you and your servants." His voice implied that he thought it a ridiculous idea. Most lords were happy for their servants to be given a stable at best.

I took against the official immediately. I knew that I was becoming a grumpy curmudgeon and I did not care. Men would take me for what I

The Battle for France

was. "That is correct." I turned to Rafe and James, "See to the horses and meet Michael back here."

The official gave me an ingratiating smile, "We have stable hands, my lord."

I snapped, "And we look after our own horses!" I saw the smirk on the faces of the two household guards. They knew my reputation.

Michael and I were led by a flushed official to the Great Hall. I saw that it was filled with other knights and the common factor was that we were all knights of the Garter. My fears had been groundless. I suddenly realised that it was June and that there was a ceremony. Someone must have died and would be replaced. I remembered that both John d'Abrichecourt and William la Zouche, who had been knights of the Garter, had died. I wondered who would be replacing them. I recognised many of the knights for they had been at Agincourt. Some had stayed either at Northampton or Weedon when they had been travelling through the country. I was not the last to arrive but nor was I the first.

King Henry came over to speak to me, "William, I was sorry to hear of your wife. Lady Eleanor was always kind to me when I lived with you. I had the Archbishop say prayers for her soul when I heard of her death."

I nodded, "She is with God, my lord."

He made the sign of the cross, "That is true. And how are you coping? I have yet to take a wife, but I should imagine that having been married to her for so many years it would be hard to live in a home without her."

I nodded almost unable to speak for the emptiness of Weedon still weighed heavily upon me. Michael and the others tried to entertain me, but I missed the comfortable silences with Eleanor when we sat before the fire. It was not words I needed, it was my wife and I had spent many nights regretting the times I had been taken from Eleanor for duties which now seemed inconsequential.

Many called King Henry a cold man, but I never found him so. He was a demanding king who did not suffer fools but when he realised that I was upset he merely put his hand on my shoulder and said, "Mayhap this gathering will take your mind from your loss. We are to appoint two new knights of the garter."

"And who are they, my lord?"

"Robert Willoughby and John Blout; both are brave fellows and that is what we shall need if we are to retake France."

He had brought up the subject and so I asked, "And when do you plan an attack?"

He grinned, "Ever the warrior! The Emperor Sigismund has been working with the Pope, or one of them at least, to have our claim and authority recognised by the church. I have emissaries at Constance where the Emperor has convened a meeting, and they are making great strides. You know I have them using English rather than French! That is a victory eh? It will take the rest of this year, but it is almost complete. I plan on crossing to Normandy next August. I will issue the indentures in February. We shall need one year of service from the men who will serve."

"That long?"

He misunderstood me. He thought that I meant the length of the indenture, but I had asked why was he waiting. He was allowing the French to regain their strength.

"I will not repeat the mistakes I made at Harfleur. I will take with me enough men to get the job done. Now that Burgundy is almost an ally, we can apply pressure from two sides." He looked intently at me. Many men found that intimidating for the scar he had earned at Shrewsbury gave his face a cruel and lopsided look. I had seen the wound when it had happened and all I saw now was the young prince who had fought so valiantly for his father. "And you, Will, can I count on you?"

I sighed for I had foreseen this, "King Henry, you know that I would give my life for you, but I am an old and half-crippled man. I can ride a horse and I can wield a sword, but I am more than sixty years old."

He looked surprised, "Really? You always seem younger to me. But age is no deterrent. The Earl Marshal, William Earl of Pembroke was in his seventies when he served King John."

I nodded, "Then I will serve but Your Majesty would be wise to use my mind rather than my arm."

"However I use you, it will ensure victory! That is some time off. For now, let us revel in the victory we shared which brought us to this happy place."

Despite myself, I enjoyed being at Windsor. I was with real soldiers. True almost all of them were noble-born and came from far above me in terms of status but they treated me as an equal. They knew my worth on the battlefield. There was genuine condolence from them too which made me feel better. For Michael, it was an eye-opener. He served the nobles, as did the other squires but here he was serving the elite of England. When we had pulled him from beneath the pile of bodies, he had been more dead than alive, and his prospects were slim. My men and I gave him a life and purpose. I suppose I was prouder of that than even the victories I had enjoyed. My world was far from Christian and yet I had done a Christian act. Now he had been elevated to serve at the table of the King!

The ceremony took a day and the King insisted that we all hunt with him. It was then that I saw my limitations. The King did not intend to make it hard for me, but he had us hunt on foot and with my lame leg that was hard. It was fortunate that Rafe and James, as well as Michael, accompanied me. When I stumbled and almost crashed to the ground, they were there to help me before I could be made to look foolish. Of course, I brought nothing down but the pain and fall apart it was a good day. We laughed and we bantered. We cheered the King when he made a good kill and the evening celebrations took me back to happier times at Weedon.

I promised the King only that I would be at Southampton in a year's time and that I would serve him in France for as long as I was needed. The others had enjoyed their sojourn at Windsor. Rafe and James always liked to visit the castles of the great and the good. They were inveterate gamblers, but they rarely took chances. They gambled on feats of strength or skill and both had fuller purses than when they arrived. For Michael, he came back with ambition.

"I know that I am your squire but is there hope that one day I might become a knight?"

I remember how Eleanor had bemoaned the fact that it took so long for me to become a knight. I would ensure that Michael did not have to wait as long. "There are tests which you must pass and skills which you need to learn but I see no reason why not."

"I am better now with a sword, lance and shield than I was, and I can use a pole weapon well, can I not Rafe?"

"Aye, Master Michael, as good as any!"

"It is not those skills which you will need. You must be able to speak French and to play the rote. You have to sing."

"How did you manage that, my lord, for I would learn?"

I felt guilty. I could not sing nor play the rote. I only spoke French because I had served in France and then the court only spoke French. "We will begin with the easier ones first; I shall teach you French!" I was now an important man. If I could not bend the rules a little then what was the point of power!

Reaching home was sad. This was the first time Eleanor had not greeted me at the door with Peter the doorman. My dogs did but that was not the same. My housekeeper and my steward had food, ale and wine ready but it was my wife!

The summer was rich with growth and produce. Many of my men became fathers and that was a good thing for their offspring would be the warriors who followed King Henry's son to war. He had not yet married but there was talk of his marrying Katherine Valois, the daughter of the King of France. To me, it seemed ridiculous for King Henry had fought and defeated her father, but this was diplomacy and politics, neither of which I understood. I was asked to be godfather to some of the boys who were born to my men at arms and archers. It was not just for the fine presents I gave them, it was a genuine affection for me. I was told this by my two touchstones, Rafe and James, both of whom always spoke the truth to me, no matter how uncomfortable it was.

I had communicated with Sir Ralph at Middleham Grange by letter and I was unsurprised when a letter arrived from him. This time it was not news but an invitation. His son, also called Ralph, was to be married and I was invited. It was to one of the daughters of Ralph Neville, the Earl of Northumberland and one who was related to the royal family through his wife, Joan Beaufort. Lady Elizabeth Neville was one of the younger daughters and it was a mark of the esteem in which Ralph was held. Red Ralph, his father, had been the man at arms who had trained me, and I knew he would be in heaven filled with pride. He had served with my own father in the Blue Company. Some of my men at arms and archers asked to come with me not to attend the wedding but to see some of Sir Ralph's men; they were shield brothers. There was a time that my sons would have wished to do so but, since Eleanor's death, they appeared to have got on with their own lives. My grandson had briefly served with me and I still got on with them but... I lived with the hurt. Had Eleanor been alive then she would have done something about it, but I just blamed myself.

Gone were the days when I stayed in inns or simply camped. I was a Knight of the Garter and I either stayed in castles or one of the many monasteries and nunneries which were happy to accommodate one of King Henry's brothers in arms. Our last stop was in the mighty northern city of York. A bastion against the Scots it had both an Archbishop and one of the most powerful Sherriffs in the land. Henry Bowet was the Archbishop, and I knew him from the time he had been a clerk to King Richard. He had not aged well and when I went to speak to him, out of courtesy, I was shocked at his deterioration.

He chuckled at my face, "Sir William, do not let this weary old body dismay you. My mind is as sharp as ever and if I have to be carried on a litter when I travel the County then so be it."

"Then I am happy, Archbishop."

The Battle for France

"I was sorry to hear of the death of your wife. I never enjoyed the company of a wife and it must have been hard to lose her after so many years."

"Aye, it was." I did not want to talk about it and so I changed the subject. "How is the border these days?"

"As you know King James is a minor and that never bodes well for that troubled country. He lives with the King quite happily but that isolation from his people allows those with ambitions to be king to plot. So long as they just plot and plan to take over Scotland it does not bother us. Another viper will come along to swallow them but some of these troublemakers choose to try to make war on England. I believe it is a way to make them look more manly and heroic. Bishop Langley keeps a close watch on them but Berwick and Norham are not peaceful places. I fear that some Scottish lord will take advantage of the King's distraction with Normandy. They did after Crécy you know? One of my predecessors helped to defeat them. I am too weak to fight but if they come then I shall use my voice to help defeat them."

I had always liked Henry and the older he became the more endearing were his qualities. I had a pleasant evening with him, and we spent most of it speaking of King Richard and his wife Anne. We both agreed that had she lived and, perhaps, borne him children, then England would be a different place. The old man was wise, "Of course, William, blasphemous though it may be, if there had been children then would our present King rule? Would we have won at Agincourt or Shrewsbury?"

I sipped the excellent wine which had been provided, "The past is the past, my lord and we cannot change it. The stone that was thrown into the pond when Queen Anne died ripples on and on. Would Hotspur have rebelled against the King? I believe that Henry Monmouth would have become a great warrior whatever happened."

The Archbishop laughed, "Of course he would, you trained him!"

I shrugged, he was right, "And imagine if he had fought with Hotspur at his side then Agincourt might have been an even greater victory, so great that...well who knows. I am a plain bluff soldier, my lord, and I was taught to fight the enemies before me and not wonder, what if."

He nodded, "But two old men like us, at the end of their lives, can speculate, can we not? It is a gift that we are able to do so. Think of all those who are not afforded the luxury of looking back on a life of service."

As we headed on the last part of the journey to Middleham Grange I thought about my conversation with wise old Henry Bowet. He was right. My wife and I had lived a longer life than most people and I knew none who had been married as long. I had been looking at it as an ending. My life did not end with Eleanor's and I thought back to her last words. She had been telling me to live and to start a new life. There would never be a woman to take her place and my family now no longer needed me, but Michael did. King Henry obviously did. If I was to die in his service, then that would be meant to be. As the Archbishop had said, it was a blasphemous thought, but I had seen too many twists and turns on the battlefield which had no other explanation.

I smiled and turned to Michael, "While we are here, Michael, we shall see if we can acquire you a courser."

He looked around. The landscape here in the north looked wilder than around Weedon, "Here?"

Rafe laughed, "Do not judge by the land in the south, Master Michael. Here they breed the best horses in the whole country. The palfrey you ride was bred here."

James added, "And they brew better ale too. It must be the water."

For my men, this was like coming to their second home. Sir Ralph looked the same as he had when last I had seen him except that he had begun to put on weight again. I dismounted and we embraced. There were no words for he had been my squire. His son had been my squire and died at Agincourt. I had fought alongside his father. In many ways, Ralph was more family than my actual one. The looks we exchanged were like the tomes of books I had seen in the Archbishop's library.

Old Edward was still the steward and I heard him speaking behind us, "Come, Rafe, you know where the stable is to be found and then we will take you fellows to your chambers!" I heard him chuckle, "Not as grand as you are used to, but you are in the north now and amongst real men!"

Rafe laughed, "Aye, old man but we can still drink like real men so that we will be the last men standing."

I stood apart and Ralph said, "I was sorry to hear about Lady Eleanor."

I nodded, "We both know of loss and it matters not if it is in the heat of battle or from an insidious disease which confuses the leeches. Enough of that, Eleanor would not have wished it, and this is a celebration. Ralph has done well for you are now related to one of the most important men in the land."

He laughed, "There speaks the man who many say is the King's right hand! But you are right. Yet the marriage is one of love and not politics. My son and the lady are in love. She is the second youngest daughter and they met when she came to view our horses. She loves animals and, like my Anne, has a good heart."

"As did your mother."

"Aye." He made the sign of the cross for his mother had died when we had gone to wreak vengeance on the child killers. "The Earl has given a generous dowry, a small manor towards Reeth way and I am not a poor knight. They will raise horses."

Anne, his wife opened the door, and I went to embrace her. She had aged since the death of Walter, but I saw that she now had joy in her eye. As we entered the hall I said, "And how is the wound?"

My wound was a visible one, I limped. Sir Ralph had been cut and stabbed in the side. He had bled heavily, and one never knew the effect of such a wound.

He smiled, sadly, "If the King asks for volunteers for France, I fear I would be of little use to him. I can raise my arm with my sword, but I have no confidence in the blow I might strike."

I nodded for I knew what that meant. When a warrior hit with a weapon, he had to believe that the strike would be true and if not then that lack of confidence would result in his death. "Then you war no more. That is good for you have done more than your share of fighting for this land and its kings. Enjoy your manor!"

It was an ending and a beginning. The Earl had not only given his daughter's hand in marriage he had also conferred a knighthood on Ralph's son. There would still be one of Red Ralph's line to go to war. I saw Michael looking enviously at young Ralph's new spurs. His day would come and soon. The wedding was held at Middleham Castle. My men, of course, were not invited but this was the north and Anne and Ralph would celebrate the marriage later at the Grange. My wife had trained me well and both Michael and I were dressed well for the marriage. The Bishop of Ripon performed the ceremony in the Great Hall. I saw that Ralph was right, Lady Elizabeth Neville looked lovingly at the newly knighted Ralph every moment of the ceremony. This was that rarity amongst the high and the mighty. It was a marriage which was not arranged for political reasons. It made me think of King Henry. He was pursuing a princess of France and the reason was most assuredly political. Ralph's son would be happy. Would King Henry if he ever managed to arrange the marriage?

There was a feast after the ceremony but mindful of the ride back to the Grange I drank sparingly. The bride's father, the Earl of Westmoreland and Ralph Neville sat next to me while the guests were entertained by troubadours and mummers. I was older than the Earl, but we had fought together on many occasions. I deferred to his rank, but he deferred to my experience.

"Well, Strongstaff, do you go to Normandy with King Henry next year?"

I nodded, "And you?"

He shook his head and spoke quietly, "Things have not been right between us since the Southampton plot. My daughter was married to Sir Thomas Grey of Heaton. There was no suggestion of my involvement but…" His voice trailed off. He had not been at Agincourt. He took a deep drink from the goblet. He might be an Earl, but he had not been chosen to be a Knight of the Garter. "I shall, of course not only send good men but keep a watch on the north. I may no longer be Warden of the North, but this is my land. Sir Ralph and his sons are good men and there are many others just like them."

"I spoke with Archbishop Howett in York. He said that the Scots are not to be trusted."

"And he is right. When the King was in France last they tried to invade England. I sent them packing at Yeavering."

"Yet here you are far from the border."

He smiled, "The Romans left us good roads and Prince Bishop Langley and I have close links. If the Scots even begin to dream of invading, then I take men north and that is normally enough to discourage them. It has been many years since they inflicted a defeat on us. You would think they would have learned, eh?"

I nodded. The Archbishop of York had told me that the young King of Scotland, James, was held by King Henry for his own protection. Scotland was ruled by a Council of Regents. "Who is the power, north of the border, my lord?"

"The Earl of Douglas, Archibald."

"He lost an eye at Homildon Hill did he not?" I remembered him from Shrewsbury where I had defeated him. He had been held by King Henry for a long time before he was ransomed.

"He did and was hostage after. He bears a grudge against England and if there is any trouble then he will be the cause of it. Still, he has been quiet for a while and his daughter has just married the young Earl of Buchan. Perhaps that will dampen his ambition."

I looked at the Earl, "But you think not!"

"I think not!" They were ominous words.

Chapter 2

I had no reason to return to Weedon and I enjoyed the company and so we stayed for a month. We enjoyed good hunting and I was able to spend longer with Sir Ralph. Men who have been close to death and survived have a different view on the world. It was a wild landscape and I enjoyed riding it. We visited Richmond Castle, now a crown castle and one of the most spectacular castles I had ever seen in England. The sheer cliff which led to the river below meant that an attacker had only one approach to take the castle and that was across two ditches and past a mighty barbican. The siege at Honfleur had taught me to examine all castles with a view to taking them and the rock upon which Richmond was built would put off any attacker.

Bearing in mind my conversation with the Archbishop perhaps this was meant to be. A few days before I had decided we had imposed enough upon Sir Ralph and his good lady wife, word was brought that the Scots had been seen gathering north of the Tweed and manors had been raided. The Earl of Westmoreland raised the north. We were told almost immediately, and Ralph summoned the men he would need. A messenger reached us to tell us that the Archbishop was travelling north first to Durham and, it was said, north to face the Scots. The Archbishop was true to his word and the church was with us.

Sir Ralph and his son joined the Earl and the men of the valley to head north and, I, of course, added my men to the army. Had I chosen to return home or wait at Middleham Grange then none would have blamed me. Honour and the memory of the dead of the north made me go. The other reason was Douglas. I had defeated him and captured him at Shrewsbury, and I knew even now, I had the beating of him. My presence might make them slink back north. The archers and men at arms I had with me were keen to go for they hated the Scots. We were not indentured, that is to say we would not be paid but they were still keen to go. They had little treasure, but my men would forego that to defeat the enemy who took every opportunity to side with France and to cause England trouble. Michael too was eager to go. I had brought my standard north for the wedding and he would get to carry it in battle.

The Battle for France

The one hundred and twenty miles to the River Tweed took us four days. The slow pace was partly determined by the fact that we had men on foot as well as the Archbishop in his wagon. Messengers were sent constantly to keep us informed of the progress of the Scots. They appeared not to be invading but raiding and I deduced that they wanted us to come north so that they could defeat us in battle. The Earl was the military leader but he constantly involved me in the discussions. We learned that farms along the border had been raided. Animals had been taken and men were slain. Thus far the Scots had not taken captives and slaves. That showed that they knew the consequences. We would cross the border and hunt down any who did that.

"It will be Douglas who is behind this attack. Why do you think they have not yet crossed in numbers, Strongstaff? You have a sounder military mind than any. Why do they wait?"

I waved a hand behind me at the long line of men. There were less than seven hundred but over one hundred were knights, many of them had joined us at Durham. Another two hundred were men at arms and the rest were either trained archers or men who used the bow every Sunday at the butts. "He does not know who comes for him. He lost at Homildon Hill and Shrewsbury. He would not face King Henry and he might baulk at you leading the army but if it was a minor lord or one without experience then he might risk a foray into England. The Scots cannot afford another defeat, but they seek a battle. They hearken back to their two victories which sent ripples through the land, Stirling Bridge and Bannockburn. Each noble is desperate to be the new Wallace or a Robert the Bruce and be the hero of his people!"

"Then if you are right our mere presence might dissipate this rebellious fog for the Scots are now a vassal people. An invasion of England would be tantamount to treason."

Sir Stephen and his men joined us at Morpeth. Sir Stephen might not go to war in Normandy or France, but this was his home and with a wife and a baby on the way, he would fight harder than any. Along with Sir Will of Stockton and Sir Oliver the Bastard, three more of the knights I had trained were with us and that gave me even more confidence.

By the time we spied Norham, the bastion of the north, our numbers had been swollen by another three hundred men, mostly archers. Norham was a strong castle but not a huge fortress and most of the knights and the army were forced to camp to the south of the castle. I was accommodated along with Bishop Langley of Durham, Archbishop Howett, and the Earl. We were apprised of the situation.

The Battle for France

"The Scots are at Berwick, my lords. They have an army of two thousand or more men although less than eighty are knights. They are led by the Earl of Douglas and his young son in law James Stewart, the Earl of Buchan. The young earl is keen for glory and Douglas has revenge upon his mind. If they can I believe they will attack us." The castellan was an old knight. Service on the border made all men so but Bishop Langley only appointed his most reliable knights to the perilous position, and I trusted his judgement. He added, "Their army outnumbers this one by more than two and a half times." Beneath his words I heard a warning. We could not afford a defeat.

The Earl asked, "And have they shown any indication that they intend to attack in force?"

"They sent men to try to cut the road south and all the farms which are close by have been evacuated. I sent them to Bamburgh, Rothbury and the other strongholds."

Although the Earl was the leader, he looked to me. I had fought at Agincourt and I was the one whose advice he sought. "Sir William, you have more experience of war than any man in this castle what say you?"

"I do not think that Douglas will expect the army that we have brought. It is not the numbers which will make him think twice it is the quality of what we have brought. Two prelates and this host of knights should be enough to daunt him. If we march on the morrow to Berwick and array for battle, he will either fight us or withdraw. If he fights us and attacks, then we win."

"You are that confident about an army which is largely made up of yeoman and is smaller than the one the Scots have?"

I laughed, "Ask the French what they think of the yeoman of England! Our archers will widow them! Trust in the bow and the men who draw them. Our men, even the farmers, practise every Sunday. The bow will have the beating of the Scots."

And so it was agreed, we would beard the wolf in his den.

We rose at the third hour of the day and the army gathered outside Norham. With a Bishop and an Archbishop along with their holy banners and relics then the mass which was held was even more special than normal. The Archbishop then stood on the wagon which was his carriage, and he addressed the army, "Men of England, the north, today we face an enemy who has ever plagued us. Know that God is on our side as he always has been. We have the right. This land we defend is God's land, the land of the Palatinate and King Henry. The Scots have no right to the land south of the Tweed. Fight hard this day and we will prevail. God is with us!"

The Battle for France

The cheer they gave must have been heard in Berwick and when the army moved off the handful of miles to Berwick I had never marched with an army in such good spirits. At Agincourt, we were weary and starving. We had been surrounded and thought we fought our last battle on the October day in France. The Archbishop might have been an old man, but his inspiring words were worth a hundred knights and the relatively tiny army which marched to Berwick feared no man and certainly no Scot.

By the time we reached Berwick, it was daylight and their scouts, not to mention our noise, had alerted the Scots who were deployed in serried ranks across the river. We waited until the one-eyed Earl who led the Scots, with bared head and open hands came to the bank of the river to speak with us. I saw the young Earl of Buchan by his side along with half a dozen other nobles. I recognised some of the liveries from Shrewsbury. The four of us went to speak to him. The Earl's squire carried his banner, Michael mine and two priests the banners of York and Durham. Even if they did not recognise us that told them who we were.

The Earl of Westmoreland spoke, "Douglas, you have defiled the land of England and we demand satisfaction. Either pay reparations or this day will see your army slaughtered for we would give battle for the honour of England."

He laughed, "We outnumber you, Neville. It is your men who will bleed."

I heard the Archbishop sigh. He was weary from the long journey north and so I intervened, "Douglas, have you not left enough of your body and blood in England already? If King Henry had not stayed my hand, I would have slain you in Shrewsbury when you begged for your life."

Although a river separated us, I saw that I had angered the nobles who were with him.

I laughed as they raised their fists, "Douglas, tell these boys who are with you that I am Will Strongstaff, champion of three kings and no Scotsman has ever had the better of me. I had a good breakfast and if any of your cockerels wish to try my arm then I am ready."

That angered his nobles even more, but Earl Douglas raised his hand, "Peace! So Strongstaff you are still alive. Are you a cat that has nine lives?"

I smiled and waved my hand, "Unlike you, Earl Douglas, I have all my body parts and we have your King too but he is not our enemy and he hunts with King Henry and views him as a friend. This is not the behaviour of a regent. Your charge is far from here or is this a way for you to have him eliminated so that you may claim the crown?"

That struck a nerve as the nobles all looked at their leader. His reaction confirmed that he had ambitions to take the crown. "King Henry has honour, and he has promised that King James will not be harmed."

"And I did not say he would be, but does this gain his release?"

That was the moment when the fight went from the nobles. The men might still have been happy to fight but the nobles now looked at their leader with fresh eyes.

The Earl of Douglas nodded, "You are right, we must do all we can to win the release of our King. Prince Bishop Langley, I beg you to send an envoy to my castle and reparations will be made. Does that satisfy you, Earl Ralph?"

I was now ignored but I saw enmity in the eyes of all the nobles as they glowered at me. They would not forget this moment nor the insults I had given.

"It does. Now withdraw!"

The Scots were humiliated. I heard the shouts and cries from ordinary warriors who begged the chance to fight us. One or two turned and dropped their breeks as an insult. In many ways, I wish they had but their leaders took them north, away from Berwick. The Earl turned to me and shook his head, "Did you mean it Strongstaff? I mean you are no longer a young man. Would you have fought them?"

I looked him in the eyes, "I do not make idle threats, my lord. A man that does has lost already for it takes but one to call his bluff and he would die." I smiled, "I may no longer be a young man, Earl, but each day I practise and I have tricks I can use."

He shuddered, "I am pleased that you are not my enemy!"

Instead of returning to Middleham my men and I went to Morpeth with Sir Stephen. He wished us to meet his family and to hunt with him. I bade farewell to Sir Ralph and his son and went with our men to Morpeth. It took just one day for we were all well mounted and knew the road. Stephen had improved his home and now it had a ditch, a good wall, solid gatehouse, and a tower. His wife was younger than he was and, I think a little daunted at what she perceived as elevated company. I tried to put her at ease, but I knew my reputation and grey hairs made me seem unlike any knight she had seen before.

We spent a pleasant two weeks with Stephen. I felt guilty, briefly, for this seemed like a lazy man's life. I had mocked those knights who spent their hours hunting and enjoying themselves. Yet here I was doing exactly the same but, I confess, I did enjoy the life. We only left

The Battle for France

Morpeth because I felt we were imposing on the family and Stephen's wife could never relax whilst I was there. We had two hundred and seventy miles to travel. Durham and Middleham would be good breaks as would York, Lincoln and Sheffield. I would be welcomed at all of them and I would be able to pick up the new horses from Ralph. The journey from Morpeth to the bridge at the New Castle would be the most arduous as it passed over the North Tyne and the road was neither straight nor particularly safe. There were ten of us in the column of twos. We had two sumpters with supplies and clothes. My archers were Matthew the Millerson, Christopher White Arrow, Harry Fletcher, and Walter of Sheffield. The two men at arms were Uriah Longface and Gilbert of Ely. Even though we were travelling through ostensibly friendly land the fact there were so few of us and our experience meant that we had two archers ahead of us and two bringing up the rear. Rafe and James led the sumpters.

Michael had grown in the time he had been with us, but he was still the youngest by a considerable margin. He was old enough to be knighted but still not yet twenty. He was excited about the hunt we had just enjoyed and was looking forward to taking his new warhorse back to Weedon. I allowed his idle chatter fly over my head and the others were watching the sides of the road. We were too far from Morpeth for help from my friends when the ambush was sprung. We were crossing the Maglin Burn which passed through a wood. Perhaps Matthew and Christopher were complacent, I know not but the first we knew was when Matthew gave a cry and almost fell from his saddle.

Christopher shouted, "Ambush!" as his leg was pierced by a crossbow bolt. None of my archers could use a bow from the back of a horse and they did the only thing that they could. They drew their swords and attacked the ambushers. It took time to reload a crossbow. Harry and Walter were at the rear and they had the time to nock an arrow and ride to our aid. Rafe and James let go of the reins of the sumpters and joined the rest of us as we drew swords and charged the enemy. We had not ridden with helmets, but we were mailed, and we had coifs about our heads. We did not ride down the road for that invited disaster. Instead, we peeled off left and right. Whoever had ambushed us were men on foot and our horses were a weapon we would use.

The swordsman who suddenly saw me jump the ditch had a small buckler and the curved sword favoured by Scottish highlanders. My leap not only disconcerted him, but my horse's hooves also clattered into his knee and he fell backwards. Even had I wanted to, there was no way that I could steer my mount away from him and the rear hooves smashed his skull to a pulp. My leap had broken the line of ambushers and when my horse landed, I wheeled to the right and was able to bring my sword down across the neck of the spearman who wore a familiar livery. He had a mail coif but my sword was sharp and I knew how to hit hard. The way he fell, suggested that I had broken his neck. I did not stop to examine it for I had no idea how many ambushers there were. A crossbowman was trying to reload quickly and, in his haste, dropped the bolt. I showed him no mercy and my sword split his head in two for he just wore a leather cap. I heard cries and shouts and then the familiar sound of war arrows flying through the air. Only two of my archers were able to use their bows but that was more than enough, and they sent arrow after arrow into the Scots who had waited in ambush. If an ambush is to be successful, then in the first moments an ambusher needs to hurt those they attack. Only two of my men had been hurt. I saw Michael, close to my right, charge towards a mailed man at arms. Michael had been taught by the best and as the axeman raised his two-handed axe to hack into Michael's mount my clever squire jinked effortlessly to the other side and brought his sword over his horse's head to almost take off the axeman's head.

 The sound of hooves galloping off told me that the encounter was over, the survivors had fled, and I shouted, "Weedon, to me!"

 All my men appeared but I saw that my two scouts were hurt and as they fell from their horses Rafe and James raced to attend to their wounds. I dismounted and said, "Michael, fetch the sumpters and any horses you may discover." He rode off. "The rest of you, bring to me any who still lives." I had my suspicions, but confirmation would be useful.

 By the time Michael returned and the dead had been examined, it was clear that none had survived. That was to be expected for a man fighting for his life could not pick and choose his blows. "How are Christopher and Matthew?"

 Rafe smiled, "Hurt but the embarrassment of being ambushed outweighs any thought to their wounds."

 Gilbert said, "We killed eight, my lord, and there were another seven, at least, who escaped. We captured three horses."

 I nodded and touched the body of the warrior with the livery, "I know who sent these men. It was James Stewart, Earl of Buchan. The three legs of Man and the fleur de lys are his livery. We must have upset them at Berwick."

 Uriah said, "Do we head north for vengeance, lord?"

I shook my head, "No, for we are too few and he will be safe in the highlands by now. Our paths will cross again, have no fear and I have a long memory. Share their treasure amongst yourselves."

When we reached the New Castle I told the Sherriff there of the attack and he promised to send men to fetch the bodies. Their heads would adorn the gates of the city. They would be recognised, and the Scots would know, even if the survivors did not return to report their failure, that William Strongstaff was still alive. We stayed at Durham and with Will of Stockton too. The wounds Matthew and Christopher had suffered slowed us down and that added to their embarrassment. The others were merciless in their comments. Christopher and Matthew would never be complacent again! When we reached Middleham Sir Ralph and his family were concerned about my safety.

His son said, "My lord, they may try again."

I shook my head, "Morpeth is close to the border, young Ralph. They must have followed us and when they saw us stay with Sir Stephen planned their ambush. They could not have picked a better site." Smiling I said, "I suppose I should take it as a compliment that this young Earl sees me as a greater threat to Scotland than your father-in-law, young Ralph."

Despite my protestations, Ralph and his sons insisted upon escorting us to York. Archbishop Howett was of the same opinion as I when we reached York and I told him of the attack. He had his healers ensure that Rafe had done a good job on the wounds and then the two of us dined again. He chuckled, "You know, William, it is a sort of joke is it not that two old men defeated the Scots with words and not with iron? I roused the English soldiers and you roused and then defeated the Scots with words. King Richard chose his men well. I wonder what England would have been like had he and the Queen had children."

"That, my old friend, is my fear for King Henry. At least King Richard had a wife and was trying to father children. King Henry does not even have one bastard to his name, and he appears to have put all of his hope into marrying Katherine Valois!"

"I can see the sense in that. It gives King Henry an even greater claim to the throne of France and remember that Katherine's sister, Isabelle, was the child bride of King Richard."

I nodded, "And little good it did him."

The Archbishop was a clever man, "But William the plan was sound. Had the King not been usurped by Bolingbroke and Isabelle and he had children then France might be ours already." He smiled, "And I have heard that Katherine is a beauty. She is the youngest of King Charles' children and many say the best."

The Battle for France

The Archbishop sent a dozen men with us as far as the Roman Road. It was not necessary, but the presence of the armed men made our progress through the crowded streets of York and the roads leading to it easier. Our journey down that great thoroughfare showed the effect of the King's indentures. Warriors and horses were already on the move as they headed to the camps close to the ports where we would take ship for Normandy. It was still many months before the fleet would take his army across to Normandy, but a one-year contract necessitated a great deal of work. Lords who had huge estates and manors not to mention castles would have the logistical problem of garrisoning all their castles and yet ensuring that they took good men with them. Then there were the swords for hire who would see the opportunity to make money from an attack which would involve chevauchée. They would be leaving lesser paid posts to offer their services to King Henry. Fletchers and bowyers would have to manufacture many thousands of bows and arrows. Horses would be needed to carry tents and supplies. The bombards we would take would have to be made and the foul-smelling powder secured.

Rafe and James had already offered their services to me. They would not be fighting but they would be the best of armed servants. As we had headed to Weedon they had explained their reasons. James spoke for the two of them, "Rafe and I began our service to you with Kit Warhammer. He was but a youth then. When we were both hurt, we thought we would be discarded as so many old soldiers are but you not only gave us a home, you gave us the chance to be part of your retinue. We do not fight in the mainlines but we are armed and, as Agincourt showed, sometimes even the servants have to fight."

Michael asked, "Do you not wish families?"

Rafe laughed, "We are too set in our ways. James and I have sired, I do not doubt, bastards aplenty but no woman would live with either of us!" I smiled for they were, in many ways, like an old married couple. They enjoyed each other's company and the house they shared reflected their martial and practical life. Everything was functional and the only things they regarded as beautiful were their weapons.

Michael would be the only warrior I would take who might have to fight and I hoped that it would not come to that. He was still a squire and whilst, as the ambush had shown, skilled, there was still work to do. In addition to the warhorse we had bought for him I had a new courser. Ralph had bred him especially for me. With age came weight and Hercules was a powerful horse who would be able to bear me, plated, into battle. I would not have to worry about the armour I wore. I had a good weaponsmith and he had made the armour which had protected me at Agincourt. The poleyn which covered the knee had needed to be replaced and this time there would be extra protection for the back of my injured knee. Michael would also need better armour but that was because he was growing. Both of us would have a gorget around the neck. Our helmets might be open faced but our vulnerable necks would be safe.

Once back at Weedon the months flew by. My son Henry came to speak to me for he said he had felt guilty that I had been neglected. I had seen him so infrequently that, at first, it was awkward. It was strange to be talking to my son without Eleanor being there and it was only as we eased into a more comfortable conversation that I realised the importance of her presence.

"Father, I am sorry that you have seen little of us, but I have been busy." The sentence faded lamely, and I saw his eyes lower to the ground. I know not what had prompted the visit but unlike me he had not thought out what he would say.

I, on the other hand, knew how to use words and I made it easier for him by giving him an answer which eased his guilt. Eleanor would have wished me to. She did not like discord. "Son, you have your family and your own life. I have tried to be a better father to you than mine was to me and I know that your mother did all that she could to bring you up well. You have to live your own life. You have chosen your path and it is a good one for I can see that you are happy and prosperous."

His face flushed, "And you did but I did not come with you on the last campaign to France and you were hurt… you almost died!"

I smiled, "I nearly lost my leg was all."

"When I was growing up all that I wanted was to be like you." He paused, "The friend of kings and a warrior who seemed invincible was a dream. Then I came to war and saw the reality. When I married…"

"I know and that makes you, a better man. I had others who fought with me and they chose to be there. They enjoy war and combat. You do not and that is a choice your mother liked. She knew that her sons were safe."

"But I was not there to protect you!"

"Nor was your brother but I was glad that you were not there. The first knight I trained, Sir Henry, was there, and he died. Sir Ralph who was a squire to me, almost lost his life. I need no protection for I was the champion of three kings. My life has been one of service to the royal house of England. Yours and your brother's, thankfully, are not!"

He sat back in his chair, "Then you do not resent the fact that we do not follow you to Normandy?"

There was honesty in the air and so I spoke truly, "All that I resent is that my sons, daughter and my grandchildren are strangers to my home. Since your mother died none have visited. Was I such a bad father that I am shunned?"

He shook his head, "No, father! You were the best of fathers and ..." his voice trailed off as he realised he had no good reason he could offer as an excuse. "We will remedy that now!"

Shaking my head, I said, "I fear that it is too late for that."

"No! I will bring my family next week and I shall speak to Alice and Thomas we..."

"I leave for Southampton in three days and I have much to do before I leave. When I return then we shall turn a new page, eh?"

"But that will be a year hence!"

I nodded, "I know."

Silence seemed to fill every nook and cranny in my hall. My wife was no longer there, except in spirit, and silence took her place. She would have said something. When Henry looked up and spoke, I saw fear in his eyes, "And what if you do not return?"

I sighed, "Then, my son, there will be no turning of the page, merely the closing of the book!"

When we parted the embrace we shared lasted a long time and I felt guilty that I had put such gloomy thoughts in Henry's head. I did not think I would die in Normandy, but I was no fool. I would be the oldest knight in King Henry's company and as my last wound had proved, I was mortal!

Chapter 3

My men and I were accommodated at Southampton Castle and our horses stabled there. King Henry had already arrived for that was his way. He had a newly built carrack, *'Jesus'*, and that meant he not only had an army to organise he had his new ship to fit out. I saw little of him for those first few days, but that allowed me to study maps of Normandy. I found them in the library where an old clerk organised them. Peter was full of information and just pleased that someone wished to look at the work of a lifetime. Some of the maps were ancient and had been used by the third King Edward when he had destroyed Caen the first time. I looked at rivers and the castles which defended the crossings. I had no idea what King Henry had in mind except that he wished to retake Normandy from the French. I could understand that for his ancestors had come from Normandy to take the English crown! I was loath to take the valuable maps from the library and, as we had time, Peter and I copied them.

When we had finished, he said, "My lord, I realise that this is an imposition, but would it be possible for you to add details to these copies? I know that they are incomplete, and I strive for perfection."

I liked Peter. He was older than I was, and his ink-stained fingers would never be clean for they had a lifetime's ink and work ingrained upon them. My body had a lifetime's wounds. We had much in common. We both served others and did the best that we could although in Peter's case it would pass unnoticed. There were many such servants of the crown who devoted their lives to others. Peter would die alone and without family, His legacy would be the maps he made but no one would remember him. "Of course! And if I can find any maps when we take castles…"

He beamed like a child being given his first wooden sword, "My lord such a gift would put me forever in your debt!"

"No, Peter, we are in your debt for your maps will save lives!"

I was invited to the council of war convened by the King when his senior leaders arrived. I knew them all for they had been with us in Wales when we had fought Glendower and at Agincourt. These were King Henry's band of brothers. The Dukes of Clarence and Gloucester

The Battle for France

were two of his younger brothers. The third, John Duke of Bedford would rule England while we were away. The King trusted his brothers! Then there were the Dukes of Exeter and Norfolk and the Earls of Warwick, Westmoreland, and Salisbury. I was a mere baron, but none looked down on me. I had earned my place at this council many times over.

"My friends, we are about to embark on a great adventure. We will be emulating my great grandsire, King Edward, and his son the Black Prince. We began two years ago to claw back our land and now we shall finish the task. We have the right and God on our side and as we showed at Agincourt, we have the skill." That brought a round of table banging from some of those assembled. I just smiled and the King nodded and smiled back. "This time we shall not be alone. I have had communication with the Duke of Burgundy, and he will support us but only when we have a large part of France under our control. It is an incentive to fight hard!" He smiled and the scar on his face gave it an almost comical aspect, "I think that Normandy is a large enough piece of France, eh?" That brought laughter from all. "We will land at the River Touques. The Earl of Dorset holds Harfleur on the north bank of the Seine and since our great sea victory, it is secure. I would make the southern bank ours too and to that end, we will take Caen rather than Rouen first for the French will anticipate an attack at the great city of Rouen. They think they know how we fight but we shall prove them wrong." The smiles on the face of most of his lords turned serious for this meant a siege and if Honfleur had taught him anything it had shown King Henry that taking a French town was never easy. Once we have taken it, we will drive south to Alençon and take the towns and castles along the way. We will not be returning home for winter. I intend to stay until the following summer, at least."

He sat back to allow those words to settle in. His brother, the Duke of Gloucester said, "But how, my lord, shall we take the great city of Caen? I have heard that they have rebuilt the defences since our grandsire destroyed them. It will cost us men, before we even begin to head south."

The King said nothing, and I knew that this was a test. No one spoke until I coughed and said, "I have spent some time studying the maps and you are right, Your Grace, they have rebuilt the defences, but they left in place the buildings that were there before. They have a new town on one side of the river and a bridge joining the two. Whilst the defences are not to be dismissed lightly both the walls and the castle are overlooked by the two abbeys built by King William and his wife. His and hers could be used to mount artillery. The trick would be, King Henry, to take them both before the French knew what we were about."

King Henry smiled, "And that is why you were chosen by the Black Prince to protect his son, Strongstaff. You have a mind like a steel trap when it comes to matters military. You have read my mind for I wish us to be as swift as lightning. The last attack was leaden, and I allowed us to be held up. This time I will use our horsemen and mounted archers to surprise and shock the French defenders."

I was then asked for the maps and I had Peter bring them. It made me smile that although every knight had been in Southampton Castle before none of them knew of Peter's existence. He corroborated all that I said and took great delight in identifying the features on his map.

When he had satisfied them and left the King said, "We have, I hope, no plotters this time." I saw Ralph Neville flush, but the King ploughed on. He cared not for the niceties of men's feelings. "However, I want all of you in this room to ensure that no word of our plan reaches the French. They will know that we are sailing but I hope that they will think we go to the Seine. I want them to put their armies close to Rouen so that we have a free hand in the rest of Normandy."

We spent a week going through his plans and the King showed how far he had come by organising three battles which were balanced and equal. He planned on attacking both sides of the city and dividing our forces equitably. I felt proud of the King I had helped to train. I had done the same with his father and King Richard but neither had proved to be the leader and the planner that was Henry Monmouth. I became hopeful about the outcome of this war. My wife had been right. I still had a purpose and with my family no longer dependent upon me, I could become, truly, the King's Counsellor.

We sailed on the carrack *'Jesus'*. It had been specially built for the King and was the largest ship in our fleet. When King Edward had fought the Castilian pirates, we had been forced to use the ships of the Cinque Ports. King Henry had decided to build ships and we had the beginnings of a navy. Rafe and James stayed with Hercules and Michael's new courser all the way to Normandy. They knew better than any that warhorses, whilst brave as any in battle, could be skittish and nervous at sea. The two of them would keep the animals calm. I stood at the bow castle with Michael and the Earl of Westmoreland.

The Earl spread his arm at the fleet which followed us, "This is a measure, Strongstaff, of the power of our King. We rule the land and soon we shall rule the seas."

I shook my head, "My lord, this is the third King I have served, and our problem is not with the man who rules the land but Parliament which seeks to hamstring him by denying him funds. Think of the money which the King has made for those peers. Yet they are penny-pinching and miserly and question the need to fund our army in Normandy."

He laughed, "You do not think much of them then?"

I shook my head forcefully, "They turned on poor King Richard and the throne was stolen from him. If I had my way I would do away with them altogether."

He looked surprised, "King Richard was a tyrant!"

I shook my head, "With respect, my lord, he was not. He made mistakes but all men do, and the mistakes were forgivable. What they did to him was not."

"And yet you served his murderer Henry Bolingbroke."

My voice became like hardened steel, "That is a lie and I will draw sword with any man, no matter how high in rank, who says so."

I heard Michael and the Earl's squire take a deep breath. The Earl however just said, "I withdraw my words then, Strongstaff, but it was what I heard."

"Then you heard a lie from his enemies. I was there, and King Richard starved himself to death and that cannot be laid at the door of Bolingbroke. It was those who feigned support for King Richard and then stabbed him in the back who are to blame. There are some men I never forgave. Thankfully, God took most of them and that shows his judgement. I helped kill many of those at Shrewsbury. I wanted vengeance rather than ransom!"

"I did not know, Strongstaff." He rubbed his beard and stared ahead. "You are a most interesting man, and I am glad that I am not your enemy. Sir Ralph tells many tales about you and I can see that none are exaggerated."

The lookout shouted, "Land ho! The mouth of the river is in sight!"

I knew that there was a small castle at the river mouth but as King Henry had predicted the French were not expecting us to land this side of the Seine and besides the castle had no guns. As we disembarked the gates to the castle were opened and the garrison surrendered. As on our last foray those who welcomed the King were treated well for, after all, he was returning as the rightful ruler. These were his people we were liberating from French misrule. The town was soon filled with soldiers wearing the red cross of St. George. King Henry had learned from his first foray into France. We rested the horses although scouts were sent on captured horses to establish the defences of the town of Caen. It was less than thirty miles from us. As on our last campaign, King Henry issued orders that no priest, woman nor child was to be harmed in any

The Battle for France

way and the only Normans we were allowed to hurt were those who opposed us. He had hanged men two years previously for pillaging and disobeying him and this time his orders were obeyed.

We spent five days resting our horses, gathering forage and wagons for the guns, and preparing for a siege. Thomas, the Duke of Clarence, was just thirty years old but he had learned much in the Agincourt campaign. Even so, the King was aware of his lack of experience at this level and the King summoned me and his brother to a meeting.

"We need these two abbeys in our hands. Thomas, I am sending Strongstaff here to advise you. Heed his words for I have ever done so, and the result is that we are on the brink of victory."

"Yes, brother, I will do as you ask!" His voice did not sound as though he was happy about the command. He was young and thought he knew it all.

"God speed and I will follow with the rest of the army and the guns."

As we left, I said, "My lord, my presence is merely to give you my fifty years' experience of war. No insult is intended by either your brother or myself."

"Then I command!" His voice sounded almost petulant.

I sighed with resignation, "Of course! All your brother asks is that you take the two abbeys. If the French have fortified or mined them, then we may have Honfleur all over again and we would not wish that, would we, my lord?"

His face showed that he knew what failure would bring. He might be sent back to England. King Henry was a fair man, but he could be a ruthless king. "Aye, Strongstaff, and with your advice we shall succeed."

We had no baggage train but the lances the Duke led had squires, men at arms, archers and servants with them. All were mounted for the Duke led elite knights. Rafe and James rode with the servants while Michael and I were with the Duke in the van. The Duke had heeded my suggestion that we arrive after dark and catch the French unawares. The ring of sentries the King had placed around our forces had ensured that the odd French scout was captured. The French might know where we had landed, but they were blind as to our intentions. This time there had been no Grey or Scrope to betray us.

We reached the first of the religious houses, Abbaye des Dames, after dark. The Duke and I dismounted and left our mounts with our squires while we went, with his son, Sir John Clarence, to see how to gain entry. The two abbeys had been built almost four hundred years earlier and they had grown in size. That we were not expected was

The Battle for France

obvious for the gates were not barred. Indeed, they were open and the Duke and I simply walked in. I could hear singing; it was one of the services and there were no priests to be seen.

"My lord, we have this one! Invest it now and I will take half of the men to the other, the Abbaye des Hommes."

He nodded, "Even if we have but one abbey my brother will be happy. My son and I will stay here while you send in the others." His son was barely fourteen and yet a knight. I had been remiss not to knight Michael.

I left by the door and sought the Earl of Salisbury, Thomas Montagu, "My lord, we have this abbey. I need half of the men here to take the other!"

The Earl was a decisive man who had been forced to fight for his lands after his father was executed for treason. He was close to the King and intended to remain so, "Of course, Strongstaff." He gave me fifty of the best knights who remained, and I was grateful for that.

It was now dark and the time I had spent with Peter paid off for I was able to pick a route to the Abbaye des Hommes which overlooked Caen Castle, without being observed by any of the sentries on the town walls. Had we galloped then it would have alarmed the populace, but they just heard horses walking along the cobbled streets which led to the twin of the abbey now occupied by the Duke of Clarence. As we neared the abbey, I heard the distinctive sounds of a service but there was a priest at the gate. I dismounted and walked up to him.

"Yes, my lord?" Michael and a dozen of the knights were behind me and perhaps the priest had poor eyesight for he appeared not to see them.

I pushed the door open, "I am Sir William Strongstaff, and King Henry of England, the rightful Duke of Normandy, has sent me here to claim back this abbey for it is his by right." The priest saw the knights appear behind me and his eyes widened. "I promise that none will be harmed. Take me to the abbot." His shoulders slumped in resignation and he nodded. I turned to Sir John Cornwaille, "Secure the gates, Sir John and send a rider to King Henry to tell him that we have his abbeys!"

With Michael in close attendance, I followed the priest to the church in which the abbot and the rest of the priests were holding a service. I realised that it was the one before they would eat their evening meal. Our arrival coincided with the end of the service and the abbot was leading his priests from the church when I opened the door.

"I am Sir William Strongstaff, and this abbey is now returned to its rightful King and Duke, Henry Monmouth of England and France! Do

The Battle for France

not resist and none will be harmed, you have my word!" There were just two armed and armoured men before them, Michael and I but the Abbot nodded his acceptance. We had our two bastions!

By noon the next day the King had arrived, and light guns were being carried to the tops of the two abbeys. The bombards were too heavy for such a move. The knights were replaced by gunners, archers, and men at arms. Both abbeys were outside the walls of the town and as soon as they realised that we had taken them, the French belatedly barred the gates to the town after those who were able fled from the suburbs to take refuge inside the walls. As they were deemed to have resisted their rightful king then King Henry allowed our men to take what they could from them. It was lawful looting.

I was commanded to join the King, the Earls of Warwick, and the Earl Marshal to the west of the town. It was surrounded by the Duke of Gloucester to the south, the Earl of Westmoreland to the north and the Duke of Clarence to the east. In one masterstroke the most important town in Normandy, outside of Rouen, was cut off from the rest of the Dukedom. The siege began. The defences of Caen had been rebuilt and our guns pounded away at fresh stonework. The French had guns too but thanks to the elevation of the two abbeys the French guns were soon neutralised, and the castle and the town walls were slowly destroyed. While guns were more effective than the old trebuchet and mangonels, they were slow and had to be regularly cleaned. It took two weeks for us to make breaches large enough for us to attack. Honfleur was ever in the King's mind. Each night the two of us along with Norfolk and Warwick would survey the walls to determine if the time was right to attack.

Richard Beauchamp, the Earl of Warwick, feared that the French would send reinforcements and that we had to use all speed, "The breach is enough now, King Henry. Let us assault them."

The King shook his head, "Warwick, when we attack and put the lives of our men in jeopardy then the attack will be from both sides. When my brother has made the same progress as we then we will attack. Do you not remember Honfleur?"

John de Mowbray, who had been there and walked with us, nodded his head, "Aye, Your Majesty, and our scouts have yet to report any movement from the French. King Charles seems frozen with fear. We still have time."

I spoke, "They remember Agincourt. The King lost many of his supporters in that battle and Burgundy threatens him. France is riven with a civil war between Burgundy and Armagnac. Whoever rules France for King Charles will hope that disease helps his cause again.

There is one thing, though. At least here we do not have the fever-ridden marshes that we endured at Honfleur."

"We wait!"

Each day Michael and I rose and went with Rafe and James to view the progress. It was slow going. "Will we be in the attack, Sir William?"

Before I could answer Rafe said, "He shouldn't be, Master Michael, but he will. The King will not hold back, and Sir William will be there to protect him."

"Do not mind Rafe, Michael, but he is right. So long as the King goes forward then I am honour bound to be at his side. I would have stayed at home if that was not my intention, but you need not worry. You will not be needed."

"Staying at the rear did poor Walter little good. I will be at your side."

He was, of course, right and he had good plate and mail. We would not have to attack until the walls of the town were breached in a number of places and the opposition would be more like to be the citizens of Caen rather than knights. The knights would be in the castle and the mighty donjon of William the Conqueror. The King decided that his entire army would attack simultaneously on the fourth of September. There were sufficient breaches to enable us to try to take the new town which had been built in the wake of King Edward's destruction of the town. As was our practice we were awoken in the third hour of the day and attended a mass. No soldier liked to go into battle unshriven. I wore an open-faced bascinet as did Michael. Our necks were protected by two new gorgets. I confess that I was worried about my knee. I did not want it to fail at the wrong time. Rafe bandaged the knee before we donned my mail and plate. It would just add extra protection, but it stiffened the leg and made clambering a little awkward. I chose a poleaxe as my weapon of choice. I could hook and stab those above me and with both a hammer and a blade, it was a deadly weapon, and I could hurt any that I met. I still preferred my sword, but the poleaxe seemed to suit my name. Michael just held a broad headed spear. Rafe and James would wait at our defensive line with my standard. My livery was upon the jupon I wore.

We lined up in the darkness. The French defenders of Caen would know we were coming. The Mass we held in the dark, the jangling weapons and the fires preparing food would have told them that something was happening. The attack was preceded by the cannons on the two abbeys firing into the darkness to enlarge the breaches and to clear them of defenders. In the darkness, they were almost firing blindly

The Battle for France

but the gunners had been firing at exactly the same spots for some days and so each gun sent five balls towards the walls and then a horn was sounded, and we advanced.

It was as I had expected, they anticipated the attack and seeing the King's standard then their defence was the strongest close to our breach. King Henry's courage had never been in doubt and it was he who charged and led us. I was, perforce, slower than he was for I was more than twice his age! I tried to keep up as he ran towards the hole we had made in their wall. Our archers were with us in the attack and they did their job well. Crossbow bolts could hurt us, and the archers eliminated the men who tried to hit the King and his knights. Attacking the breaches eliminated the danger of fire and oil but we had to negotiate fallen masonry. My slow pace meant that King Henry had already slain his first Frenchman by the time I reached his side. One of his men at arms lay dead, a huge rock had crushed his skull rendering him almost unrecognisable save for his livery.

Ensuring that I had firm footing I swung the head of the poleaxe at the two men trying to attack the King's right side. My right side was protected by an agile Michael. In contrast, I would be as an unmoving rock! The head of the poleaxe struck the left arm and side of the first Frenchman. His arm was chopped in two and the head gouged through his mail to tear a long gash in his side. Screaming the man fell and in doing so knocked the other to the ground. My weapon was long enough for me to jab the spike up into the groin of the fallen Frenchman and their falling allowed King Henry to slay the man he was fighting and take a step into the breach. I joined him and from the corner of my eye saw Michael's spear dart forward to end the misery of the groin struck Frenchman.

The French were like a tide but the fact that the town was attacked on all sides diminished the quality of their attack. They had numbers but most were ordinary Frenchmen sometimes led by their lord but often with rudimentary armour and poor weapons. They died but, in their dying, they slowed us down and blunted weapons. After an hour of fighting, we had barely progressed beyond the wall and then we heard a wail ahead. The Duke of Clarence had made a bridge of boats and crossing the river had fallen upon the rear of the men attacking us. At the same moment, the Earl of Warwick led an attack which secured the fort of St. Pierre, another obstacle guarding the bridge, and we were able to attack the Old Town. If any of the men with the King thought that this would become easier, they were wrong, and we had to fight street by street. They were narrow and the Frenchmen, fighting to protect their homes and their land died fighting to the last. There was no

The Battle for France

surrender. Once we reached the Old Town, I dispensed with the poleaxe for I needed my sword which was of more use in the narrow streets. The King had lost most of his protectors and it was down to Mowbray, Michael, and me to guard him.

While the men we fought were either men at arms or the ordinary folk of Caen, they fought ferociously. One Frenchman, from his build he had to have been a blacksmith or the like, roared at us as he and what looked like three of his workers burst from their shop and ran at us with hammers and chisels. The tools would be as deadly as any weapon. The King still wielded a war axe, and the sledgehammer was longer. I stepped before the King, swinging my sword as I did so. Michael still held his spear and he jabbed at the man next to the smith as I hacked into the forearm of the blacksmith. In my left hand, I held my rondel dagger. As my sword cut through to the bone severing tendons my dagger drove up under the smith's chin and into his skull. Sir Mowbray, the Duke of Norfolk, blocked a blow from a sledgehammer and then used his own dagger to slash across a French throat. It was left to King Henry to bring his axe down and split the skull of the last Frenchman who had burst from the workshop.

The Earl of Warwick and some of his knights appeared behind us and surveyed the bloody scene, "Is all well my liege?"

The King grinned, "Aye for I had three heroes to protect me. Strongstaff, your squire deserves to be knighted for his deeds!"

I nodded, "And when I deem him ready, my lord, he shall be!"

That was our last combat of the day. The French who were able fled into the castle and our men took to pillaging Caen. They were mindful of King Henry's orders and only the men were killed. All the rest, priests, women, children, the old, were allowed to leave.

Rafe and James were amongst the first to join us and they quickly found us a good house with food, wine and beds as well as a small stable. It was perfect. They evicted the three archers who thought they had found a comfortable billet. No one argued with my two former men at arms. We closed the door and sat down to a good meal.

Michael was excited, as he had a right to be, "James, the King said I should be knighted! What do you think of that?"

I answered for James by shaking my head, "You did well, Michael, but you are not yet ready for knighthood. There is still work to be done."

Michael was a modest man and he nodded, "I know, lord. I was just pleased that the King noticed me."

"You did better than you know for many men who were chosen to protect the King fell. You did not."

After we had eaten, Rafe and James left the house to fetch our horses. They were as protective of our expensive animals as we were.

The next day I was summoned along with the other leaders to meet the King outside Caen Castle. We could no longer use the abbeys to bombard the castle and so while the guns were moved closer to the walls, we held a parley with the defenders.

King Henry was, as ever, decisive. He stood fearlessly within crossbow range and commanded rather than asked, "If you surrender to me then I will allow your warriors to leave with their horses and weapons. If you do not, then death will be your only reward."

The Governor of Caen spoke, "A kind offer, King Henry, and if we are not relieved by the twentieth of September then we will accept your offer."

The King nodded, "So be it but we shall bombard your walls in any case."

"Of course."

Such was the way we made war. It was fought between gentlemen who followed certain rules but once those rules were broken then the gentlemen could become barbarians.

We withdrew to the large merchant's house which the King had commandeered. "There is little point in attacking the walls. It will be a repeat of Honfleur."

The Earl of March asked, "And if they do not surrender on the twentieth, my lord, what then?"

His voice was icy, "Then we destroy the walls and slaughter every man in Caen Castle."

I knew that he meant it, but the defenders had little option other than to surrender for our wall of lances around Caen meant that it was unlikely that the French would have had the time or the men to come to the aid of William the Bastard's city! When the date came for the surrender the Governor of Caen and the garrison were happy to comply for our guns had pounded them relentlessly. They left with their arms and their horses but not their treasure. The city was filled with the gold and silver of the surrounding area. They had thought Caen was safe. They were proved wrong. King Henry was generous, and all his nobles shared in the bounty. My men and I were well rewarded for our effort. All of us became even richer.

Chapter 4

Even as the garrison surrendered, the towns of Bayeux and Lisieux sent messengers to tell us that they surrendered without us having to attack. Caen had been such a powerful city that the smaller towns who were close by knew resistance was futile. We then headed south towards Alençon. King Henry took Argentan, Sées, and Verneuil with little fighting but Alençon itself decided to resist us and so King Henry ringed the town and began to blast away the walls with his bombards. The resistance of Alençon did not last long and with November approaching and after garrisoning the captured towns the King planned on taking us north, back to Caen. We were in the castle of Alençon holding a council of war when we were visited by Duke John of Brittany. He had not fought against us at Agincourt but his brother, Arthur de Richemont, had and we had captured and ransomed him. The King did not look apprehensive, but his brothers did. Was this a prelude to a declaration of war?

The King was mindful of the delicacy of the situation and just the Earl of Warwick and I were present for the meeting. Even his brothers were kept without. Duke John was wiser than his headstrong brother. He had taken advantage during our first campaign and had seized some French land. His presence was soon explained.

"King Henry, I will be blunt with you for I understand that you are an honest King who appreciates plain speaking."

The King nodded, "Then some truths are spoken about me. Go on, Duke John."

"You are now on the very borders of Brittany and I have to ask, what are your intentions?"

Silence, like a heavy frost, lay over the table. When the King spoke, his smile dissipated the silence and warmed the room, "Why to secure Normandy, which is mine by right and then seek the French throne which is also mine by right! I have no intention on taking Brittany for we have no claims upon your land and never have!"

The Duke smiled, "Then that is good. I feared you had ambitions for Brittany."

"Then that sounds like the words of my enemies."

The Battle for France

"Perhaps I can be of assistance to you."

"You would ally with me?"

He smiled, "King Henry, you know that my brother bears a grudge against England and the knights who captured him. I can keep him on a leash but only if I am seen to be neutral. No, the help I can offer is political rather than military. Know you that I am allied to the Duke of Burgundy?" The King nodded. "It would not take much to persuade him to ally with you. He and Bernard, Count of Armagnac, are sworn enemies. John the Fearless is at Dijon. I could send two loyal knights of mine to escort one of your emissaries to speak with him if you wish."

King Henry was decisive, and he showed it that day. Without missing a heartbeat, he turned to me, "Sir William, as I recall, Duke John gets on well with you."

"I believe so, Your Majesty." I was being unduly modest for I had, when serving Henry as Prince of Wales, saved the life of the Duke of Burgundy. I had been offered the title Count of Arles, but I had refused as it would have meant swearing allegiance to Duke John and instead, I had been made a knight of Burgundy and given the manor of Sunderda in Brabant. I had yet to visit the manor but the money I received each year was useful.

"Then you shall go." He turned back to the Duke of Brittany, "It is good that we are allies for we have a common enemy in France." The two leaders then spent two days celebrating this erstwhile friendship.

The Duke's visit delayed the King's departure north. I awaited the arrival of the Breton knights and the King planned his route to Caen, "We did not reduce Falaise when we headed south. We will take that before wintering in Caen. I will send to the Duke of Bedford for more men and funds to pay for the army."

One of the contradictions of this campaign was that while we had taken a fortune from the French already that money went to the lords and nobles. Of course, the archers and men at arms lined their own purses but it was not pay, and the Treasury in London would have to pay for the lances in France.

The Earl of Warwick said, "My lord, Falaise is the strongest castle in Normandy. We cannot mine it for it is built upon solid rock."

"Richard, that is why we must destroy it for how can we control Normandy if we have such a fortress at our rear? I know not how we shall do this but do it we will!"

The two knights and their men arrived as the King and the army were preparing to head north. Sir Guy and Sir Richard were young; they looked to be an age with my son Henry, but they were both admirers of

The Battle for France

King Henry. While Rafe and James prepared our horses King Henry took me to one side.

"This time, Strongstaff, you do not go with bishops and earls. Know that I trust you and your judgement. Get an alliance with Duke John. If you do so then you will, once more, have served the crown of England. I will be in Caen when your business is done!" He paused, "Unless, of course, Falaise proves to be a difficult nut to crack."

As I mounted Hercules, I reflected that the King had dismissed the journey both to and from Dijon as though it was nothing! We had a three-hundred-mile journey through the land ruled by the enemies of England. Duke Charles hated the English and John the Fearless even more for John the Fearless had ordered the murder of his brother, Louis. The two Breton knights might be useful, but I would have to be the one to plan a route which would see us get to Dijon in one piece!

They had with them their squires and six of the Breton light horsemen. Despite their youth, Sir Guy and Sir Richard knew of the dangers which we might face in Orléans. They also knew of my reputation and deferred to my grey hairs immediately they spoke, "My lord, it will be a longer journey but if we head to Le Mans and then the north bank of the Loire, we can make our way to Bourges." Sir Richard shrugged, "The whole of this land knows of your courage, my lord, but if the men who control the land now that the Duke of Orléans is a prisoner in England hear that you are close to his land then they will not rest until they have you. You are valuable and could be used to persuade King Henry to exchange you."

I knew that would never happen; the King was too ruthless for that but it made sense to go in disguise. I smiled and nodded, "You are saying that I should hide my standard and wear a plain jupon?"

Sir Guy looked relieved, "It would be safer, my lord."

I was quite happy to do as they suggested. I had no false pride. I could not serve King Henry if I was a prisoner. I was helped in the disguise by Rafe and James. Neither looked like the servants of an English lord they looked like a pair of brigands. The detour would add four days to our journey, and I wondered if that would be problematic. In the event, the next few days were relatively pleasant. The two young knights were good company. Both wished to take part in a war, but their Duke was a clever and pragmatic man, and he did not risk war while the fate of France was in the balance. King Henry had won at Agincourt, but the King of France was still the major ruler in the land. Duke John was waiting for King Henry to win and then he would choose his side. I think that Sir Guy and Sir Richard hoped for an adventure on the road. It was autumn and whilst not as dramatic as in England the land still had a sort of beauty. Here many trees kept their green leaves over winter but the ones which changed colour looked all the more dramatic for that.

The Duke had given us a ducal pass and that meant we stayed in fine castles through Le Mans and the other Breton towns captured by Duke John. The Loire, too, was littered with magnificent residences and Blois especially was a daunting fortress. It was as we were leaving that Rafe rode next to me. Hitherto he and James had allowed me to converse with the knights while they chatted to the light horsemen.

"Lord, it may be nothing…"

I laughed, "Rafe, I have learned to trust your instincts and I do not doubt that whatever this is, it will be something. Speak!"

"I saw a face I recognised as we were passing through the town gate. He was coming through. It was a face I remembered from Agincourt, a French face."

"There were many French faces that day!"

He nodded, "And normally I would have ignored the coincidence, lord, but the man stared at you and it was not a pleasant look." Few Frenchmen would ever give me a pleasant look, but I knew that Rafe had more to say. "He wore livery, my lord, red and white bars with black figures on the white."

I remembered the livery. I had slain Robert de Beaumesnil in the battle. "Thank you, Rafe. If he was going into Blois, then that means he cannot overtake us."

"I thought you should know, my lord."

I was silent for we were heading east towards Burgundy and our detour, whilst it had taken us away from the French held territory, might prove to be costly. We could not be overtaken but a French rider could reach the lands of the Duke d'Orléans quicker than we could reach Dijon. Rafe had spotted one man but there could have been others who had seen me who did not wear livery. My presence close to King Henry at the battle had drawn the attention of many Frenchmen, noble and soldier.

"Gentlemen, thus far we have had a leisurely journey but now I am keen to make all haste."

"Of course, Sir William, but why?"

"Let us say I sense danger on the road and my mission is too important to risk failure."

We then began a race and I fear I was the one who suffered the most. My knee ached, especially when the rain began to fall. My waterproof cloak kept my upper body warm and dry, but my knees had to bear the brunt of the rain and the hard riding. Each night, when we stopped, I could not wait to dismount. When we reached Nevers, we were close to the end of our journey and the city was an important one for there was a cathedral with a bishop. We would have one more stop before Dijon and that would be Beaune. We examined every face for recognition, but we saw none. We would not relax our vigilance but each mile closer to Dijon meant we were nearing safety.

We left the next day to the accompaniment of steady rain. It was almost wintery rain and chilled me to the bone. We had left a roaring fire and a good breakfast. I realised I was getting too old for such adventures. A few miles from Nevers we passed through a forest which would stretch, we had been told, for almost twenty-three miles. James became the advance scout. He was older than the Bretons, but he had a nose for an ambush. The road twisted and turned through trees which had been copsed for winter, but which still canopied the road. When I saw James stopped in the middle of the road with a drawn sword I reacted immediately.

"Don your helmets, draw weapons and leave the sumpters where they are. Sir Guy, order your light horsemen to prepare their throwing javelins."

"But Sir William, your man has merely stopped."

I put my open-faced bascinet on my head and fastened the leather strap. "And drawn his weapon." As if to make the point James turned and began to trot back towards us. He did not gallop as though frightened and that meant he was trying to lure the men he had seen closer to us. I heard hooves in the distance. I had brought my shield with me and I reached down to put the guige strap over my arm. I drew my sword. "Michael, take the right. Sir Guy and Sir Richard flank us if you please."

I could tell that they were confused but they did as I asked and when their squires joined us, we had six men across the road. The drainage ditch which was full of autumn rain would give us some protection from the side. Here was where I missed my own men. I knew not what the two knights and their light horsemen might do. How would they react? There would be just four of us that I could count on.

James reined in and said, calmly, "Armed horsemen, my lord. They have drawn weapons. I drew the horsemen back here in case they had crossbowmen in the trees."

"You did right. You and Rafe guard our backs."

I saw the horsemen and they were mailed and plated. If we had brought longbowmen then I would have felt comfortable facing the eight men at arms and ten light horsemen who approached us but as it was, I had two untried knights and three squires. I would have to try to talk our way out of trouble. The eighteen men reined in across the road. It was barely wide enough for the six of us and they were a jumble of men and horses. The flooded ditch separated them into three groups. I did not recognise the livery, but I saw spurs on at least three of the men at arms and knew that they were knights. Rafe and James would be looking for danger from the trees.

"Gentlemen, you bar the road. I ask you, politely to let us pass. Our quest is a peaceful one."

The knight in the centre whose livery was three red stripes and three blue ones with yellow birds laughed, "Since when was Sir William Strongstaff peaceful? You are a killer and today your reign will end."

"Perhaps but before we do test our arms before God let me know the name of the arrogant knight who speaks to me thus."

"I am Sir Louis de Chartres and a cousin of Robert de Beaumesnil. I am here with my familia to wreak vengeance on you for you murdered him."

I shook my head, "That is a lie and guarantees your death, my friend. I slew your kinsman in a fair fight at Agincourt."

"I was there and saw you strike him when he lay on the ground."

"He had not surrendered!"

"And you did not ask him!"

I smiled for I had the measure of this man, "Then if you were that close why did you not seek vengeance there and then? The reason is simple, Sir Louis, you were too busy fleeing, like so many other Frenchmen that day, for your life." I pointed my sword at the knights with him. "This is the man you follow. Like many others that day he fled even though there were more Frenchmen standing at the end of the battle than English."

I do not know if it was the pointing of the sword or the insults, but Sir Louis de Chartres put spurs to his horse and launched himself at me. I had yet to fight on Hercules' back but as we had travelled barely half a dozen miles that morning, he was eager and ready and when my prick spurs touched his flanks, he leapt at the Frenchman. The French knight obliged me by riding at my sword hand. He bore a spiked mace and he intended to batter me to death. My leap took me ahead of Michael and Sir Guy and I had room to swing my sword. His mount had a metal headpiece, and I sliced my sword in an arc over the top of the metal. At the same time, I brought my shield over to counter the blow I knew was coming towards my head. His shield stayed on his left and as my sword hacked into the plates which protected his middle, I did not expect to pierce them, but I knew that I would hurt him. His mace struck my shield and slid its face to catch on my saddle.

I wheeled Hercules to the right and pulled back my hand. I was close enough to see the plates of his fauld which were articulated and covered his back. I rammed the tip into the gap and pushed up. The sword struck mail and I pushed harder. As his horse and Hercules were going in the same direction, I had the time to force the sword through the mail links and gambeson to stick in his flesh. He shouted in pain as my sword grated off the bone and then he jerked his own reins around, freeing my sword. The coins we had spent on Michael's plate now bore fruit. He was fighting a squire who just had a leather brigandine and even as I wheeled Hercules again, I saw the French squire fall from the saddle. One Breton horse was riderless, but I forced myself to turn my attention back to Sir Louis. If I could defeat him then the Frenchmen might cease the attack.

Sir Louis was angry, "You have no honour, you struck me in the back!"

I laughed, "Then try to be a more skilled knight and face me. Come on, boy! I am an old man and I have forgotten more tricks than you will ever learn."

He lost control again and charged towards me. This time I danced Hercules to the right so that we were shield to shield. His mace was less effective whilst my sword had a point. As I punched with my shield I lunged with my sword. My shield made him reel while my sword tore through one cheek and out of the other. He now had two bleeding wounds. He swung his mace at my shield. It was a good strike, but my shield was padded, and the blow did not hurt me overmuch. Neither of us was moving our horses any longer. In my case, it was because I did not need to and in his, because his horse appeared to be weary! My disadvantage was that I could not stand to bring my sword down upon his. I think he realised that for he stood to use his mace to its greatest effect, on the top of my helmet. My hope was to use the gap in the articulated fauld or skirt. My first blow must have weakened it for as I lunged and held my shield above me the tip of my sword penetrated to flesh once more. I had been right. He did intend to crush my helmet and skull with his mace. This time the mace not only hit my shield it struck my head, but my coif and arming cap saved me. I drew back my sword and saw the blood. His hit with the mace had encouraged him and he stood to finish me off but this time he brought his shield to protect his fauld. As he raised his arm, I saw my opportunity and I lunged up and under his armpit. He had no protection there for he had no besagew and my sword slid up into soft flesh. I tore it out sideways and severed something vital for he dropped the mace. I punched hard with my shield at his face and he was so distracted by the wound that he did not see it coming. He tumbled from the saddle but the right sabaton caught on the stirrup and the horse started to run.

If I thought that the falling knight would end the combat, I was wrong. Although three men at arms and the light horsemen fled the others continued to fight. Another of the knights hacked away Sir Richard's sword and came directly for me. He had an open helmet and he screamed obscenities as his horse lumbered towards me. He had a war axe, and I knew he intended to use it on my helmet. I gave him every opportunity to do so by riding at his right, but Hercules was fitter and as I spurred him his burst of speed confused the knight. He started his swing, but my sword was already tearing across his teeth and up into his skull. The force was so much that his helmet flew from the back of his head. That death did end the battle for the rest turned and fled.

I turned to see the cost. Two Breton horsemen lay dead and Sir Guy was slumped over his saddle. Rafe, James and Michael appeared unharmed. All three French squires lay dead as well as one of the men at arms. Rafe and James were already stripping the dead.

"Gather the horses and take the plate from the dead!" I dismounted, sheathed my sword, and said, "Well done, Hercules." I walked over to Sir Louis whose horse had finally stopped running and was grazing. When I reached him, I saw that I had not killed him, his horse had. His skull was caved in where it had struck the bole of the tree. There would now be another knight seeking vengeance on me!

We did not reach Autun until dark. We were now in Burgundy and my name meant something. I told the Seigneur of the attack and that the bodies lay in the woods. He nodded, "The knight, Sir Louis, and his men spent the night here. I am sorry Sir William. Had I known…"

"You could not have known. We have some of our dead to bury."

"I will speak with the priest and it shall be done."

Sir Guy's wound had not been serious, he had suffered a blow to the cheek from a mace. Nothing appeared broken but a healer tended to him. Sir Richard had been silent on the journey to Autun. "Our adventure almost ended badly."

"Sir Richard, for two of your men it did. Did they have family?"

He shook his head, "I do not know. I will find out."

"There are two sets of plate. Sell one and give the proceeds to the families if they had any and if not then give the coin to your men for they fought well."

The Seigneur insisted on an escort for the rest of the journey. We arrived safely at Dijon and, forewarned of our arrival Duke John the Fearless was waiting for us. His face was grim and I thought it to do with the attack on me but it was not, "I am glad you are here, Sir

William! I need you at my side. The Queen of France is in danger and we must rescue her!"

Chapter 5

I was getting old. I was confused by the Duke's words. Why should the Duke of Burgundy expect an English knight to rescue the Queen of our enemy? Then I remembered. There had been rumours around the two of them and I held my tongue as I waited for the Duke to explain.

"You know that I have no love for Queen Isabeau and that she hates me?"

I decided that honesty was the best policy, "My lord, I am a simple soldier. Ask me about war and I will give you an answer but in such matters as this..."

"You are honest, Strongstaff, I had forgotten just how honest. My avowed enemy is Bernard Duke of Armagnac. He has poisoned the mind of King Charles and accused a young man of adultery with the Queen of France. I think it is because his brother did commit adultery with the same lady and he was killed for it. Sadly for the young man and the Queen, King Charles had a rare moment of sanity and the young man was tried, tortured. and then flung in a sack into the Seine. The Duke of Armagnac has imprisoned her in Tours." He paused, "She has appealed to me for help. Her father, the Duke of Bavaria, is powerless to help. I intend to ride to rescue her."

"And why do you need me, my lord?"

He lowered his voice, "I was accused of the murder of the Duke's brother, Louis. I need you to give an honest account of what happens when I rescue her. Even your enemies respect your honesty."

"And if I had not arrived?"

He smiled, "I knew of your journey from the moment you set off. I did not know that you would take so long to get here. I expected you sooner."

"Then you know of my mission?"

"King Henry would have an alliance, aye I know and if you help me then we will have an agreement and King Henry will have Burgundy as an ally against the snake Bernard of Armagnac."

Without doing anything I had succeeded but I was like a dog with a bone, "And why should you rescue a Queen who, by your own admission, means nothing to you?"

The Battle for France

He smiled and I saw the cunning and clever leader who was almost as powerful as the King of France, "Queen Isabeau is the Regent. She is the most powerful woman in Europe. You are a soldier, Strongstaff, and I admire your skills. I am a leader who needs your skills to make his land great."

I was in more familiar country here; the treacherous behaviour of kings, dukes and counts, "Then I shall join you."

So it was that we barely had one night in Dijon before we left with eight hundred Burgundian knights to ride the two hundred and forty miles to Tours. I realised then that it was fortunate that we had not done as I had first intended and gone to Tours. The knights all knew me. I had ridden to battle with them before and I wondered if that was another reason for my inclusion. My reputation amongst Burgundians was the same as it was amongst the English. The Duke was fearless, but I had been involved in more battles. It was as we rode that I realised the Duke commanded almost as many knights as had fought at Agincourt for King Henry. This would be a powerful alliance and I began to believe that King Henry would succeed in his ambition, he might be crowned King of France.

I rode, of course, next to Duke John and that meant that Michael was relegated to the rear with Rafe and James. The Breton knights were also with the baggage but that meant I had no worries. My squire would be safe there.

"Duke, is the Duke of Armagnac in Tours?"

The reckless Burgundian laughed and shook his head, "I would that he was but the coward hides in Paris. Put him within reach of my arm and he will be a dead man."

"Then who guards the Queen?"

"Why, his knights of course. I brought far more knights than I need. I do not think that they will resist us but if they do…"

I counselled caution, "Duke, you do not wish to have to besiege the castle, do you?"

I could see, for he slowed down as my words sank in, that he had not thought it through. "Of course not, but they would not dare to bar their gates to me, would they?" The end of his sentence told me that doubt had entered his mind.

"You are no friend to the Armagnac faction, are you? I do not think they will allow you to simply ride in without a fight."

"We are ready for a fight!"

"But not a siege!"

The Battle for France

He was silent for a while and when he spoke, I knew that he had accepted that a romantic and chivalrous ride to rescue the Queen would not work. "And what do you suggest?"

"When I served King Richard, he liked to read tales of the ancient world and he told of one story. One band of Greeks were fighting another, I think a kidnapped princess was involved. They persuaded the Greeks hiding her to accept a gift of a wooden horse. They did not know it was filled with warriors. When night fell, the men escaped from the horse and opened the gates."

"I have heard the story, but we have no time to build a wooden horse."

I sighed, "It is a symbolic story, Duke John. I will be the horse. The men guarding the Queen will have heard of me, but they will not know the Breton knights. We have the plate armour we took from the knights who tried to kill us. We can dress my two servants in the armour, and they can say that they captured Strongstaff. I am sure they will admit us and throw me in some deep and dark place. Then the gates can be opened by the two Bretons, and you will have your fortress."

"That is a risk."

I knew that it was and I was taking a huge chance but no matter what happened my sacrifice would mean that King Henry had his alliance and that was all that mattered. "You are willing to be England's ally. It is worth the risk."

He nodded, "Then know that I will rescue both you and the Queen and King Henry shall have the stoutest of allies." I believe he actually meant his own words.

We had time on the journey to plan it all, including the signals. The last day of our journey the Bretons and my men rode with us and we halted five miles from Tours. A dozen of Duke John's bravest knights would take off their jupons and follow us and seek accommodation in the town of Tours. They would take the city gates to allow Duke John and his men to take the town. My sword had been taken from me, but we had concocted a story that when my squire and servants were slain I had surrendered and given my parole.

As we rode towards the mighty city which, along with Saumur, controlled the movement along and across the river my two Bretons chattered away for they were excited at this quest. Sir Guy, now fully recovered, and Sir Richard, were delighted to be involved. This had been their dream when they had begun and to be party to an attempt to rescue a Queen was every young knight's dream. Rafe and James were happy to be dressed as knights. They did not see a problem. The only one to express doubts was Michael.

The Battle for France

"Surely, they will see through this, lord!"

"It is obvious to us because we concocted the story. They will see what they expect to see. Sir Guy and the rest of you will play treacherous Bretons who have betrayed their Duke. The Duke of Armagnac is a master of such treachery." I turned in the saddle, "Remember the priority is to get Duke John and his men into the castle. If we do not manage that then all will be a failure. Do not worry about me. Once I am taken away, forget about me and my fate, I will look after myself." I had a dagger in my boot and no matter what the French believed I would not have given my parole.

James said, "We will rescue you, my lord, and we will admit the Burgundians. If they harm one hair of your head…"

I laughed, "Whoever commands in the castle will wish to keep me whole, if only to allow the Duke of Armagnac to use me to bargain with King Henry."

We reached the gate before dark, as we had intended, and Sir Richard played his part well. "We have captured the Strongstaff, King Henry's adviser is ours!"

The reaction was all that I could have hoped. The seneschal was fetched and the gates to the citadel opened. Sir Richard was embraced as though the French had won the war. "Welcome! We heard that this monster was loose in our lands, but we never dreamed… how did you take him?"

"We were assigned to take him to Duke John of Burgundy, but we thought that the Duke of Armagnac might pay us more!"

The look on the face of the seneschal told me that they had swallowed the bait. "And he will! He is not here but I shall send a ride to Paris immediately! Come." The seneschal suddenly looked at me. "He gave his parole?"

Sir Richard beamed, "He surrendered to me!" He cleverly used his words so that neither his nor my honour might be compromised. For myself I cared not. I did not believe in honour the same way as those raised as knights. My honour was of a different, more down to earth type and involved the men alongside whom I fought.

"Then you are destined to be a great warrior. Sir William, you are now my prisoner. Do not try to escape!"

I said nothing but I scowled to hide the smile which was forming. The plan was working.

The seneschal, Geoffrey de Vierzon, was an older knight than my Bretons but still much younger than me. He must have been at Agincourt for he mentioned the battle from the first moment I was escorted by two of his men to the small dining room in the castle. "The knight who was at Agincourt has fallen far, Sir William. Here the memory of that October day will be erased forever. Agincourt will be forgotten. We have you and soon we shall have your King!" He nodded and the two guards pushed me unceremoniously into the small dining room. "This shall be your cell until we have a suitably high chamber arranged and I shall be your gaoler until then. The Duke himself will wish to come and take charge of you. You might as well sit!" Turning to the guards he said, "One of you wait without and the other guard the door. This knight has no honour and needs to be watched! He murdered two knights at the castle of Agincourt and is treacherous." The table was just six feet from a roaring fire. My cloak had been removed when I had first entered the castle so that all could see there were no weapons for me to use. The two chairs were at opposite ends of the small table.

"Yes, lord."

The sentry who watched me had a mail hauberk and carried a pike. The seneschal had a sword and a dagger. I had said nothing in reply to the insults for I was trying to work out what part of our plan was being put into operation. The Bretons along with my three men would need time to get to the main gate without being seen. They would also have to wait until the town gates were taken and Duke John had gained entry. I could afford to take these insults for a little while longer.

"You are silent, Sir William. I hope that you are not planning an escape for that is impossible. When we have eaten, and your cell is ready you will be taken by the four men who will guard you until the Duke is here. One will watch in your cell and the others without. You will be the ransom to fetch back the Duc d'Orléans and are worth more than all the gold in Paris!"

There was a knock on the door and the sentry opened it a little, "The food, my lord."

"Have it brought in. We need to feed Sir William. We must keep him in good condition until we exchange him."

Three servants brought in wine, goblets, bread, cheese, and ham. The ham was already carved, and they were being careful not to allow me a weapon which I might use. When they had gone the seneschal poured me some wine. It was the heavy red wine they made in Chinon and I would have to drink sparingly for it was powerful. The seneschal had no such reservations and after pouring a large goblet for himself he drank it in one and then refilled it, "I drink to the fates that have delivered you into my hands. Your famous luck has deserted you, Strongstaff!" As he poured himself another he nodded at my untouched goblet, "Not drinking? I expected more from you, Sir William, or are you only belligerent when you have your cutthroats behind you?"

The Battle for France

I sipped the wine and spoke for the first time, "I am just storing up these insults, seneschal. All will be answered and repaid. You might as well use your tongue now while you can."

He paused mid drink and I saw fear in his eyes. I was neither cowering nor begging and he was worried. He looked over at the sentry, "Do not take your eyes off this one!" He finished his second goblet and poured a third.

I tore off a piece of bread and smeared some soft cheese upon it before placing a thick slice of ham on the top. I ate slowly but my eyes never left the seneschal, and I could see that I had unnerved him. My eyes bored into his and there was no fear in mine. I knew that my reputation as a defender of kings was legendary and the thinning grey hairs on my head must now have seemed of less consequence for my eyes were being used as weapons. When I had finished the food and drunk a little of the wine I smiled and said, "You seem a little worried about an old greybeard, Sir Geoffrey. Of course, if you survived Agincourt then that means you know how to run away quickly!"

He banged the goblet down on the table and some splashed out, "That is a lie!!

I nodded, "You were ransomed then?"

He sat and drank the wine, "I was not ransomed."

"Yet you are alive! The ones we caught we ransomed and the rest we killed... apart from the many who fled!"

"Murderer! You and your King killed those who had surrendered."

"Just as your barbarians killed the squires. War is not pretty, seneschal, and any who think it is are fools themselves." I had bought enough time. The seneschal had drunk heavily. Even as my last words sank in, he filled his goblet again. I stood, "Is there a garderobe in this chamber?"

The seneschal became a little more alert and pointed to the north wall where I saw the entrance to the hole and wooden board, "Sentry, keep your pike point in his back."

I shrugged. I genuinely needed to make water, I was an old man but I also needed to be on my feet. As usual, the moment I stood and began to walk my injured knee complained and I naturally limped. It would soon wear off, but I saw both the sentry and the seneschal notice and they started to relax a little. There was the usual whistling wind rising up through the passage of the garderobe. The sentry did as he was asked, and the pike point touched my back. I made water and felt all the better for it.

As I turned the sentry moved away and the seneschal waved him to the door. I exaggerated the limp as I headed back towards the table. In the distance, I heard noises. The sentry heard them too, but the seneschal did not. The sentry went to the door and I saw him listen. I stopped and lowered my right hand as though to massage my knee. Neither sentry nor seneschal saw anything untoward in that and I was able to slip the rondel dagger from the boot. The dagger had a large round pommel and, as the increasing noises crystallized into the sound of clashing steel, I raised my hand and brought the pommel of the dagger down on the top of the seneschal's head. He fell to the floor before the sentry could react and swapping hands with the dagger, I reached down to draw the seneschal's sword. The sentry shouted for his companion and lowering his pike ran at me. I suspect the other sentry was distracted by the noise of fighting which could be heard. The pike was not the weapon for the small room. I placed myself behind the table forcing the sentry to negotiate the unconscious seneschal.

"My friend, put down your pike for I wish you no harm!"

The sentry laughed, "Old man, I will not kill you for Sir Geoffrey needs you for the exchange, but I will cripple your other leg!" He lunged at me with his pike. As he did so the door opened. I did not turn but he glanced that way. I swept the pike head towards the fire with the seneschal's sword and then lunged with the rondel dagger. The distraction of the door was fatal. The dagger entered the sentry's throat and I ripped it to the side. The blood hissed and sputtered as it hit the fire and his body fell into it. The second sentry now called for help, but he too faced the same problem. To get to me he had to negotiate a body and a table. This one, however, would show more caution for he had seen me dispose of his fellow.

"Sentry, I will make the same offer to you as I did to your poor friend here. The castle has fallen, and my friends are here. Put down your pike lest I kill you too. I do not take prisoners. You either surrender or you die. It is that simple."

The sounds of fighting could now be heard more clearly. Duke John and his knights were in the citadel of Tours Castle and the outcome would no longer be in doubt. He had eight hundred knights. The sentry, however, must have had a great sense of duty. He came forward purposefully. The body in the fire began to smoulder and suddenly the hair and beard of the dead sentry flared into flame. The air was filled with the stench of burning flesh. The pike's shortcomings now came to my aid. Instead of lunging at me with the spike as the first sentry had attempted, the second sentry tried to split my head in two. As he raised the pike the top caught on the ceiling of the small chamber and that gave me the chance I needed. I whipped my sword horizontally and it sliced through both hands. I saw at least two fingers fall to the floor as

The Battle for France

blood spurted and the pike fell from the damaged hands. I pulled back my right hand and punched the man in the face with the hilt and pommel of the sword. He fell atop the seneschal.

I wasted no time in getting out of my cell and I hurried as fast as my injured leg would allow me into the corridor. It was empty but I could hear, from the Great Hall below me, the sound of fighting. I hurried towards the grand stairs. These days I could not run. The stairs were wide enough for five men abreast. As I reached the top of them, I saw a block of French knights falling back before Duke John. Michael, Rafe and James were close behind him. There were twenty knights and Burgundians who would die for the French had the advantage of height.

I shouted, "Hold! The seneschal has fallen! I have his sword. Surrender for the castle has fallen!"

Men ceased fighting as French faces turned to look at me. One French knight, I recognised his livery as being similar to Sir Louis whom I had slain on the way to Dijon, suddenly raced up the stairs to me. He had a sword and dagger in his hands, and he was much younger than I was, yet I knew what the outcome would be. If he had been more experienced, then he would have hacked at my unprotected legs. It is what I would have done but he wanted to hit my head and that gave me all the time in the world to bring my sword down diagonally across his neck. The blow was struck with such force that the head was almost hacked from his torso. The knight hung there for a moment and then tumbled down the great staircase. His bloody body crashed into the French knights.

Duke John seized the moment and shouted, "Throw down your weapons and you shall live. I want not the castle but Queen Isabeau."

That, and the falling torso, did it and weapons struck the wooden staircase.

The Duke grabbed a French knight by the arm and said, "The Queen, where is she?"

The bloody corpse had just stopped next to the knight and he pointed up towards me, "Along that corridor and up a narrow staircase."

The Duke ran up and as he passed me, said, grinning, "Once more I am in your debt, Strongstaff!"

Some of his knights followed him while the rest herded the captured knights. I shouted, "The seneschal is in the room with the burning body!" I walked down the stairs.

Rafe was smiling and shaking his head as I reached him, "All you had to do, my lord, was wait for us to rescue you! A burning body?"

I shook my head, "I did not intend it, but you know me, Rafe, I cannot sit idly by while men die for me!"

We went down to the Great Hall where the bulk of the fighting had taken place. I saw few bodies. In a confined space it is hard to manage to kill an armoured knight. Sir Guy and Sir Richard were there. We had just drunk a couple of goblets of wine when Duke John led Queen Isabeau and her ladies into the hall. Every man bowed as she entered. She was stunningly beautiful despite the fact that she was closer to fifty than forty, but she was also the most dangerous woman I knew! Duke Louis had died because of her as well as her tortured lover and now knights, both French and Burgundian, had died.

"I hear, Sir William, that it is you to whom I owe my gratitude. It seems that I will be forced to ally with my enemy, King Henry, whether I wish it or not!"

I kissed the back of the proffered hand, "Your Majesty, it is up to you. I was aiding King Henry's new ally, the Duke of Burgundy, but I was pleased to help rescue a lady in distress. You are under no obligation to me."

She smiled, "So not all Englishmen are as cold as the fish they eat! A gallant knight; how refreshing!"

We stayed for three days. The Duke wrote a letter for me to take to King Henry and my men took the horses and plate from the knight I had killed. When we dined with the Queen, I realised that she saw Burgundy and King Henry as the lesser of the evils facing her. The Duke of Armagnac effectively ruled France and she would have us eliminate that threat before she would revert to being our enemy. I explained all of this to Michael and the Breton knights as we headed for Falaise where King Henry was still besieging the castle.

Michael shook his head, "I do not understand all of this, my lord. Whose word can a man trust?"

I smiled and sadly shook my head, "That, Michael, is something you can never guarantee. I trust King Henry."

Rafe nodded, "Aye, lord but that is because it was you who brought him up and not his father. There was a king who could not be trusted!"

I reprimanded him, "Do not say that in the King's hearing!"

Rafe smiled, "I would only speak thus in the hearing of men I trust! There is a lesson for you Master Michael. We are a band of brothers."

Chapter 6

We reached Falaise at a crucial moment in the siege. Mining had proved impossible and so King Henry had the men using pickaxes to dig out the rock foundations of the castle. He had learned lessons from Honfleur, and the men were housed in log huts which were covered in turf and the clever king had organised a daily market. It meant there was less disease and a certain amount of comfort. The Governor of Falaise, Oliver de Maunay, had repeatedly sortied from his walls to try to slow down the siegeworks. King Henry believed he hoped for help from the rest of France. With all the other castles garrisoned and in our hands help would not be forthcoming.

We arrived when it was daylight and both fighting and mining were in progress. The King took me to one side as the action of the day ended. With the town in our hands, he had commandeered the mayor's house and that was where the two of us, with the Earl of Warwick and his two brothers, could speak of my mission and the progress of the siege. It was January and Christmas had simply not existed either for the men at the siege of Falaise or, indeed me.

I told the King, first, of the rescue mission. I left out the attack on the road for it was of no relevance to the campaign. The King was pleased, and my account of our Trojan Horse made him smile, "One day Strongstaff, your clever trickery will be your undoing, but we could not have asked for a better result. We have a good ally and the Queen of France herself supports our cause. I am, once more, in your debt. I should not be surprised for I saw all of this when I was the callow young Prince Hal but your ingenuity constantly surprises me."

I was then informed about the proposed attack. It had taken almost a month to undermine the walls, but they were about ready to fall. Fires would be lit beneath them and while it might take some time the walls would, eventually, tumble into the ditch and the Governor would have little choice but to surrender.

"And then, King Henry?"

"I will retire to Caen while I have my three armies raid the Cotentin, the land close to the Breton border and take all the land which lies close to the Seine. The Duke of Bedford is sending us more men and twenty-six thousand pounds to pay the wages of the indentured men here. It may be that the majority wish to serve another year. This war is profitable for all." He was right. We had lost far fewer men and taken far more land and prisoners than we had in the Agincourt campaign. Few men had deserted and there was a hopeful mood in the camp.

It took two days for the fascines to be rammed in the holes which had been dug for them. We had enough archers to keep the French from the walls and we lost not a man while doing so. The entire army was armed and ready to attack as the fires were lit and thick smoke, followed by flames, began to rise. The effect was spectacular. Although the fires did not bring down whole walls, they brought enough down to create a path to the castle which the French could not now defend. The fires were lit before dawn and by noon we were ready to charge. The horns sounded and we raced across the open ground. Our archers sent so many arrows that we reached the fallen walls unharmed and I followed King Henry up into the castle. There was a mighty donjon at Falaise, but the mining had destroyed part of it and Oliver de Maunay had no choice but to surrender. Compared with Caen it was an easy assault, if there is such a thing and the three men we lost were almost insignificant

King Henry, however, was angry for this was his castle and we had ruined it. I was with him as the Governor handed over his sword, "And you, petty little man that you are, will be my prisoner until you have raised enough ransom to pay for the damage that was caused. You should have surrendered for this defeat was inevitable!"

De Maunay's head sank for he knew that King Henry was right. King Henry had learned from Honfleur and we would not be caught out again by a poorly managed siege! The army spent less than a week at Falaise and the three columns left to enlarge the territory we controlled. The Cotentin was important as Cherbourg was a good port. The King returned to Caen which had not suffered much damage when we had taken it. He sent for me a day after he had walked the walls and spoken to the garrison he had left.

"Strongstaff, I need you to come with me and some handpicked knights."

"Of course, my lord, but where do we go? Your brothers and the Earl are busy making Normandy secure. What is there left for you to do?"

"While my brother Clarence distracts the French with his moves towards the Seine, I would find a place to cross the Seine. All our efforts this past year are to be able to threaten Paris and Rouen. When the Duke of Bedford fetches the reinforcements in the summer, we will

The Battle for France

be stronger than we were when we first landed and took this great fortress. Thanks to your efforts the French are now weaker than they were. The King of France is no threat, but Armagnac remains to be a problem and with the Queen of France and the Duke of Burgundy on our side then I am confident that when we can bring the French to battle, we shall succeed but I need a crossing which will not cost me men!"

"Then I will go with you but is this not a great risk?"

He smiled his lopsided smile, "It is, Strongstaff, but so was giving the command of a third of the army to a fourteen-year-old at Shrewsbury. That paid off and so will this. I cannot see the protector of kings allowing anything to happen to me!"

I gave a mock bow, "I thank you for your confidence, but I am now an old man."

"An old man who is still one of the greatest warriors in England."

The four knights he took with us were all young and keen to impress the king. None of us wore livery. These days knights often went abroad in plain armour without even the short livery coated jupon. He took two squires with him but no servants. Rafe and James had that task. Fifteen of us would be a small enough number not to arouse too much interest and yet we would be able to defend ourselves should we find that we were in danger. This was not the campaigning season and the Duke of Clarence would be drawing French blades to his column.

He left the Earl of Salisbury in command of the forces at Caen. The Earl and the King were close, and he knew the plan. He would also wear the King's livery to maintain the illusion that the King was in the castle. We slipped out before dawn through a gate guarded by household knights. With plain cloaks, we would blend into the wintery landscape. We knew that for the first day we would be in the land already cleared of the French. We would be in land that was safe and when we reached French land we would have vanished. As the Duke of Clarence was to the north and east of us, we headed due east.

I rode next to the King and this time Rafe and James both acted as scouts for they were better than the knights and squires who rode with us. "The closer we are to Paris, my lord, the more chance there is that the French will be there in numbers."

"I know, Strongstaff, and I thought to find somewhere we can cut the Seine in two. I want Rouen isolated from the rest of France and Paris cut off from the sea."

"Then we head to Elbeuf, my lord. If memory serves it is not a large castle."

The Battle for France

He nodded, "But can we cut the river there? It is a start, I suppose, and we must begin somewhere."

As with all journeys, it is those first steps which set the mood. King Henry was in a philosophical mood. That was partly the fact that he had no nobles with him. The young knights had yet to become politically motivated, they were just excited to be guarding the king, and I was like a comfortable pair of buskins. The other reason was that he had lived in my household for a time and when he had been King Richard's guest he had come to know and trust me. He had barely known his father, Henry Bolingbroke, whose ambition had exceeded his abilities. His son was not like him.

"We have a chance to become the masters of France, Strongstaff. I can feel it in my bones."

I could be honest with him, "You are blessed, my lord. Poor King Richard was beset by enemies who would stick a knife in his back, and he had those like de Vere the Earl of Oxford, who feigned friendship but sought to bring him down. Your father, too was beset by enemies. You have men who support you and you have a land which is at peace and supports you. God has given you this opportunity and I do not think that you will shun it."

He nodded, "I forget, sometimes, that you have been close to we kings in this struggle for a crown and you are right. Any foes I have are foreign." I said nothing. "John the Fearless, can I trust him?"

I shook my head and laughed, "Not for a moment! The Queen of France has allied to him and she struck me as a most dangerous woman. The Duke is fearless, but he is ambitious, and he hates the Duke of Armagnac. King Charles is no threat, neither is his son but the Duke of Burgundy? If he takes over Paris and therefore France, then any alliance you have with him will be as nothing. He sees you as a friend, but the crown of France will be dangled before him by Queen Isabeau and she truly terrifies me!"

"Yet you like him."

"He is a warrior and fights well. I like all such men for I grew up with them. There the similarity ends. These grey hairs come from having lived through battles, wars, and plots. I am a little cynical, but I believe I know the character of men and the Duke of Burgundy has ambition. With the Queen of France at his side then he has the chance to rule France." I paused, "Is that not why you have not taken a bride yet, King Henry, and seek the hand of Katherine de Valois?"

His head whipped around, and I wondered if I had gone too far, "You frighten me sometimes, Strongstaff. You seem to read my thoughts. Is wishing to marry Princess Katherine a bad thing?"

The Battle for France

I shrugged, "I am the wrong man to ask when it comes to women, my lord. I married Eleanor for I fell in love with her and she had nothing. Yet she proved to have more within her than any could have known. I was lucky."

"And I am a king and do not have that luxury. I have to think of my country first and last and how I can serve it. If that means a loveless marriage, then so be it."

"You are more like King Richard than your father. King Richard fathered no bastards and neither have you."

He nodded, "I liked King Richard and I am of your mind. He was much maligned! As for bastards, they can be a problem. I will save my seed for the Queen of England, my heir will have no threats from elder unlawful siblings!"

After that we rode in silence. The King, I knew, would be digesting my assessment of his new ally. He would put his mind to devising strategies which might neutralise any threat from Burgundy and Queen Isabeau. I would have said he was a perfect king, but I knew there were flaws which even I could not see.

Empress Matilda had endowed many abbeys and monasteries in Normandy. The King knew of one which lay close to St. Georges and we sought shelter there. Although we were in disguise the scar on King Henry's face made him recognisable and I am sure that the abbot knew who we were. I could tell that from the deference he showed. I hoped that he was like many churchmen, pragmatic. As the King was in disguise the abbot could, if it was discovered that he had sheltered the enemy of France, deny all knowledge of his identity. He was quite a knowledgeable man and we learned much when we stayed with him. Now that the Duke of Burgundy had become an ally of the Queen, Paris was now filled with his Burgundian and French supporters. There was a small-scale civil war going on in the city between the supporters of both parties. He said little when he heard the news, but I knew that it would please the King. Until the reinforcements reached us, we were still vulnerable and if Duke John could wrest control of France from the Duke of Armagnac then he could break the alliance and make war on us. I believed we would still win but Duke John was a more formidable foe than either the Dauphin or Duke Bernard of Armagnac. Dissension in Paris would also keep nobles and knights there. Their eyes would not be on the Seine!

The next day we headed for Elbeuf. The castle there was on the south bank and therefore an easier prospect to assault. We reached the outskirts of the town by mid-morning and rather than riding towards the town and castle we rode along the river. We needed somewhere that would enable us to block the passage of the river. We were aided in our quest by the murky nature of the day. There was a late winter mist which masked most of the riverbank in grey. We could still see across the river although the other bank was hard to make out. What we were looking for was the flow of the river.

King Henry shook his head, "It seems to me a little too wide here. We cannot ford it. We will move on to Pont-de-l'Arche."

We had to ride around Elbeuf rather than risking going through it and it meant we reached Pont-de-l'Arche in the late afternoon. Rafe and James had the foresight to have brought both food and drink, not to mention blankets but the King and the household knights had not.

"Your Majesty, let us see if we can find some building which will afford shelter."

King Henry nodded, "It has been many years since I did this, Strongstaff, one forgets. We are in your hands."

We rode down the deserted road until I spied a gap and we headed down the track which led to the river. The farm track had been used in the past but there was no sign of either ruts or footprints. That told me that either the building whose gloomy shadow we saw ahead was unoccupied or a hermit lived within. I waved Michael, Rafe and James forward. They dismounted and ghosted into the dark. I sensed nervousness amongst the household knights although King Henry seemed oblivious to danger. We both knew that here we were relatively safe. We were beyond the town and hidden from river traffic by the dark. There would be more danger on the morrow when we scouted the river.

One of the King's squires, John Page, actually jumped when Michael appeared from nowhere. I saw the smile on my squire's face as he spoke, "The farmhouse is deserted, my lord. Part of the roof has fallen in and there is no food but there is enough roof for shelter and Rafe and James assure me that we can light a fire for warmth."

I nodded, the King ruled but I commanded my men, "Is there a stable?"

Shaking his head, he said, "No, but there is a barn."

"Then lead on."

John Page said, to the King, "How does his squire do that?"

The King nodded to me, "John, you should spend six months with Sir William here. What I learned in the time I was with him stood me in good stead. I was never as good as the rest of his men but there was a time when I could sneak around like one of Sir William's archers."

The house was dirty and had been abandoned for some time but there were no corpses. Dead bodies meant rats! Rafe and James were

The Battle for France

good foragers and they had managed to find dried kindling and wood to light a fire in the room which faced the river. We would not be seen, and a warm fire was always as good as a hot meal. We did not have a great deal to eat as what had been intended for four was now shared by all but as Red Ralph used to say, '*it filled a hole*'. There was little point in being complacent, however, and we kept a watch. We woke before dawn. In my case, I needed to make water and in the case of the young knights, it was the discomfort and the cold which woke them.

The day was relatively bright, and we could see across the river. The view from the deserted farm was not hopeful as the river seemed as wide as at Elbeuf but further east it offered some hope for the north bank appeared a little closer. We skirted the town and kept to the fields, taking shelter behind hedgerows. We saw a few men working in the fields. Some were planting crops while others were preparing the ground. The sight of knights appeared not to alarm them, but I urged haste. The sooner we were back in Caen the better. When we reached it we saw that the crossing was better. There was an island and that meant we could make a barrier of logs and protect it with archers.

Not long before noon, the King was satisfied enough to allow us to head south and west again. He was keen to see what dangers lay in that direction. I was happy as it never did to repeat a journey when in enemy territory. It was in the late afternoon when we met the French patrol. Their jupons bore the sign of Evreux, but they were heading away from that city. The twisting nature of Norman roads meant that Rafe and James saw them moments before they themselves were seen but we had warning and cloaks were thrown back to allow us access to our swords and shields. Michael and I had our shields on our arms as soon as Rafe raised his hand to give the warning signal. King Henry too was swift, but his knights stared ahead as though mesmerized.

There were ten men in the patrol. It was led by a knight with eight men at arms in attendance. They looked to be escorting two priests, by their garb. There were servants with four horses. Rafe and James rode back and took their places behind us with Michael. Our experience in Burgundy had helped us to react as though we were one.

We had ridden with our helmets on. It was not just for protection, it also disguised us. The French knight had a visor on his sallet helmet. The men at arms wore kettle helmets. They were all armed with spears while the knight's squire had a lance and I saw more lances on the sumpters. Perhaps the knight was on his way to a tournament; the reason was immaterial. We had a problem, and it was up to either the King or me to solve it. We waited until the knight was close enough for conversation. As was the custom we rode on the left, as did the French

The Battle for France

so that our hands could draw weapons if it was necessary. None were drawn as we spoke.

"Well met, my lord." It was King Henry who spoke and his French, as one would expect, was perfect but the French knight had sharp ears. "Who are you that travels the roads which belong to the King of France?"

King Henry looked at the priests, "I hope, father, that we may pass peacefully. It is too fine a day for violence."

The knight appeared ready for a fight, "You have not answered me, Englishman!"

I did not like the tone and I answered, "I pray you to speak in a more courteous tone, Frenchman," I spat out the word in the same manner as the knight, "or you and I will cross swords. It is many years since I was at a tournament but I fancy I could still unhorse you."

The King turned, "Peace, William, this French knight means nothing by it, do you sir? And to answer your question, we are travelling from Pont-de-l'Arche and heading south. There, are you satisfied?"

In answer, he drew his sword, "No, for I believe you are the enemies of France! Take them!"

His men had spears, but none had lifted their shields. His squire was encumbered by the knight's lance while at least five of us were ready and armed. King Henry did not hesitate but rode at the French knight who had also forgotten to raise his shield. He had a shock when King Henry's sword rang against his. It sounded like a bell ringing the alarm. Michael and I rode at the men at arms who were busy trying to do two things at once; lower their spears and raise the shields. The sooner we reached them the greater our advantage. Rafe and James also beat the English household knights to the first blows in anger. Michael, thanks to the movement of the King, reached the French knight's squire. The youth did not know if he should use the lance or discard it and, in the end, did neither. Michael was remarkably merciful, and he hit the youth in the face with his shield. He fell from his horse, stunned. The man at arms who came at me was better prepared and he lunged with his spear. I deflected it with my shield and then hacked through the spear haft with my sword. Despite my years, I still had fast hands and my sword was at his throat before he could think about drawing another weapon.

"Yield or you will die, and this is not a day for death!" He nodded and raised his right arm.

Another man at arms obviously thought that Michael was an easy target. He had no spurs and no beard, The Frenchman charged at him, but Michael had learned to be a good horseman and he danced his horse out of the way and then swung his sword around to smash into the man at arms' back. He had a breastplate but no backplate and I saw his back arch as he threw his arms into a crucifix. It was at that point that King Henry flicked away the French knight's sword and pricked his gorget with the tip of his own sword. The Frenchman nodded and said, "I surrender!"

I could see that King Henry was angry and I rode my horse next to his, "Well done, my lord!" My deference told the Frenchman that Henry was an important man. I turned to the priests, "Perhaps had the church counselled peace then you would not have injured men whose hurts need attention."

The words were enough to calm the King and he nodded, "Well said, Sir William, let us ride and perhaps you have learned a lesson Sir Frenchman, do not be so hasty to draw weapons for you know not whom you face!"

We had a relatively quiet ride back to Caen and our one stop was in a priory. The household knights were the most impressed by Michael. After all, I had a well-deserved reputation, having been the bodyguard for kings but Michael was a squire and the way he had dealt so adroitly with his two opponents made him the centre of their attention on the way back.

As Caen loomed into sight the King said, "Come summer we shall begin our attack. Let us hope our enemies allow us the time!"

They did not but when moves were made they were not against us!

The Battle for France

Map of Paris and its environs

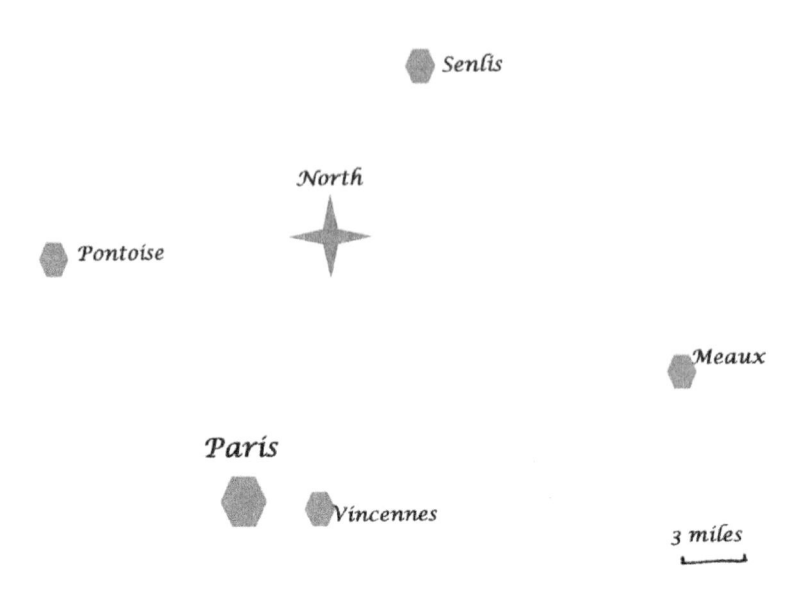

Senlis

North

Pontoise

Meaux

Paris
Vincennes

3 miles

Chapter 7

It was May when the populace of Paris arose. Many said it was at the instigation of Duke John, but it could just as easily have been Queen Isabeau. The mob went on the rampage destroying the property owned by the Armagnac faction and killing those that they could lay their hands upon. Duke Bernard was murdered! When the bloodletting had ended then Duke John restored order and put the King into the care of his wife. There he would be protected both from his illness of the mind and his enemies. The Dauphin fled but his only ally appeared to be the fourteen-year-old Duke of Anjou. Although one enemy had been removed, had he been replaced by a more dangerous one?

The three parties sent to raid had returned and the news prompted King Henry to mobilise his recently reinforced army and to head north and east to Pont-de-l'Arche. We had more guns now, as well as sappers and miners. Knights would not play a part yet. We besieged the town and the castle. This time we had the experience of Falaise and Caen behind us. The disaster that had been Honfleur was forgotten. We built bridges of boats to connect our camps and the cannons were sited all around the walls. The bombards began their daily relentless bombardment, and the walls began to crumble. It took us just three weeks to reduce the walls enough for the French to surrender. We lost barely a handful of men during the assault. We had enough men to garrison the captured castle and still leave a mighty force to head to Rouen.

The Duke of Clarence had sent scouts ahead to assess the problems which might face us. The town and castle were even more formidable than Caen. Before we reached its suburbs, we knew that the town had five miles of walls and that, unlike Caen, the defenders had ruthlessly destroyed the suburbs outside the walls and used the rubble to repair and improve their defences. There were six gates which would need watching and even before we reached them the King had allocated the men who would guard and watch each gate. We had a chain placed across the river so that the town was effectively cut off from the rest of France. The harvest had yet to be collected and as the town could not be supplied then the people would starve.

The Battle for France

The siege began on the last day of July. Guns were brought up, but it soon became clear that even Nicholas Merbury, our master of ordnance could do little against the French bombards and fowlers. The French artillery was mounted on the walls and along with their crossbowmen prevented our guns from being close enough to do any damage. For the first month, we tried to move them closer, but it could not be done. We had lost men thanks to the outlying fort of St. Katherine and the Earl of Salisbury begged permission to reduce it. He finally captured it at the start of September, but he lost many men in doing do. I had asked to help but the King kept me by his side. The battle was a harsh lesson for the Earl but one which helped him later in the campaign. He learned how to fight! The siege then began in earnest and after the first attempts to take the walls ended in failure the King decided to starve them into submission. We captured some of their men and they captured some of ours. It was from the prisoners we took that we learned the identity of the two men who led the enemy garrison. Guy Le Bouteiller was the titular commander of the forces but, according to our prisoners, Alain Blanchard, the commander of the crossbowmen, was the real leader. It was he who angered King Henry. The Master of Crossbows had hanged the men he captured from the walls. These were not nobles, who could be ransomed, but ordinary men and it angered not only the King but also all the other soldiers for it told them of the fate that they could expect. It did not bode well for Rouen when it would eventually fall. We knew it would fall from the demeanour of the King which changed when the first prisoners were hanged.

The hangings stirred the King into action. He summoned his leaders, me amongst them, and we held a council of war. "I am determined not to suffer another Honfleur. I have an army of seven thousand men, and I will not bleed them away. No more attempts will be made on the walls. The people will starve to death and it shall be ours in the fullness of time." The Duke of Exeter, Sir John Holland who was the King's uncle, looked uncomfortable and was about to speak when the King silenced him with an imperious hand, "I know what you are going to say, that the men will become dispirited and we shall have desertions as well as disease." The Duke nodded. "That will not be the case. I intend to create three columns of one thousand men. Each day one will ride forth to ravage the countryside and fetch in food for us. Each column will ride a different route. I intend to change the men in the columns regularly so that all men have an opportunity to ride forth and to pillage the land. The owners of the land are in Rouen and, as such, are my enemies. They will suffer! The leaders of the three columns will not change. Warwick you, and Sir William Strongstaff shall lead one

The Battle for France

column. My brother Clarence a second and Gloucester a third. I urge you not to harm churches, priests nor those who do not bear arms, but any other resistance must be crushed. This is my land and until all bow their knees to me then they must pay the price for such disobedience."

For the Earl of Warwick, this was just what he had been clamouring for. He did not like enforced idleness and I knew why the King had made us joint leaders. He wanted my caution to counterbalance the reckless Earl. The King's brothers were given the honour of the first two chevauchée and we had to bide our time. However, we were given the chance to ride along the river which gave us a better road and more opportunities. Holding the river further upstream we knew that there would be no castles to bar our way and with a thousand horsemen, we could cover a large swathe of the land. That first raid took me back to Castile when I had been with the Blue Company. We took animals and early crops. The farmers and their families fled at our approach and although the King might have frowned on it the ordinary soldiers were kept happy when they were allowed to loot the houses and farms. What little treasure the people had was unearthed and wine, as well as knick-knacks, were taken. It had the effect the King desired. The camps were filled with happy men. The only ones who would not get to ride and raid abroad were the gunners and servants. For the rest, men at arms and archers they knew that once a week they would get to leave the camp and have the opportunity to fight and to become richer. No matter what the priests might say soldiers like to fight. Rafe and James were typical of the bulk of the army. They liked nothing better than to defeat French in battle, if they could not fight the French then the Scots or the Welsh would do. Their forefathers had fought at Crécy, Neville's Cross and Poitiers. They had fought at Agincourt and they feared no enemy save disease. They came with us on the raids with sumpters to carry back the loot we took.

As October drifted into November so we began to raid further afield. The Earl of Warwick was keen to get close to Paris which lay just seventy miles away as the crow flies. In the middle of November, we were given the opportunity to make a two-day raid. The King allowed the Earl and me to raid as far as Pontoise which lay just sixty miles away. The King had not taken the decision lightly and he had taken me to one side the day before we left.

"Strongstaff, I am allowing this deviation from my plan for two reasons. Firstly, you are with the Earl and I know that you will curb any aggressive tendencies. Secondly, the French will not expect this. For the last week or so we have brought in less and less. The French are withdrawing. I think that Pontoise is far enough from us to make the French feel safe."

"Do not worry, King Henry, the Earl appears to value my opinion. I am confident that he will do as you command." The King and the Earl were close, almost like brothers and the King did not wish to lose a dear friend. I was being told to guard the Earl of Warwick.

Our raids had drawn us closer together and I learned that he knew the King of France having stayed for eight days with him ten years earlier. His knowledge of Paris and the lands around was invaluable. I confess that I liked him for he was a brave leader and despite his eagerness for action was mindful of the responsibility of leading men into battle.

The first day we raided the north bank of the Seine opposite Vernon. There we found a castle. It would have been foolish to try to take the castle, but the Earl and I decided to destroy the bridge across the river which would make the castle less secure. Having taken the suburbs which were on the north bank and the people having fled across the wooden bridge which went first to an island and then to Vernon the Earl took half of the men, mainly the men at arms, to take what they could from the houses while I led the archers and some of the knights to take the bridge. The French had made a problem for themselves as the river was too wide for us to use our bows from the north bank but from the island, the bridgehead at Vernon was just one hundred and fifty paces away. It was well within range.

We ran unopposed to the island and some of those who fled before us risked hurling themselves into the river rather than face our blades. I had half the archers cut down some of the undergrowth on the island and pack it beneath the bridge while the rest of the archers, protected by the shields of the men at arms rained arrows on those fleeing towards Vernon. Our arrows were so accurate that they felled men on the two towers at the bridgehead. The crossbow bolts sent in return were ineffective for we had shields protecting our men and so the French sortied in an attempt to save the bridge. Despite the pleas for me to stay behind the archers, I was in the front with the other knights. It was not in my nature to let other men fight for me. The French sortied for they saw what we were doing and men at arms raced from the bridgehead to attack us.

The Captain of Archers was Jenkins, a Welshman. I would have preferred my archers to be behind me, but the Welsh Captain did not let me down. The war arrows we had used on the people fleeing were of limited use against the armoured men who ran from the bridgehead.

The Battle for France

"Bodkins!" There was the slightest of delay as archers switched missiles. In that time the Frenchmen came to within forty paces of us. "Release!"

Some of the French, the knights especially, had good plate and even bodkins did little damage, but some of the others wore mail or had gaps in their plate and those fell with arrows sticking from them. Others were hit and were wounded. Those who fell impeded the ones who followed and when the ragged line struck us, we were ready. The men at arms and knights who had survived and were at the fore all bore pole weapons, but we had our shields. The French, who knew what they were about, smashed their weapons into the shields to render them useless. The French knight with the red diagonal stripes on his jupon was one such and being amongst the first to reach us was able to swing the poleaxe and smash into my left arm. The shield, whilst a good one was not intended to take such a blow and I felt it crack and split as my arm was numbed. He had an open bascinet such as I wore, and I saw him grin when he heard the crack. He pulled the poleaxe back to use the spearhead to ram it at me. I did the one thing he did not wish me to do, I stepped forward and punched with my broken shield as I did so. His stab with the spearhead had less power and although the shield split, I used my sword to ram into his nose and up into his brain. His body juddered and he fell. The archers had cleared the far bridge and the survivors of the attempt to shift us fell back. I pulled the sword from the corpse and looked for more enemies.

Rafe shouted, "Ready to fire the bridge, my lord!" It was his way of ordering me back.

I saw that we had blunted their attack and Captain Jenkins' archers were still felling Frenchmen. "Fall back!"

The Earl of Warwick echoed my command and we fell back with our archers who still afforded us the cover of their war arrows as they loosed and nocked as they walked backwards. Four men stood at the end of the bridge leading from Vernon and lit that section before running back over the road to the shorter section leading to the north bank. With flames licking the other section they had the time to light a good fire. It was possible the French might be able to save some of the bridge leading to Vernon but not the shorter section. Another French castle which lay south of the Seine was in danger of being isolated and taken. We watched the flames bite into the wood and then retired to our camp.

We ate well in the suburbs north of the ruined bridge and the Earl was in ebullient mood. "You know, Strongstaff, I believe that we might be able to reach Paris."

I nodded, "And it is a fine city to view, as you know well, my lord, but this chevauchée is not ready to take on the French defences. All that our arrival will do will be to alert the defenders."

He nodded, "Nonetheless we will stop only when we see the walls of the city and the spire of St Denis."

I would go along with that, but I would resist any attempt to do more. Another bridge might be a bridge too far.

We ransacked and torched two more villages before we reached Pontoise and it was there that we saw the enemy. The Duke of Burgundy had raised an army. Word had reached him of the siege, and he had acted. All pretence of an alliance now lay in tatters and if nothing else the news would reach the King earlier than had we not done as the Earl had suggested. As soon as we were seen the French and Burgundian soldiers were summoned to form up. I turned to James and Rafe, "Ride back to the King and tell him that the French have an army and," I pointed, "they have a new Oriflamme. They mean war! Tell him that the French army is led by Duke John the Fearless. He will know what that portends."

They nodded and Rafe said, "No heroics, eh, Sir William?"

Pontoise lay on the River Oise and both the town and the castle guarded the bridge and road which led to Paris. The army led by Duke John was obviously on its way west. Perhaps they had hoped to surprise King Henry. At least we had a warning.

"What do you advise, Strongstaff?"

I turned and smiled, "With ten thousand men facing I do not advise a reckless charge!"

He laughed, "Even I am not foolish enough for that."

"Then I suggest we talk. I know John the Fearless and I have done him some service in the past. I think he will let us talk first. He may decide to be belligerent, but any delay will help King Henry prepare defences. We have a few hours until darkness and if we talk, he will have to wait until the morning to head to Rouen."

He nodded, seeing the wisdom in my words. We had made this journey in two days, but Duke John would need at least three to reach Rouen and by then the King could have turned his artillery to face the new threat. "You think he means to relieve the siege, Strongstaff?"

"I can see no other reason to raise an army. We shall see."

I turned to Michael, "Unfurl the banner. We will ride bareheaded with the Earl to speak with the Duke who would be king."

"Aye, Lord."

"Captain Jenkins, have your archers dismount and prepare to cover us if they decide they wish to have a battle."

The Battle for France

"Yes, my lord! Archers dismount, horse holders, take the horses to the rear. Plant your stakes!" Every archer carried a mallet and a sharpened stake. At night they would make an improvised fence and they afforded some protection from charging horses. The mallets were also useful when it came to dispatching Frenchmen! This way the stakes, sunk into the soft earth, would offer protection to our archers.

The Earl's squire unfurled his banner and with helmets hanging from our cantles we rode across the one thousand paces which separated us. Behind us, we heard the hammering as stakes were driven into the earth. They would be freshly sharpened only if the French formed to attack. We were travelling across fields planted with beans. I reflected that if the French did attack us, they would find the beanfield harder to cross than we and they would be destroying a crop. The burghers of Rouen might be ruing that they had destroyed their own crops to deny them to us, now they were starving.

The Bishop of Beauvais along with the Constable of France, the recently appointed Charles, Duke of Lorraine accompanied the Duke, but I knew that any decision would be made by John the Fearless. They reined in and Duke John grinned broadly, "I can see that King Henry holds you in high standing, Sir William, that he sends you to negotiate a surrender!"

I smiled back and shook my head, "You misunderstand, my lord, King Henry is of the opinion that France would be better ruled by him than one who seeks to sleep his way to the crown."

The insult was deliberate. I did not want the Duke to be comfortable. The Duke of Lorraine had only recently been appointed as Constable of France and he had been the Queen's appointee. That he was a favourite of the Queen might mean discord between the leaders. We had discovered the connection with the Queen when we had taken the suburbs of Vernon.

John the Fearless' eyes flashed angrily, and he shook his fist at me, "It is good that you have done me service before now. Any other would lie dead."

"Do not let that stop you, Duke John. You know that I fear no man, least of all one whose life I have saved twice. Of course, if you do not draw your sword then I will have saved your life three times!"

He smiled, realising what I was doing. "You are trying to provoke me and make my men charge your forest of stakes and die like my brother and so many others did at Agincourt."

I leaned forward and said, "Duke John, here we bring but seven hundred archers. When you find our army know that there are more than six thousand and each one has a hundred arrows. Have you enough men?" I saw doubt in his eyes, and I pushed him further, "This is a divided country you wish to take. The Dauphin and Tanneguy du Châtel have a French and Armagnac army. What happens when we defeat you? Will they take over Paris and Dijon?"

There was more than doubt in his eyes now and he nodded, "You understand France well, my friend, especially for an Englishman. Bishop, will you be our emissary to King Henry to see if there is a peaceful solution to this?"

I could see that the priest was not happy, but he nodded, "Of course, my lord." He looked pointedly at the Earl of Warwick rather than me, "I have your word, Earl, that I will be treated well?"

"Of course, Your Grace."

The Duke nodded, "You know, Strongstaff, that this means you have lost the manor I gave you?"

I smiled, "What is a manor when *I* still have honour?" I emphasised the word, "I did not break a promise. You were the one who said he would ally with King Henry." I tightened my cloak about my shoulders, "But I have seen Queen Isabeau and know that she can turn heads and twist men around her little finger. I thought you were more than that. It seems that I have been guilty of a misjudgement!" I held his gaze until he dropped it and jerked his reins around.

We turned the army around and headed back to Rouen. With the Bishop protected by our priests and the Earl's familia the Earl and I spoke. "You took a risk there, Strongstaff!"

"Did I? Tell me, my lord, what would have happened had he charged us?"

"As you said our archers would have rained death upon them but that is not the point. We could have lost men and you have lost a manor and its income!"

"Not as many as they would have lost, and it was worth it to hear the doubt in his voice. He fears Armagnac and, surprisingly, the Dauphin. That was worth the loss of a manor." I shrugged, "I had never even seen it anyway!"

We were met twenty miles from Rouen by the Earl of Salisbury with five hundred men at arms. He looked relieved when he saw that we were whole, "The King thought this the best way to give warning of an attack."

The Earl of Warwick nodded, "There will be no attack, not, at least, until the Bishop is returned to Beauvais where Duke John awaits."

"Nonetheless we will wait here."

"And how goes the siege?"

"They are starving, that much is obvious, but they are holding on!"

When the King saw us approach, he brought his own negotiators to speak with the Bishop. First, he spoke to the Earl and me to discover both our thoughts and our words. When the Earl told him what I had said, he smiled, "It is good that you never change, Strongstaff, and I think you chose the correct approach. If they fear the Dauphin and Armagnac, then it means that they are less likely to be in a position to attack us. To do that they need to be united. You have both done well. Rest for we shall have need of you soon."

Rafe and James had found us a house which we used and Michael and I went directly there for the times when I could ride for four or five days non-stop were long in the past. I was weary and needed both a bath and food. "Have we food?"

Rafe laughed, "Of course we have, my lord. We managed to forage on the way here. We relieved a rich merchant and his family of a leg of ham and a round of cheese. They were keeping it for Christmas."

"You did not kill them!"

They both looked offended, "My lord! of course not. Perhaps they were frightened by tales of Englishmen, I know not, but once we spoke English, they could not wait to give us food and have us leave!"

They were good cooks, as was Michael, and we had a fine meal. They forgot to mention that they had also relieved the merchant and his family of a small barrel of wine. Our Christmas would not be as mean as many. The negotiations lasted just two days and the Bishop of Beauvais returned to the Duke with the same terms I had offered, give the crown to King Henry or face further fighting.

At the end of the first week of December the gates opened and hundreds of poor people, mainly women and children and a few old ones were ejected, and the gates slammed shut behind them. King Henry acted swiftly. He rode to the ditch on his horse, "You go no further than the ditch!" They cried piteously and appealed to King Henry who showed his ruthless side, "I did not put you here, your commander did. If he surrenders, then you will be fed!"

A priest stood on the gatehouse and shouted, "I curse you, King Henry, by bell, book and candle! Your soul shall rot in hell!" That single action upset and angered the army more than any wound which might have been inflicted in battle. The priest had damned King Henry's soul!

Even though they were our enemies the plight of the poor upset many of our men and that first night dozens of them sneaked down to the ditch and risked a crossbow bolt to give them food, water and kindling for a fire. After three such nights King Henry heard, and he forbade it to continue. I was the one charged with ensuring that his orders were carried out. I had twenty of his personal guards with me and none of the charitable soldiers wished to risk the King's wrath. I did my duty and spent three hours there. While I did, I spoke with an old man who appeared to be their unofficial leader.

"You know why the King behaves this way?"

The old man had a crippled right hand which he held up, "Aye, lord for I was at Agincourt and I was a soldier. If he feeds us, then Guy Le Bouteiller will throw more out, and the siege will last longer." He shook his head, "It is not right, lord. We were ordered to find ten months of food. Where could we find that? The four thousand Burgundians eat well enough!"

I nodded, "I will speak with my King. He is not heartless."

All that I managed to persuade King Henry to do was to feed them on Christmas Day. For my part, I gave the rest of the ham to them. A Christian could not eat knowing that the poor were starving. I believe that more than half of the poor were saved by that single Christian act. I am not sure if all those who were evicted were poor because some of the men watching them thought that three had been soldiers who left the ditch and fled. When in early January a priest came to speak to the commander of the garrison of Rouen it was confirmation that he had formerly been in the besieged city for when the man was admitted he did not return. Perhaps the horse he rode fed the garrison for an extra day or two.

I was not at the walls the day that the citizens contacted Sir Gilbert Umphraville. I had the loose bowels which often preceded dysentery and death. When King Henry sent for our leaders Rafe told them that I was indisposed. As the pursuivant left, somewhat shaken by Rafe's response, my former man at arms said, "The King has other knights who can fetch and carry for him! Now begone before you feel the strength of my arm!" He turned to me, "You have done enough, my lord, and we will see you well before you are tasked with such service!"

They gave me a soldier's remedy. I was fed eggs cooked with cheese. I know not where they found the eggs and I had equal measures of the sweet red wine which comes from Portugal mixed with brandy. There was little point in objecting. I had three of them to contend with. The remedy worked and after three days my movements were almost normal.

As soon as I was able, I went to speak to the King to tell him why I had been absent. Rather than anger, I was greeted with real concern, "You are well, Strongstaff? Had I known you were unwell I would not have disturbed you."

"Aye, my lord, and I am sorry if Rafe caused offence."

He laughed, "Rafe was it? My pursuivant was shaking when he returned. Would that I had a thousand Rafes fighting for me."

"And how goes the siege, King Henry?"

"We shall know in three days. Some of those within Rouen said that they wished to surrender but the soldiers within said they would wait until relieved. It was agreed that if no relief had come by the nineteenth then they would surrender."

"And will they?"

He smiled, "Aye, we have smelled the burning flesh from their dead. The siege has begun to bite, and the Duke of Burgundy has miscalculated. He should have come to their aid and now the city of Rouen will pay the price."

The siege had taken far longer than he had expected, and I feared his anger. I risked censure, "My lord, what retribution can the citizens expect?"

"This is my land and unlike the Duke of Burgundy, I will not make enemies of my people. I will allow any soldier to leave once they have left their arms. If any of the citizens will not swear allegiance to the crown, then they shall be evicted too."

"That is all?"

He shook his head, "Alain Blanchard will be hanged for his murder of prisoners and I shall imprison that priest! He upset my men!"

Chapter 8

The King was as good as his word and fewer than four hundred of the folk of Rouen refused to swear. They were sent from the town with just the clothes on their backs. The head of the Captain of Crossbows adorned the gatehouse until the birds had pecked all the flesh from it and the skull was unrecognisable. The next months saw the completion of the campaign and, except for Mont St Michel, the whole of Normandy was King Henry's. We had not taken France, but we had gone a long way to doing so.

Envoys were sent to the Duke of Burgundy and the King and Queen of France. King Henry wanted to negotiate not just peace but a bride! I, of course, was deemed unacceptable to be the emissary and I was quite happy not to be given the task. A meeting was set up at Meulan just twelve miles from Pontoise. I was with the King but in the background and I heard of the discussions second hand through the Earl of Warwick.

In the evening we sat in the house we had commandeered and drank the good wine the merchant who had lived there kept in his extensive cellar, "The King wants Katherine, and she is a pretty young thing."

I remembered when her older sister, Isabella, had been the child bride of poor King Richard. Katherine was twelve years her junior and bearing in mind her mother's reputation I wondered if King Charles was the father.

"And he will water down his demands?" I knew King Henry but I wondered if his desire for a bride and an heir might have mellowed him.

The Earl laughed, "No, Sir William; we keep all the lands promised in the last treaty as well as full sovereignty over Normandy. Besides that, he demands a dowry of eight hundred thousand gold crowns!"

Shaking my head I said, "The French will not agree."

"It all depends upon the Duke of Burgundy. I believe he might agree but he fears that, if he does then his French support will turn against him. He sent men to Rouen, but they failed to relieve the siege. The French are fickle and while the Parisian mob has handed him power, they can just as easily turn against him."

The Battle for France

He was right and terms could not be agreed. We returned to Rouen and a further meeting was arranged for July. As we rode back King Henry was in a belligerent mood for he was an astute leader who knew how other men's minds worked. "Duke John is playing for time. He thinks I will send my army home. We will not for we now have money to pay our soldiers and more will soon be coming from England." They might not have had much food in Rouen, but they had a full treasury and King Henry's generosity did not stretch to letting the French army and the lords leave with anything more than their lives. All had been searched before they were allowed to leave, and it was not just weapons which were taken but also any coins.

I confess I wondered about asking the King if I could return home. My brief bout of illness had left me weaker than I wished, and I was feeling my age. When I mentioned it to Rafe and James they were all in favour. We had profited from the war and the loss of my manor in Brabant was insignificant compared with the chests of treasure we had gathered.

Michael seemed disappointed, "My lord, I think you are still needed here. I was with you at Pontoise. No other could have done what you did. The King needs you but if you would go home then I will follow."

Perhaps it was the oysters I ate with my meal but that night, as I had a fitful sleep, my wife's spirit came to me. She said nothing in the dream, for I knew it was a dream, but she stroked both Prince Hal and Michael's head and her smile told me that I should stay. She had loved them both dearly: Hal as a surrogate son and Michael as a grandson. Having made the decision, I threw myself into the appointed tasks which King Henry gave to me. We would be riding, when we went to war, in one battle. We had too few men to divide our forces. Even if the civil war did not end and the two parties kept apart each element would have had more men than we. We prepared for war and I joined with the King and the Earl of Warwick in poring over the lists of men and animals. War to us was a business. It became more and more apparent that the French would not meet in July and word reached us that before July there was to be a meeting in Paris between the two parties: the Burgundian and Armagnac factions. The Dauphin and du Châtel would meet close to Paris on a bridge across the river. King Henry declared the truce over. We were going to war!

The natural place to head for was Pontoise and as the Earl of Warwick as well as I had been there we rode with the van and King Henry. Our rapid movement, for we were all well mounted, caught the French by surprise. As we approached the town the gates were still open as refugees had been fleeing before our advance. There were just five

The Battle for France

hundred knights and men at arms in the vanguard but with the King, his brothers, the Earl and me leading the men we were the equal of any and the Duke of Burgundy had taken his best men with him. Hercules had proved himself to be a great warhorse. He had become better with each passing month as we came to know each other. Now, as we raced towards the open gates, even the King and the Earl's mounts struggled to keep pace with him. Armed men were trying to close them but the press of bodies trying to get within was too great. The sight of Hercules powering towards them made some hurl themselves at the gates which prevented their closure and I managed to ride through them, followed a heartbeat later by King Henry and the Earl of Warwick. I reined Hercules around and aimed his head at the nearest man at arms. He stopped trying to close the gate and drew his sword to hack at me. I pulled back on Hercules' reins and his forehoof clattered into the man at arms' helmet. It was a good helmet, but the blow killed the brave Frenchman.

We had the gate but now crossbow bolts were sent at us. There were still refugees in the gateway, and they suffered some of the casualties. One bolt hit my cantle, and another pinged off the side of my helmet. Until our archers could reach us and dismount then the crossbows could hurt us. The only advantage we had was that they were slow to load.

Turning in my saddle I shouted to the Earl and the King, "Follow me, my lords!"

The gateway was now filled with our men and we had entry into the town but if King Henry was hit, as King Richard had been two centuries earlier then all was lost. I spurred Hercules and, while swinging my sword, I led the King and his nobles into the narrow streets of Pontoise. There was a bridge at the far end we needed to take and crossbows could not be sent at us while we were in the narrow streets. By reaching the bridge we would secure entry into Paris and made it less likely that the King would be hit. As we rode through the French town which until a day or so earlier had been Duke John's headquarters, the populace used everything that they could to slow us. They threw stones, jugs, pots, anything, in fact, which might hurt us. To men in plate armour, they were nothing and they bounced off doing no harm whatsoever. The galloping horses forced the French defenders to leave the narrow street and we did not even have to use our swords.

As we reached the bridge gate, I saw that it was defended, and the armed and mailed men who were there were trying to close it. This time we would have to fight for we needed the gate open so that we could secure the bridge and prevent its destruction. The bolt which hit me was a lucky strike. I was swinging my sword at the French man at arms with the spear and my sword hit the missile. It slowed it and deflected it at the same time. It struck my cheek and entering my mouth rattled my teeth. I reached up with my left hand and pulled the bolt out which, thankfully, was not barbed. My sword had made the man at arms' spear miss and as I raised my arm for another strike, I whipped Hercules' head around. It made the man at arms flinch and I brought my sword across his shoulder. Over the years I had found this an effective blow for even if it did not cut through to flesh it was often enough to break the bone there. When he fell to his knees, I knew that I succeeded in breaking it!

Hercules' race to the gate had spurred King Henry and the Earl of Warwick along with their familia and it was they who cut down those at the gateway allowing the King himself to gallop to the bridge. His household knights were in close attendance and one fell into the river when a lucky bolt from the other end found his open face. His death made the King pause and order his knights to dismount. We had the bridge, and we did not need to risk men. Our archers could clear the far end. We needed to secure the town.

Captain Jenkins and a company of mounted archers had followed as close to the King as they could and I waved them to his side, "Captain, the far end has crossbows and defenders. They have killed one of the King's men!"

"Aye lord," he needed no instructions for the archer knew what was necessary. If there was one enemy archers hated more than any other, it was crossbowmen, and he dismounted his men to lead them over the wooden bridge. Even while they were on this side some of his better archers tried an arrow at long range and when there was a scream from the far bank then I knew that the French were doomed. None could withstand our archers.

The King brought half of his knights and men at arms inside the castle, "Warwick, support the archers and gain us the north bank." He paused, "Be mindful that we will need every knight when we face the French and the Duke of Burgundy."

"Aye, my lord." I had no fears about the Earl. The reckless lord had changed in the time he had been in Normandy.

The King turned to me, "Come, Strongstaff. We still have work to do and, mayhap, the Duke left documents here which might aid us."

The King had a mind which was made for war. While others might just have thought about securing the town, King Henry was already planning what might come next. There were still many defenders in the town. Our rapid attack had cut many off from an escape. The King's jupon and his familia were like a weapon. When we appeared then soldiers who were fighting dropped their swords to surrender. Of course, I was with the King too and I still had a reputation. The raid I had led to avenge the squires of Agincourt was told by soldiers around campfires. Rafe and James had discovered that when we had captured French soldiers. By the end of the day, the town was ours and the King and I found not only a chest of coins but also a table littered with papers. Some were idle scribblings, but others gave information. The Duke had sent to Burgundy for more men. There was also evidence that he was seeking an alliance against us with the Duke of Brittany!

King Henry shook his head, "No matter what there will be no alliance with John the Fearless now. He has burnt his bridges. This will end in battle. I cannot trust the man."

"I think, my lord, that the Queen of France has ensnared him. She is a beautiful and alluring woman."

He looked at me, "You think her attractive?"

I nodded, "Just as the deadly nightshade is a beautiful but deadly flower. There was only one woman who held my heart, my lord, and she is dead. I am immune to Queen Isabeau's charms."

"But you are counselling caution in me."

I laughed, "My lord, you are the most single-minded king I have ever known. You will wed Katherine of Valois and none will draw you from her."

He began to gather the documents, "It is good that at least one of those who follow me know me and my heart."

"My lord, why should I not? I protected your family since before you were born. I have witnessed every act which affected you. Your father was not with you in Ireland when King Richard held you, but I was. It is the reason I stay here now when I am old and should be let out to pasture. I still have a task to perform!"

"Strongstaff, you never grow old! As I followed you through the gate, I could have been transported back to Weedon when I followed your banner!" He gestured towards my wound, "And now obey another order. Have your cheek tended to! You would not have a scar like your king, would you?"

I nodded and obeyed. The healers made a good job but there would be a scar there. A reminder that I was mortal.

Even while the baggage was entering the town the King was issuing orders, "Clarence, take a thousand men and get to St-Denis. Put your spearheads in the backs of the French. We will follow soon."

His younger brother was keen for more glory and he happily obeyed. We gathered treasure and food for this was not Normandy, this was France and while we were fed the French would starve. After leaving a

The Battle for France

small garrison under Sir John Page whom the King had knighted for his bravery in the charge through Pontoise, we headed for Paris. The Duke of Clarence had told us that he held the town, and the cathedral was his. St Denis was a holy place for the French and its capture would hurt them. The Oriflamme was normally kept there and there was something magical about the church. It was also a mere six miles from the walls of Paris.

I rode with Warwick, the Duke of Gloucester, and the King as we headed to Paris. The Duke was in confident mood, "We have Paris now, brother! All of France will fall!"

The Earl of Warwick shook his head, "Paris is ten times the size of Rouen and they have layer upon layer of walls and defences, culminating in the river which protects the island where they will have their final defence. We would need an army at least five times as big as we fetch to surround the town. I visited here and I know the city. The King can demand a meeting and we can try to force a battle, but we cannot besiege Paris. It has grown too big!"

"The Earl is right, brother. We can threaten but if they resolve to squat within its walls then we will have to do as the Black Prince did before Poitiers and raid the land to force them to battle." The famous chevauchée had resulted in the great victory of Poitiers and I knew that King Henry knew that and the plan was already in his mind should he need to use it.

When our army was reunited, we heard from prisoners captured by the Duke of Clarence that the royal family, including Katherine of Valois, had fled to Troyes which was close to Burgundy. We also learned that the two opposing sides were meeting to form an alliance. The Duke, the Dauphin and Tanneguy du Châtel were meeting at a bridge in Paris. That suited King Henry.

We held a council of war outside the walls of Paris in a large and well-furnished house we had commandeered, "I care not if we are outnumbered by France, Burgundy and Armagnac. They will be as divided as they were at Agincourt. We choose a ground where we can defend our flanks with archers protected by our stakes and we let their men at arms fall upon our lances and swords." Scouts were sent out to find such a piece of ground.

In the event it proved unnecessary. Duke John was treacherously murdered by Tanneguy du Châtel. The actual details were murky, and some said that the Dauphin had a hand in the murder but whatever the reason there would be no battle and King Henry now held the high ground. There was no truce but nor did King Henry campaign aggressively. We occupied Pontoise where we could threaten Paris, but the main protagonists had left. We were, effectively, the rulers of Paris and therefore, France. We need not fight for the opposition was now fighting amongst themselves. Whichever side emerged victorious would have to face us and I knew that none of them relished that thought. The King spent the next months securing the land around Paris and finding a suitable emissary to begin talks of peace. He wanted the French crown and that meant diplomacy.

I was not needed. He allowed me to go home. It was not a charitable act for he wished me to raise men. Parliament had baulked at providing more money for his quest for the French crown and so it would be up to those who were loyal to him to do so. Before we left, at the end of October, he insisted upon knighting Michael. He had done so for Sir John Page who had done less than my squire. In truth he was ready, and Michael was knighted in the Cathedral of St Denis. Only Rafe and James, from my men at arms, knights and archers were there to witness the dubbing but there were no prouder parents than my two former men at arms. They had helped to make Michael what he was. He was a modest and grateful young man, and he thanked the three of us as though he had done nothing to achieve the honour.

James shook his head, "Sir Michael," he gave the title as though it was a fine wine to be savoured, "You have done more to be knighted than any other I have seen. You are like Sir William reborn and you will be a great knight. Rafe and I are just pleased that we lived long enough to see this. We can die happy!"

Rafe, laughed, "Speak for yourself."

We were so keen to leave that we left at terces. We were just outside the city and, as we looked back the sun erupted in the sky to the east. It was a spectacular sunrise. It looked like the sky was on fire. The reds went from yellowy orange to almost purple and we were so moved that we watched it until the sun had risen. Then just as suddenly as it had come clouds filled the sky and it became grey. We turned our horses and continued north and west.

Michael said, "That was a sign, my lord."

I nodded, "And it is like our lives, Michael. We have brightness and joy, but it is over before we know it. We savoured the sunrise, savour your life too for it will be over all too soon."

He nodded as he took it in, "And yet you, Rafe and James have lived a long time!"

James laughed, "We are not as old as Sir William!"

Michael smiled, "Yet, Sir William apart, you are the oldest men I know. How is that?"

The Battle for France

James looked to the west, our home and said, simply, "We have been lucky but as every gambler will tell you, that runs out one day. No matter, Rafe and I have had good lives and better than most. I am content."

Rafe snorted, "You are a miserable old curmudgeon! Do not be the cloud to Sir Michael's sunrise!"

Laden with the booty we had taken, we returned to Calais in a long caravan with those who had either been wounded in the sieges or had completed their indenture. We reached Weedon at the start of December. We were at home when we heard that the Earl of Warwick had signed a truce between the two sides. There was, for the first time in a long time, peace between France and England. Of course, the war was not truly over for there had to be a treaty. A treaty was not something in which I would be involved. I had done as my wife had asked on her death bed and I had stood by the King. He did not need me now, at least not for a while, and I spent the first Christmas for a couple of years, back at Weedon. A newly knighted Michael and the riches we had brought back meant that my family came to visit with me, and to stay for more than a couple of days. I saw grandchildren now grown beyond recognition and that showed in their nervousness when they were near to me. They did not know this old man with the new angry scar on his face. The younger ones, especially the girls, seemed to fear me. It made me sad, but I had time to remedy that for I had finished with war, albeit temporarily.

The King's last words to me were, "I need you back here in France by the summer of the next campaigning season. That should allow you the time to find twenty archers and twenty men at arms! My brother Clarence can hold France until then." That was the time I had left to get to know my grandchildren while obeying the King's commands.

The Treaty of Troyes was signed at Troyes. The King had the support of the new Duke of Burgundy, Phillipe and, surprisingly, Queen Isabeau. That the Dauphin was not present was immaterial. Indeed, the Queen had spread doubts as to his father. She said it was not King Charles. King Henry would marry Katherine Valois and the Dauphin Charles was disinherited. King Henry would inherit the title King of France once King Charles died and King Henry promised to rule the two lands separately. The title he gained was Regent and Heir of France. King Henry was wise enough not to offend the French. He ruled through their *parlement* and their three estates. He changed not one law. All this was seen by me from afar.

The Battle for France

Chapter 9

Although a treaty had been signed I knew that so long as Tanneguy du Châtel and the Dauphin were abroad there could be no real peace and so I set about obeying my King's command and raising a company of men to fight in France. I had time and I set about recruiting carefully for I knew that this might be my last campaign. I was, so far as I could work out almost sixty-eight or sixty-nine years of age. Red Ralph had been vague about such matters. How much longer could I expect my luck to last? I heard regular news from France and Normandy. The King had quickly wrapped up the resistance. Only Melun held out and that was because it was commanded by a true robber baron, the Sire de Barbazon. There was fierce fighting in the mines, and I heard, from a returning lord who visited with me, that King Henry himself had fought beneath the castle. It was a hard siege for there were many Scots in the castle and town. King Henry asked King James of Scotland, who served with him, to demand their surrender, but they refused. At the end of the siege, there was much retribution. King Henry hanged many Scots and the men who had defied him. The Earl of Buchan who had tried to have me killed was one of the prisoners and a large ransom was demanded for his freedom.

The King and his Queen returned to England after the marriage in Paris. The royal couple spent Christmas in Paris with the King and Queen of France as well as the Duke of Burgundy. Queen Katherine was crowned Queen of England in Westminster Abbey. I did not attend even though I was invited. Such ceremony was no longer for me. If I did not need to attend, then I would not. King Henry was keen that he should make England know who he was, and he and the Queen went on separate tours of England. He was a tireless King.

Most of the men who had been on the vengeance raid had not fought for five years. I did not think that they would be coming to war with me for the ones who had wished service had joined the retinues of other lords. I had seen some in Normandy. The ones who had stayed at Weedon had kept their skills and guarded my home, but England between Agincourt and the Treaty of Troyes was a peaceful place. There is a world of difference between practising sword and bow skills

The Battle for France

and fighting. I needed fighting men, but I would heed the advice of my former brothers in arms. I still trusted their judgement.

Michael, too, had responsibilities. He needed a squire, as did I. There was no need for him to have a manor yet. He would be my household knight and count as one of the men at arms I needed. We went to the weaponsmith, once Christmas was over, to have better armour made and a set of spurs, which I paid for. He was now as near fully grown as he was likely to be. As his livery, he took mine with a hawk upon it. I liked it.

When I sent to my former men at arms and knights, I was pleasantly surprised when Sir Stephen and Sir Oliver promised to come and to bring with them a further eight men at arms. I had more than half of the men at arms I needed already, and the messenger who returned told me they would reach Weedon by March. Kit Warhammer and Karl the Dane had also had enough of a peaceful life although the fact that they had both chosen farming and wives who turned out to be scolds may have also had an influence. The two men at arms who had stayed at Weedon and been my captains were Uriah Longface and Gilbert of Ely. They both chose to come with us too. Between them, my sons and son in law sent me five men at arms. Rafe drily commented that they had not volunteered their services, but I silenced him with a look. They had made their choices and if they lived and became family men then so be it. I was a warrior and could not change my stars. John of Northampton, Richard son of James, Peter Poleaxe, Henry son of John and Reginald of Raby were all sound warriors and I learned later that they had all tired of the dull life in my son's castles.

Matthew the Millerson, Christopher White Arrow, Harry Fletcher, and Walter of Sheffield were four of my veteran archers who were happy to come and I sent the four of them on the road to return with other archers. Matthew returned within a week and had with him Owen the Welshman who, it seems, had fallen on hard times. Owen always liked a drink and had either spent or lost most of his money. However, he was an archer, and he kept his bow and gardyvyan. My other archers would bring him back to the fold. We found archers easily enough for my archers told the candidates that they would make a fortune serving me and we had more than we needed. The best of them were hired to go to France while the others were paid less and allowed to serve at Weedon.

The need for two squires was more of a problem. All the squires who had served me in the past had been known to me. They had either been my children or the children of my men at arms and knights. Poor Walter had died at Agincourt and his death still weighed heavily upon my shoulders. Michael was the exception. God had sent him to me. It was March and we still had not found two suitable candidates. Michael's came from a surprising source. Alan of the Woods had a son, Jack. He had been training as an archer and was indeed one of the best archers I had ever seen. When he had been growing and I was still at home, I had been impressed by his progress. I visited Alan to ask if his son, Jack, could come with me as an archer for I knew that he could ride. I arrived in the middle of March. I had with me Sir Michael along with Sir Stephen and Sir Oliver. They were old friends of Alan and wished to speak with him. We found my former archer in low spirits and all thoughts of asking for his help went from my mind.

"What is amiss, Alan?"

He shook his head, "It is Jack, my lord. He has suffered an injury last week. He is not himself and sees no point in life any longer."

His wife poured us ale and I could see that she was upset too.

"Tell us all!" I would not, it seems, be taking Jack to war.

"He and his older brother Stephen were copsing the hawthorn and using billhooks. Stephen was distracted," he shook his head, "Stephen is my firstborn and as lovely a youth as you could wish but he is a little slow and his mind wandered. He mistimed his blow with the bill hook and took one and a half fingers from Jack's right hand."

We all knew immediately what that meant, he would not be able to draw a bow. All thoughts of taking him as an archer disappeared. That was as nothing compared to the loss the young man had suffered. He was meant to be an archer, the equal of his father perhaps and now, although he would be able to work, for he had great strength, he was denied the one thing he was good at.

"What will he do?"

"His brother is the farmer. Stephen showed no interest in the bow. Jack knows nothing else. I taught him to ride and to use a sword. What else is there?"

We looked in silence at one another until Michael said, "If he wished, Alan of the Woods, he could be my squire."

I was the one with the swiftest mind for I saw, in an instant, that this was a perfect solution, if the young man would take it. The others, however, could not see that it was a solution. Alan shook his head, "A kind offer, Michael, but he has not been brought up to be a squire."

I laughed and waved a hand around the four of us, "Not one of the four knights in your home was brought up to be a knight! I followed the Blue Company, Stephen and Oliver were men at arms and we rescued Michael from a pile of bodies! Ask your son! Let him make the decision. It would suit both Michael and me for we have a short time before we must go to France and fight once more for King Henry."

"I can ask."

His sons were sent for and I saw immediately what he meant about Stephen who was dull-witted but had a pleasant smile. It seemed to me that he was not even sure what he had done. Certainly, Jack did not blame his elder brother. I had not noticed that when they were younger but now it was clear. Stephen would be a farmer but unless Jack chose to follow Michael, I could see no satisfaction in his life.

Both boys knew me for Alan had often brought them to see me before I went to France and fought at Agincourt. I saw that Jack's hand was still heavily bandaged. They bowed. I nodded to Alan to speak, "Jack, you are low in spirits. How do feel about serving Sir Michael who is newly knighted by King Henry himself?"

Jack seemed not able to take it in and looked from his father to me and back. Michael said, quietly, "I know the fear you have, Jack, for I felt the same when Sir William first made me his squire. You wonder if you can do the job and if anything in you is lacking."

Jack nodded, "You are right, my lord, and those are my fears for I cannot sing and I am clumsy, how can I wait on great lords? But also, I have a maimed hand!"

I spoke, "And that will not stop you using a sword although these days battles are often fought on foot with pole weapons. Your strength will overcome any infirmity."

Sir Stephen said, "Aye, Sir William is right and as for all the rest, with due respect to Sir William, all the work of waiting on lords and learning to sing," he shook his head," just nonsense. He never learned and neither did we."

I think Stephen's bluff northern accent swayed him and Jack nodded, "Aye, with my father's permission I shall be a squire."

There was joy in Alan's house for although there was danger ahead for Jack his mother and father knew that it was in his blood to go to war and men should always follow their destiny. His father was not poor, and Jack was fitted out well. He rode Michael's palfrey which was a sound horse. His father had killed and taken enough men at arms in his time to have a good sword and scabbard, not to mention a fine sallet. We had one squire.

My squire came about equally strangely. I visited Sir John of Dauentre who had been my squire and had been on the vengeance raid with me. I went to speak with him out of courtesy. He had left France before we had completed our quest and he brought back the body of Sir Henry of Stratford. For many reasons, some of which I did not

The Battle for France

understand myself, we had not spoken since then. Five years was long enough, and I went to speak with him to clear the air and my conscience. I did not wish to die in some war with bad feelings for one who had been close to me.

He had aged and that shocked me. I went with just Rafe and James who would not let me stir a step without protection. As they told me on the way back to Weedon they too noticed the grey hair. "My lord, it is good to see you. It has been too long!"

I embraced him in silence for the sight of him brought back many memories. His father had been my steward and Eleanor and I had been close to both. "It has been too long, and I should have come sooner."

He shook his head, "It is my fault, I was embarrassed, and I have a stiff neck. I felt guilt for leaving you. You had trained me, and I could not face war. I have paid the price. My nights are tormented."

"Let us put that behind us. How is your lady?"

He shook his head, "She died two years ago."

He had not told me and that was a measure of the fracture. "I am sorry. She was a fine lady and both Eleanor and I liked her."

"I know and I was sorry to hear of Lady Eleanor's death."

"And your children?"

"They are well but Rufus, my youngest, is a problem."

"How so and is there aught I can do to help?"

"Come into my solar for there may be." He turned to his housekeeper who hovered close by, "Have rooms for Sir William and his men prepared."

Once seated in the solar, his steward poured us wine. Dauentre was a rich manor and provided me with my greatest income. Sir John also did well from it. "My other children are happy with a life of peace. I no longer even have a squire and therein lies the problem with Rufus. He wants to be a warrior. My sergeant at arms has trained him and, no doubt filled his head with stories of when we served with you. He is wild and I have had to chastise and punish him on many occasions. He starts fights with other young men. Even now I have him on his knees in St Cuthbert's church to atone for breaking another's coxcomb. When night falls, he will return but he will not be repentant."

I smiled, "Then I can help! I need a squire and immediately. I sail to France with King Henry."

It seemed he heard not the first part but just the second. "Am I needed, Sir William?"

I sensed the fear that I would answer yes in his voice and I shook my head, "As I learned, to my cost with Sir Henry, better to leave behind those who do not wish to war. I have the men I need."

He looked relieved. If a man did not wish to fight, then if you took him to war he would die.

"It is kind of you to offer to help with my son, but he is not like me, nor Ralph, nor any of your other squires. He is my son but he is arrogant. You and I saw many young nobles just like him, my lord. I would hate to think of you wasting your time."

"Are you saying he is not worth the work?"

"Never, Sir William, he is my son and I love him dearly, but I see his faults and his flaws."

"Then perhaps I need to atone too. I have been, as you say, lucky with my squires. This may be a test from God to make my last squire, a good one."

When Rufus came in, I saw a young version of John. It took me back to the keen young man who was desperate to please me. I also saw the anger on his face and in his eyes. He balled his fists when his father called him over. He was bursting with something inside. His father was right, he was unrepentant. He scowled at his father and then saw me. He adopted a less belligerent look and uncurled his hands.

"Rufus, this is the knight who taught me, Sir William Strongstaff."

His whole demeanour changed in an instant. His eyes widened and he bowed, "I am sorry, Sir William, I did not know…"

My voice was stern, "That is obvious else you would not have shown your father such disrespect in his own hall. I am not the one who needs the apology."

"I am sorry, father."

John had always been a most polite and pleasant young man and I saw it now as he smiled and forgave his son directly, "Of course, Rufus, and I accept your apology."

I shook my head, "If he was to be my squire, Sir John, he would have much to learn." I saw now the Herculean task I would be setting myself. Every other squire I had trained had been easy. They had been obedient and pliable. Perhaps this one would challenge me for his father was right he was like every other young noble who had been brought up to think that he was better than everyone else. His good looks and the skills inherited from his father would have compounded the problem. I would have to take him apart and then rebuild him. Would I have time left to me to complete the task?

"Rufus, Sir William here needs someone to go to war in France with him and I have said that your dearest wish is to be a squire."

"It is father! I want that more than anything! Thank you, Sir William, to be trained by the man who trained kings and then guarded them… there is no greater honour and I swear I will work hard."

"I have not said yet that I will train you. From what I have seen you may not be worth the effort. If your father was not the magistrate here, then for your crimes you would have been punished more severely than spending a day on your knees in a church!" Had I slapped him I could not have hurt him more. His face fell.

"But my lord, I was only that way because I could not train as a squire."

I nodded, "So to get your own way you deliberately cause mischief?" He could see that the hole he was digging was becoming deeper. "If, and I repeat, if, I am to train you then you should know some things about me. I grew up not like you, a pampered and spoiled noble. I was a camp brat who had to forage for food and was beaten almost on a daily basis. My friends are not nobles but men who are of common stock, archers, spearmen, mercenaries. I do not indulge myself in fine food but eat whatever the most common soldier is given. I work long hours and I expect no reward. My squire, as your father will tell you, works equally hard."

His face lit up, "I understand, and I accept all of those terms."

"And do you also accept that like Walter of Middleham who died at Agincourt, death is as likely an outcome as glory?"

He took pause and steeled himself, "Aye, I do."

"Then I shall try you. If you fail to live up to my high standards, then you will be returned to your father."

"You will see, Sir William, I will impress you!"

Sir John held out his arm to me, "Thank you, Sir William. I am in your debt and perhaps you can succeed where I have so patently failed."

"You have not failed. When he was growing up, I took you from him. I failed you and the youth has failed himself. Let us see if I can make up for my failure."

"He has a good sword and a bascinet as well as a mail hauberk, chaussee and a brigandine. He can have my courser for he is well trained and hardy."

"He will need a sumpter too. I shall provide the surcoat and jupon and now, Sir John, I have an appetite and Rufus can begin his lessons."

Sir John smiled and Rufus looked from me to his father and back.

His father said, "What he means, Rufus, is that this night you wait at the table and eat when we have finished!"

The realisation set in. He had been on his knees in a cold church all day and now he was told that he could not eat for hours more. I could almost hear his stomach rumbling.

The next day, as we rode home, I deliberately ignored him so that he had to speak to Rafe and James. It was all part of his education. I had

The Battle for France

seen young men like Rufus all my life. De Vere, the Earl of Oxford showed how they turned out if they became lords with power. Rafe and James had seen many squires. He would have to be special to be better than Michael had been, and I heard him trying to impress them with his deeds in Dauentre. They did what I knew they would do, they picked at him with their rough humour and took away any illusions he might have held. He failed to impress them and it was a most miserable young man who began to unpack his things back at Weedon. Rafe and James made no attempt to help him and it was left to Jack, Michael's new squire, to help him out. That was no bad thing for they would both learn together. In many ways, they were a perfect combination. Rufus knew how a squire should behave and could teach Jack the niceties of table service while Jack knew about horses and weapons. Perhaps this was meant to be.

As it turned out my early return with Rufus was fortuitous for three days later King Henry and his household knights rode in to my courtyard. Had Eleanor been alive then she would have blamed me for his sudden arrival as though I should and could have divined it. The King would take my hall as he found it. However, when he dismounted and then entered, he seemed distracted. He had lived in the hall and I had expected some comment, but he was preoccupied and went directly to the main hall where he sat at the table, "Rufus, find Jack and Alfred, my steward. Fetch food and drink."

The two of us were alone in the hall. Michael was training with the new men at arms. The King looked at me bleakly, "My brother, Clarence, is dead!" My natural reaction was to ask how but I knew the King would tell me in his own time and way. "He was a foolish young man and perhaps I should have left Warwick in command, but my young brother begged for the chance. He charged five thousand dismounted men at arms and archers with just fifteen hundred horsemen. It was a disaster. Had not Salisbury been close by and extracted the survivors then all that we won with the treaty of Troyes would have been lost!"

The wine came in and was poured. I waved a hand to dismiss the three of them. Jack and Alfred turned to go but Rufus did not. Alfred was not delicate, and he and Jack forcibly took Rufus from the room.

"Where was this, my lord?"

"Not far from Angers, at a place called Baugé. Apart from my brother we lost John Grey, John de Ros, William de Ros and Gilbert de Umfraville." I knew them all and Gilbert was a particularly gifted knight. "And we lost men who were captured, John Beaufort, the Earl of Somerset, Thomas Beaufort, John Holland, and Walter FitzWalter.

The Battle for France

The losses are bad enough, but the Scots fought with the French and now our two enemies are cock a hoop. It is our first defeat." He downed the goblet in one, "And now we must return sooner rather than later. We take a ship in June; can you be ready?"

"Of course. Will you stay with us this night?"

He stood and shook my hand. Smiling sadly, he said, "I am afraid I cannot. It seems I am destined not to spend a great deal of time with my wife and she is beautiful, William. I know why I married her, but she has won my heart and I pray that my marriage can be as good as yours and Lady Eleanor." He waved a hand at the room, "This hall exudes the love and joy you both enjoyed. I wish for half as much!"

When he had gone, I sent for Michael and asked him to gather my archers, knights, and men at arms. They knew something was amiss and when I told them Michael said, "I knew that the Duke had weaknesses, lord."

The new knight said, "Aye, Sir William, had you not been with him in Normandy then who knows what other mistakes he might have made."

"He has paid the ultimate price for such mistakes and you would do well not to speak thus before the King."

Michael grinned, "Sir William, just because I was knighted does not mean that I have lost all my senses."

I knew that I was a lucky man to have such good warriors following my banner. Would Rufus end up the same or was I due my first failure?

The Battle for France

Chapter 10

We had a shorter crossing this time for we sailed from Dover but while we were waiting for the tide and the wind the first result of the defeat was made known to us. The Duke of Brittany had allied himself with the French. Baugé had shown him that we could be beaten. We no longer enjoyed a secure border. The good news we had was that the new Duke of Burgundy, Philippe, had allied with us. It was to be hoped he would not be as fickle as his father but only time would tell. When we landed in Calais, he was there to meet with us and it was decided that while he would campaign in the north, in Picardy, we would tackle the Dauphinist strongholds south of the Seine.

First, we headed for Paris. The Duke of Exeter commanded there and guarded King Charles. Since the murder of Duke John, Queen Isabeau had seemingly withdrawn from public life. Perhaps she, too, feared her son. It was from the Duke of Exeter that we learned that the town of Dreux had declared for the Dauphinists and their soldiery were raiding the outskirts of Paris. The disaster of Baugé had emboldened many places and not for the last time we spoke disparagingly of the Duke of Clarence. We did not do so in the hearing of the King for he would hear no ill word spoken of the rash Duke but those who knew such matters lamented the serious setback we had suffered. Battles were often about the confidence or lack of it. Now the French and their Scottish allies had the confidence we had once enjoyed.

We reached Dreux ready for yet another siege. There were enough artillery pieces for us to be able to surround the town with guns and to begin to bombard the walls of the town. The first cannon opened fire in the middle of July. Perhaps the King was mindful of his brother's rash behaviour for he constantly walked the siege lines to ensure that his orders were being carried out to the letter. When he came to the bombard my men and I defended to view our section of the wall, it was to chat. He spent longer with us than the others and I think I understood why; I knew that I now looked much older. War and sorrow had taken their toll. I think the King thought that I might not be around much longer. I was much older than his father had been when he had died. The King had no relatives as old as I was. When he came to speak, he

The Battle for France

talked of his unborn child. He believed it would be a boy and he spoke of his hopes for him. He spoke between the cracks from the bombard and when the foul smoke had drifted away to allow the gunners to clean and reload their weapons.

"I hope that I can give my son two kingdoms which may, one day, become even larger. Castile was once ruled by my family, perhaps it will be again." That was a vain hope. I had fought in Spain and the people there were even more treacherous than the French and Scots.

I smiled and shook my head, "I fought there, King Henry, and there is nothing worth fighting for. I left many friends in that land. Is not France and England enough?"

"You may be right." He stared at the walls as the bombard cracked again. "King Richard failed in Ireland. There seems a place we could take as my ancestors did." He nodded towards King James of Scotland who had been his prisoner but now fought alongside him. King Henry had done the same with King Richard in Ireland. "King James there is keen to fight in Ireland. Perhaps I should return him to the Scottish throne although that nest of vipers are even worse than the men of Armagnac and France!"

"King Henry, do you not yearn for some peace and time with your new bride?"

"I do but you taught me too well, Strongstaff. I have a sense of duty and besides, I am a warrior. I do what I do well, and I fight and lead men. When we have taken this nest of rebels we will head for Chartres and see if we can bring the Dauphin to battle and end this rebellion against our rule. Then I might return to England for a while."

"You need to watch your son or daughter grow, King Henry. Poor King Richard was denied that joy and I missed being with mine when they were young and full of laughter."

The guns pounded every day, and the walls were slowly reduced. For Michael and me, it was the opportunity to train our squires. Jack took to the training easily. He had a second chance to be a soldier and he grasped it with both hands although one was partly maimed. Rafe and James both knew what it was to overcome a wound and they helped the son of an old friend. They used soldiers' remedies to toughen the skin and helped develop techniques to hold weapons. He responded well.

Rufus, in contrast, seemed to resent the attention which Jack received. I had been forced to chastise him when the two had first begun to serve us for Rufus tried to command Jack as though he was an inferior. Jack was a kind youth and used to being considerate to others. It had been when we were in Paris that I became angry and had taken

The Battle for France

Rufus out to the courtyard of the Louvre Palace. "What is it that you do, Rufus? Why do you order Jack to do that which is your duty?"

"He is happy enough to do it!"

"That is because he has something you do not, a kind nature! Your status is the same. If I catch you shirking your duty once more then I shall ship you back to England."

The fear in his face had been clear and he had begged, "You need me as a squire!"

"Do not presume to tell me what it is that I need!"

"Please I beg of you, do not disgrace me with a return to my father! I promise I shall change!"

I had spoken in a cold and icy voice, "And you had better for I mean what I say and as for needing you as a squire… I do not. I have Rafe and James who could easily do their own jobs and that which you do. I keep you here as a favour to your father who was a real squire and not a spoiled noble."

He had begun to change that day, although it was not an overnight event. It took weeks before I began to be half satisfied with him. Poor Jack had been so upset that Rufus had been chastised that, when he had heard of my rebuke, he had begged me not to send Rufus back. Jack was a genuinely good man, and he took it upon himself to make Rufus a better squire.

Now that we were close to the threat of fighting, Rufus had more purpose in his life and he heeded every command, obeying instantly. I also had the opportunity to observe the new men who had come to me. Sir Stephen and Sir Oliver had served with me for many years and they knocked the rough edges from the ones who needed it. Jack knew the two knights but Rufus found them intimidating for they were not as refined as the lords he had seen when growing up. Their influence also changed my squire. As we prepared, in the middle of August, for our assault on the town, both Jack and Rufus had changed. Jack was far more confident than when I had first seen him. He was skilled with weapons and was eager to try his skill. Rufus had learned that his breeding and background were irrelevant in a siege camp. He too was keen to make an attack. In the end, they were both denied the opportunity for Dreux surrendered without us having to assault the walls. King Henry punished the rebels. The nobles were held for ransom and the rich of the town fined for their rebellion. None were hanged but every weapon and piece of armour was taken, and the soldiers set to repairing the walls we had destroyed. It was a message for France. Baugé had been an aberration and now King Henry was back.

The Battle for France

To emphasise the new reign King Henry had us ride around the land between Dreux and the Seine rooting out rebels and Dauphinists. It was a good experience for our new squires and men for this was the English way of war. The Black Prince had been renowned for it and King Henry liked to emulate his ancestor. Once the land was scoured of the enemy we headed towards Chartres and the Dauphin. King Henry came to me on the night before we broke camp.

"Strongstaff, I want your retinue to be the advanced scouts. They are good at that sort of thing. Sir Stephen can lead them, you shall ride with me."

We were with the earls of Warwick and Salisbury. I saw the shock on their faces when I said, "No, King Henry, they are my men, and I shall lead them. The day I cannot lead my own men is the day I hang my sword above the fireplace in Weedon."

Instead of rebuking me, the King smiled, "I think to look after you, Sir William. You are no longer young!"

I nodded, "Aye, and my backside and knee will complain but what else does a soldier do? Besides, you need my old head to make decisions, do you not?" He nodded, "Then it is settled."

To be honest I relished the opportunity to lead my men once more. I now had my mounted archers, and they were the best in the army. We would not be ambushed. With Rafe and James leading the sumpters we were self-contained, and we had no need to stay with the rest of the army. The King had guns with him, and they would slow him down. We had no such restrictions. I had my men remove their jupons and surcoats. Our liveries would have told them who we were and while they might assume that we were English, or enemies at least, I wanted any Dauphinists we found to be in doubt. Doubt was a weapon I would use.

We were just twenty-seven miles from Chartres when Christopher White Arrow rode back to tell me that he and the scouts had spied rebel outposts on the road.

"How many are there?"

"They have a barrier across the road, and we spied ten men at arms, ten crossbows and twenty men with spears."

"They are mounted?"

Christopher shook his head, "The spearmen appeared to be on foot for we saw just twenty horses."

I turned to my knights, "Then while our archers get around this barrier, we will prepare to charge them. I wish to prevent the Dauphin from knowing how close we are until I have spied out his army. I want no one to reach Chartres with news of our imminent arrival."

The Battle for France

My knights nodded and Christopher said, "And none shall!"

My archers were all experts at using cover and they rode, not down the road, but across the fields using trees, bushes and buildings for cover. It would take them some time to get into position and we would be able to prepare. I turned and said, mainly for the benefit of the two new squires, "Don your helmets. Squires, guard the horses." I saw the disappointment on the face of Rufus. He was not happy. "Rufus, fetch me a spear." The spears were with Rafe on the sumpters. I hefted the shield and slipped the guige strap over my shoulder. I would let it hang until I needed to put my arm through the brases. "Knights you shall ride with me and the men at arms behind."

Sir Stephen said, hesitantly, "Why do you not ride in the second rank, Sir William?"

I snorted, "Do you think I am too old to charge a few Frenchman, Sir Stephen?"

"No, my lord, I just thought we might give some of the new men at arms the opportunity to tilt at the French."

Mollified, although I did not believe a word of it, I said, "Perhaps the next time. For now I need to rid myself of stiff joints and this will do that." I saw Michael grin until he saw my eyes and then covered it by pulling up his mail coif to his nose.

I deemed that enough time had elapsed to allow my archers to get into position and I gestured to my men to follow me with the spear which Rufus had just handed me. We cantered down the road. I wanted to draw every French eye to us and be curious. Had we galloped then they would have been forewarned of danger. This way they thought that they would have the edge. They would have weapons at the ready but they would wait until they could identify us, and my archers could then clear them from our path. The twisting hedge-lined road meant that when they did see us, we were just one hundred paces from them. Our spears and lances were vertical, but we all wore helmets and I saw the crossbows, behind the barrier, aimed at us. Our horses' heads were protected by plate shaffrons while their chests had good peytrals; some of leather and some of mail. The first ten bolts were sent when we were just sixty paces from them and coincided with the twenty arrows which were aimed at the crossbowmen.

One bolt hit Hercules on his shaffron, but the plate was well-made, and the bolt deflected to strike me on the upper arm. Its force spent it dropped to the ground. Another was taken on my shield and I slipped my arm through the brases. I had been lucky for I had forgotten to use them. The sound of bolts striking metal was almost musical, but the cries of the stricken crossbowmen were anything but. I saw the heads of the French men at arms and spearmen turn as more arrows were sent at them. Christopher and my archers were using war arrows and eliminating the unarmoured spearmen first. We were now just twenty paces from the barrier. The four of us had spears and we reined our horses in so that they did not impale themselves on the tree branches. We jabbed our spears as one over the top of the barricade. Mine struck the body of a spearman who had just been hit in the back by an arrow. Michael's skewered a man at arms in the face. And then it was all over. As soon as my archers began to use bodkins then the fate of the Frenchmen was sealed. Had any surrendered I would have accepted it, but it had all happened so quickly that none of them had time.

I took off my helmet and held my spear out for Rufus to take it. My archers collected the horses as my men at arms cleared the barrier. Michael took off his helmet and examined the vambrace on my arm where the bolt had hit. He nodded, "The weaponsmith was worth his money, lord. There is no damage."

I shook my head, "There is, but it is hidden and it will be slight. Metal becomes weaker with each blow. Always remember that when you fight. If you can avoid being hit, then your armour will last longer."

Each of my archers and men at arms led one of the captured horses. They were not only worth money they would be used by us to enable us to ride further. We continued towards Chartres, but we took a smaller side road which my archers found. The horse manure on the road told us that the guards for the road had used it. I guessed it would bring us closer to the French camp and we now had the advantage that any Frenchman we met would assume we were friendly as we had passed their vedettes. We spied first the towers of the city and its cathedral and then the tents of the army.

"Sir Michael, Sir Stephen, come with me. The rest stay here and watch. Archers have your bows ready in case we are attacked. Christopher, I shall want an archer to ride to the King when I have assessed the numbers we face."

"Aye, lord."

Sir Stephen said, "You have a plan, lord?"

"Of sorts. We shall ride as close as we can get to count the numbers of men. I take heart that they are not all within the city but that means our numbers will be an estimate only."

Michael said, "And the fact that they are camped without and have their horses close to them means that they might leave quickly if they are alarmed."

I nodded for Michael was right. He was astute.

The Battle for France

As we headed closer to the camp, I saw that they had no sentries. Their road sentries were their protection. I also saw many Scottish standards in addition to the ones from Armagnac. This was a large army. I said, "Michael, dismount and pretend there is something amiss with your horse." As he did so I added, "Stephen, count the standards and we will compare numbers." It would only be a rough number and we had no way of knowing how many lay within the town and castle, but it would be a guideline. Each standard would normally mean a knight and, perhaps twenty men. As some were Scottish the number for each standard might be just ten. As I counted the banners, I saw many of the ordinary soldiers from Scotland who, whilst they had little in the way of armour, were there in great numbers. Those armed with the long spear were particularly dangerous for mounted men at arms.

"Sir William, men are watching, and they have become suspicious." I looked and saw a dozen or so Scotsmen looking in our direction.

"We have seen enough. Michael, mount."

As we turned our heads there was a shout of alarm and the curious Scots ran for their horses and shouted for others to follow. We spurred our horses. It would take some moments for the enemy to saddle and mount their horses and I hoped we could build up a lead. Michael had the wit to turn and he shouted, "Sir William, five had horses mounted already. They are galloping.""

I did not want to weary our horses. We might have fifteen or so miles to go to reach the vanguard of the army. I drew my sword and looked over my shoulder. We were travelling along a good road surface and there would be little danger for us. The Scots were just fifty paces from us. All wore armour and carried swords. We could have risked halting to fight but with odds of five to three, there was always a chance, however slight, that one of us could be hurt. As we neared my men the fact that we all had drawn swords was warning enough for those archers who had followed me for years. I saw the bows bend as the strings were drawn back. When the arrows soared, I was not worried. My archers hit whatever they aimed at. I heard a horse whinny and then a man shouted in pain. I turned and saw that one horse had been lamed and two men had been knocked from their saddles. Two others had arrows sticking in mail links. They slowed. We had bought time. Another flight made them turn and head back to the camp. They would soon be reinforced by others.

"Mount! Send a rider to the King! We have their numbers, and they are camped before the town." I saw Harry Fletcher whip his horse with his bow and he galloped off.

"Do we stand and fight, Sir William?"

"No Rufus, you will learn that the purpose of a scout is to take back information. We run away every time!"

We had good horses and we had remounts. As soon as we sensed that they were catching us I ordered the men to change horses. When they did so then the pursuers, largely Scots by their shouts, drew closer and they pushed their animals even harder. At one point they were less than ten paces from the rearmost man but as the fresher horses opened their legs, so the pursuers dropped back. It was early in the afternoon when we saw a company of men at arms led by Sir John Cornwaille and his son, John, head towards us. We opened up the centre of the road and they galloped through. The men pursuing us saw them too late and there was a clash of swords. Four of them were slain and three more captured.

"Let the horses rest here, and Stephen and I will report to the King." The King was at the head of the main body and we turned our horses so that we could talk while we rode up the road.

"How many did you estimate, Sir Stephen?" I had a figure of eight thousand in my head when I asked the question.

"If they had all been French then I would have said perhaps ten or eleven thousand but there were many Scottish banners. I live near to the border and know that every petty warrior fancies himself and has a banner. The number will be nearer nine thousand."

I nodded, "That is roughly my estimate."

The King said, "Then they may fight."

I shrugged, "A large number were outside the town and the castle so that may be a reasonable assumption, my lord."

He turned in his saddle, "Have the ordinance and baggage guarded by the Duke of Exeter. For the rest let us hasten to the town of Chartres lest our prey leaves!"

Although we had ridden hard and arrived without guns, the Dauphin had decided that he was not yet ready to face King Henry despite his superiority of numbers. He abandoned Chartres to us and with it much treasure which he left. He fled south and we assumed that he was heading for Tours. When this was confirmed by prisoners caught in the road by the pursuing Earl of Warwick the King knew that the Dauphin had escaped. With a new ally in the Duke of Brittany, he was trying to build an army which would guarantee victory.

We held a council of war in the castle. "I need the opinions of each of you. We have a dilemma. We are deep in enemy territory for Armagnac and Brittany both support the Dauphin and his cause. It is hard to supply our army and if we are to take Tours, Saumur and Chinon then we need more ordinance. What should we do?"

His brother, Gloucester, said, "At the risk of sounding like my brother Thomas," he made the sign of the cross, "I think we keep our swords in the backs of this rebel army. If we do not, then they may gain even more support."

The King nodded.

"And yet," said the Duke of Exeter, "we have already lost horses and if the rebels decide to do as they did at Rouen and destroy crops to deny us food, we may have a starving army. I remember the road from Honfleur to Agincourt!"

The debate went on for some time and we were getting nowhere. I said little. The King eventually banged the table, "Enough debate. I have listened to all your arguments and I can now see that so long as some of you believe that we should fall back then that is the right decision. I propose to make the north more secure. Duke Philippe has not made as much progress as I would have liked. We will end the rebellion there and winter closer to Paris. I will send to England for more men. We return to Paris!"

That was typical of King Henry. He made a positive out of every negative. We took the treasury from Chartres and headed back to Paris.

Chapter 11

King Henry was never idle, and his riders were sent to Paris and to Picardy to find out where his army was needed. Meaux was just twenty-five miles from Paris and was a formidable castle. It was held by a warlord called Bastard of Vaurus. The garrison, apart from the rebels, was made up of Scottish and Irish. King Henry's treatment of the Scottish prisoners at Melun meant that they would fight to the very end. It was seen by the King as a key target for it protected Paris from the east and was the most formidable of the northern French fortresses. King Henry was in a positive mood as he began, at the start of October, yet another siege. The rains began and after an already wet autumn, the River Marne flooded. My heart sank when we arrived for I knew that this was Honfleur all over again; we would have a flooded siege which would only become worse as more rain fell. The difference this time was that the King had already planned his camps and his strategy. The fortress lay in a loop of the river. The town walls followed the river and were punctuated with towers upon which they had their guns. The castle lay in the heart of the town. Once we had taken the walls then we would have to take the castle. Our main efforts were at the barbican which guarded the main entrance to the town. It was there that the French had placed their bombards and we lost two of our valuable and irreplaceable guns while they were being brought into position.

The army surrounded the town and castle with camps. As the vanguard my men had chosen one which was slightly higher than many but, even so, we were wet from dawn until dusk. We used logs and, when we could find it, turf, to make log houses but we had to make them in what was soon to become a sea of mud. We were never clean! The French had artillery and they used it well. The stones they fired caused death to our men as we prepared the siege lines. Until the wooden defences were in place then we were vulnerable. There was damage to our defences before we could even put them up. Firing from an elevated position, they were able to outrange our guns. It was like Caen in reverse. There we had held the high ground and now, in this swampy part of France, the French and Scottish did. It was once we had finally built our defences and started to pound their walls that disease began to hurt us. Men died, as they had at Honfleur but in even greater numbers. One in five of the army was ill and soon they succumbed to the cold and dysentery and died. We seemed to make little progress and each day was a repetition of the previous one. The air was filled with the stink of gunpowder. Morale was already low and many men wondered at the wisdom of the siege. When the seventeen-year-old son of John Cornwaille was decapitated by a rock sent by a cannon then his father took his son's body and returned home. The departure of such a popular leader who had fought at Agincourt made the morale of the army plummet to its lowest point.

King Henry walked the perimeter to raise the morale of the men. Sir John had been his friend too and the two men had not parted on the best of terms. Sir John had been one who had wondered at the wisdom of trying to take such a bastion. After he had gone King Henry came to see me and I could see that he was clearly worried. "Strongstaff we have suffered setback after setback. We need a victory. What magic can you conjure?"

"None, my lord. I cannot bring the Bastard forth to fight us. If I could then I would."

He nodded, "Men curse the gun which killed the poor youth who died. He was, like his father, popular."

I looked across the muddy ground to the river and the small tower where the gun which had fired the fatal shot was mounted. It had not been a bombard and the gunners at the gun close to us had said that it had been pure luck, bad luck, that the small rock had decapitated the youth. An idea began to form in my mind. "I suppose..." My trouble had always been that I tried to please the kings I served but I also felt as much affection for King Henry as I did my own children, perhaps more. I did not like to see him so low in spirits. He deserved more for he was a good leader and a good king.

"Speak, Strongstaff, whatever idea you have will have more merit than the emptiness which fills my mind."

"It is just a thought, my lord, but if my men and I could fashion a raft then we might be able to sneak across the flooded river in the depths of the night and, perhaps, destroy the gun. I would need to speak with Nicholas Merbury to discover how to do this, but it may be possible, I suppose."

Having given voice to it the idea which had grown in my mind seemed even more preposterous, but the King was excited and when he said, "You are the best of men and have ever been the hope of England!" I knew that no matter what the Master of Ordinance advised I would have to do it.

The Battle for France

We had to keep it secret for if the defenders had an inkling of what we had planned then we would all die. The King and I told no one except for Nicholas. Surprisingly, he thought it a good idea and he had a man, he said, who would go with us and show us how to destroy the gun.

Once the plan was approved, I gathered my men to ask for volunteers. They all asked to be taken and that gave me the difficult task of choosing the twenty who would come with me and therefore which ones I would leave behind. I chose my ten best archers as well as Rafe, James and Sir Stephen. I left Sir Oliver to defend the place we would use to launch the raft. Sir Michael was also an easy choice for he was quick thinking. Karl the Dane, Kit Warhammer, Gilbert of Ely, and Uriah Longface were also immediate choices. I looked at the new men to pick the best of them but Jack and Rufus, when my gaze did not light upon them stood and it was, surprisingly, Jack who spoke.

His voice was calm and reasonable when he spoke but it was also firm, "My lord, Rufus and I have been happy to fetch and to carry. We have waited with horses while others fought, and we have done so uncomplainingly but you need the two of us for this task."

Michael said, "Jack, know your place!"

I shook my head, "Let him speak for this is not like Jack and if he can give me a good reason then…"

Encouraged by my words he went on, "Apart from Sir Michael all the men you have chosen are old men!"

Sir Stephen growled, "You may not be my squire, but I will happily show you that I am not!"

I smiled, "Stephen, you are old and we both know it. Not as old as I that is true but old. Go on Jack, what is your point for with age comes wisdom and experience!"

"And what of quick wits, Sir William and young agile bodies? It seems to me that if we are to ascend a tower then the two of us would be able to climb faster and more silently than the old men who will have to huff and puff."

I waved a hand to silence the increasingly angry warriors, "And you can climb?"

Jack laughed, "Aye, my lord."

I thought about it for a moment. There were risks involved and I did not relish telling either of their parents that their sons had died while serving me, but Jack was right, and they deserved a chance. I nodded. "You have persuaded me and we will use the two of you to climb the tower. Now you must make a pair of rafts and do so out of sight of all. You will return with it after dark. None shall wear plate. Mail coifs, brigandines, knives, clubs and hatchets are what the men at arms and squires shall take. Do not forget, Jack, that you shall need ropes too!"

I was left alone while my retinue left our quarters. Although I knew the risks involved, I found myself quite excited at the prospect of a night-time raid. If it did succeed, then we could not repeat it for they would guard against it. The King and Nicholas Merbury came in the late afternoon with a grizzled old gunner. He had the blackened fingers of one who works and handles gunpower. He would never be able to scrub them clean.

The Master Gunner gestured to the old gunner, "This is Jacob, and he has forgotten more about guns than I shall ever know. He is happy to come with you."

The old man chuckled, "If you are mad enough, Sir William, to try this then I shall go with you not least to tell the tale when we are back in England."

I asked, "Can it be done, Jacob?"

He nodded, "Gunpowder is funny stuff and likes to go off when you do not wish it to. We will need to take a linstock and fire. That is dangerous in itself. We have to keep it dry while getting across the flooded land and, if we are to succeed then the French will hear the explosion and come after us but aye, we can blow it up, my lord!"

The King spoke to each of my men before we departed for the river. We had half a mile to carry the two rafts for Michael had determined that was the best way to cross the flooded land. It says much about the opinion my men held of Michael that they all went along with it. The water was four times the width it normally was because of the floods. Most of it was just knee deep until you came to the river proper, but mud was beneath it. The only way to cross would be by raft.

Finally, just before we left King Henry clasped my arm, "I believe that when you succeed, for succeed you shall, then our mood will improve and with God's help we shall prevail. Keep safe, old friend."

The men who had replaced us at our front line had been warned that we would be returning and that there were to be neither fires nor lights. The French defences were in darkness. They would have sentries but the low fog which seemed to fill the river each night would help to mask us and our approach. The floods, the mud, and the river itself were the best defences and there were no other obstacles. For the last week, as we had stood our watches, I had studied the ground and knew it to be free from any man-made defences which might hinder us. They were reliant upon nature.

The cloying mud almost stopped us before we had begun but Jacob, our gunner, suggested using the branches which had been cut from the

The Battle for France

trees felled for firewood to make a brushwood path. It became easier once we walked on those. After placing the two rafts in the water we waited. It was hard to see where the floodwater ended and the river began but we were not a boat and it made little difference to us. We had more than a hundred and fifty paces to paddle. The archers who would remain on our side of the water each waited with a nocked arrow, but a hit would be highly unlikely. They were there as a last resort in case we were pursued.

We detected no movement on the small stone tower, but we all knew there had to be guards there. I nodded and we clambered onto the rafts. We did it carefully but the disparity in weights meant that as we climbed on board first one side and then the other dipped and water flooded over until we were all safely aboard. The ones on the outside had crude paddles and they worked in unison to propel us across the water. Jacob, his linstock and fire were on one raft and I was on the other with exactly the same equipment as Jacob. On each raft was a single archer with an arrow nocked in case sentries had to be silenced. The fog hid the other bank and we jolted to a halt when we struck it. The two archers with nocked arrows were ashore first followed by my men at arms with drawn swords. We would need to pull the rafts from the water but there was no point in doing so while they were laden. We stepped from the rafts as carefully as we had boarded. We drew the rafts ashore and secured them. If they floated away, then we would be trapped. The archers went first, and each nocked an arrow. They would watch for sentries.

Jack and Rufus did not hesitate. As the knights and the men at arms had dragged the two rafts onto the muddy bank the two squires began to climb the small tower. It was not more than twenty feet high but that was high enough. The knights, men at arms and Rafe and James joined us. Michael and Stephen followed the squires up the side. Rafe and James cupped their hands to boost them. The two squires were just six feet from the top when a face appeared. Four arrows slammed into the skull so hard that I heard the bones crunch and break. The sentry was dead. I thought he was the only one until another face appeared further along the tower and he suffered a similar fate. I think the second sentry could not believe what had happened. Had he shouted before he died then all would have been lost. As the two squires squirmed over the top Stephen and Michael were half-way up. The two ropes were thrown down and Jacob and I, encumbered by fire and linstock, walked up the wall. So fast was our progress that we were just moments behind Michael and Stephen. While Jacob went to work on the fowler, which looked to be newer than the ones we were using, Michael and Stephen went along the fighting platform. There were braziers with kindling placed along the wall. They passed them until they reached the next tower. They climbed the ladder from the castle side of the wall and slipped over the side. The sound of the two sentries dying was not enough to disturb any. The two knights hurried back, picking up the kindling along the way. I had been watching Jacob work while Rufus and Jack kept an eye on the two knights.

Sir Stephen whispered, "There is another cannon in the next tower and the guards are dead."

It was a risk but a risk worth taking. I too spoke in a whisper, "Rufus and Stephen come with me, I will try to do as Jacob has done. Jacob, do not light the powder until you see me return."

"You know, lord, that your gun will explode before ours and alert the guards."

I nodded, "It is worth the risk." With the linstock and fire, I hurried down to the next tower. The two guards lay in pools of blood. I gestured for Stephen and Rufus to turn the cannon so that it faced into the castle. Jacob had done so in the first tower loading a ball and packed powder around the stone missile. He had emptied almost all the gunpowder around and under the metal tube as well as most of the smaller rocks he could. He had then poured oil from the lamps over the wooden frame which held the gun and his last job had been to lay a trail of powder. I did the same as Jacob. Of course he would have done it better, but we had a chance to hurt the French. That done I waved the other two back to the rest of my men and as I stepped on to the ladder, I lit the powder. I climbed down as it spluttered, sparked, and flashed. I went as quickly as my lame leg would allow to the other tower and was just inside the safety of the parapet when the gunpowder exploded. The night sky was lit up by the explosion.

Jacob said, "Over the side my lord!"

Michael and Jack had already descended the rope and now Stephen and Rufus were following. I had just grabbed hold of the rope when Jacob joined me, and he lit the powder. I wasted no time in descending. From the castle, we heard the sound of horns waking the garrison. We had barely made the bottom when the powder went off in the tower above us. Jacob had made a much better job of it than I had for part of the top of the tower was destroyed. Stones fell from the tower on to the wall below. One missed Michael by a handspan! We now had to run.

The men at arms had already refloated the rafts and we hurled ourselves on them. Now it did not matter if we took on water for there was no pot of fire to be doused and the paddlers dug deeply in the water, this time unafraid of making any noise. We were halfway across

The Battle for France

before bolts were sent after us, but they were loosed blindly for we were hidden by the mist.

Our archers had also sent blindly loosed arrows at the fiery towers where men tried to extinguish the fires. The kindling had set fire to the wooden platform at the tops of the two towers and our archers, although at extreme range, had a target. Sir Oliver and our men at arms helped us from the rafts which were pulled ashore. I had realised that they could now be used to make a shelter from the weather and we would take them back with us.

I turned to Jacob, "Thank you, Master Gunner!"

He grinned, "That is two fewer guns for us to hit and they cannot make more powder. Had we just destroyed their powder then they would have been hurt. Tonight was good, Sir William, and I thank you for the chance to leave our position."

The King ghosted from the trees where he had watched all silently. I saw his bodyguards hidden behind him, but they allowed me to approach him. "Let us hope that this is a change in our fortunes, Strongstaff. You have done your part and now it is my turn to do mine. I shall do as I did on St Crispin's Day and be everywhere tomorrow. I want our men and the enemy to know that we are not done yet."

I know that men thought the siege at Meaux was King Henry's finest hour. I did not think so for I loathed sieges, but he was a leader and even though nobles had left to return to England he never gave up hope. The next day saw a more buoyant English camp. It was at the end of the first week of December that we heard more news which brought cheer to us all, especially King Henry. His wife had been delivered of a son at Windsor castle and the babe was christened Henry. There would be a king to follow King Henry. He was not doomed like King Richard. The news brought heart to all of those at the siege lines and our guns pounded away. That one simple adventure seemed to change the siege. Jacob was right they could not conjure more guns and gunpowder. We had replaced the guns we had lost and powder was fetched from our other castles. The artillery duel was now being won by us and the walls began to crumble. The barbican's damage was only crudely repaired, and we began to hope that this siege would soon be over. The King was as good as his word and he toured our lines each and every day to encourage our men. It took its toll and he began to look tired. Then there were a couple of days when he did not venture forth.

It was later in the month that we had the first hint that all was not well with the King. A doctor was sent from England to tend to him and although he recovered a little, he was never the same again. He spent less time at the siege but when he was there, he seemed determined to make the most of the shorter time he spent facing the rebels. He exhorted men to work harder. We were desperately short of men. Almost a sixth of the men we had brought had died of disease and others had been killed in battle. There were no reinforcements from England, and it was numbers that we needed.

In our little camp, we were lucky for none of us became ill. We may have been lucky to have chosen a disease-free piece of land for our camp or there may have been another cause. We prayed each morning to give thanks that we were still alive and at night begged God to keep us safe for another day. The attack on the tower changed one of our company and for the better. Rufus realised that he owed much to Jack. Until the raid he had, somehow, looked down on the son of an archer. I had often told him that his grandfather had been one who worked the land and his nobility only went back to his father, but it had taken Jack's plan to show him that he had been wrong to judge. It seemed that when he looked at Jack with new eyes, so he was able to look at himself. It was as though Jack was a twisted mirror which allowed Rufus to see his own cracks and flaws. I saw him, over the days which followed the raid, go about his tasks with more diligence and without carping and complaining. He had already begun to improve but the planning for the raid and the raid itself were the key moments in the change. There was more respect in his voice as he spoke to men at arms and archers. He was more considerate and when he did speak it was to ask how he might become a better soldier.

Michael also noticed and as we stood a watch on the now broken tower, he spoke of it, "Perhaps that was like St Paul on the road, lord. When we raided the tower, it was though this strange blindness to his faults was removed."

"You may be right, and I hope that it is a permanent change. How about Jack, did it change him too?"

"A little but I am happy with my squire. Like me when I was your squire, he has much to learn but he soaks up all that I offer to him. He will do well. I enjoy training him. Rafe and James did a good job with me and I try to emulate them." He turned his attention back to the tower. "And this, lord, when will this end?"

I had been giving that much thought in the month since the raid. I pointed to the water which had receded a little. It had left a muddy morass but that morning there had been a frost and when I had gone to make water, I was surprised that the ground supported my weight. "I think that we can use Jacob's method, Michael. If we spread the branches from trees over the mud, then we can make a causeway to the river proper. The rafts we made gave me an idea. If we make pavise and use the night to put them in place, then when the dawn comes our archers will be in range of their walls. It is time we inflicted deaths upon the defenders."

He beamed, "That is a good idea, lord. Why not tell the King? If we did this along the whole of the siege, then we might end the siege."

"Let us try it here first. I am happy to make extra work for our men for they will not lose heart but if others lost heart then desertions might begin. You were at Honfleur and know the effect of desertions."

Rather than just spending each day, along with the other companies close by us, just watching the walls and being too far to do anything my men enjoyed the challenge. While half of the men made the pavise we would need, the other half went to find as many branches as they could. When darkness fell, we would all begin to make the causeway and after two nights of work, we were at the riverside. The pavises were put in place and using men from nearby companies to take our nightly watch we retired early so that we could be in position before dawn. Although we only needed archers for this task, we were one company and my knights and men at arms went with my archers. We watched the dawn break and, as it turned out, it was a fine day. We had an inkling that it would be so for there had been a hard frost and that meant clear skies.

Christopher was my captain of archers and he knew all the men he commanded well. He knew their range and their strength. It was he made the decision when to loose. We saw the Dauphinists on the battlements. They had done their best to repair the two damaged towers but the flimsy pieces of wood they had used would be of little use when we assaulted. All that they could see of my men was the line of pavise and my archers were hidden. The line of men at arms and my two knights would not alarm them for the black snake of the Marne gave them protection.

"Draw!"

As the twenty heads appeared above the pavise the defenders must have realised what was about to happen but even as they shouted the alarm the order to release had been given and twenty goose fletched missiles descended upon a short section of wall. Twenty more followed and the trumpets and horns from within told me that the Bastard thought this was a major attack and was summoning men to the walls. A few desultory crossbow bolts were sent at the pavise, but another two flights eliminated them and two flights later the order to hold was given. All along our section of the lines, there were cheers for the towers and walls were devoid of defenders. If we had prepared boats, we could have crossed the river unopposed and begun an assault on the walls.

The Battle for France

King Henry arrived at noon when we were eating. We now had a front line which was closer to the walls than when we had first arrived. King Henry did not look well but he beamed, "Why did you not tell me of this plan, Strongstaff? We could have employed it along the whole line."

I shrugged, "My humblest apologies, King Henry, but I was not sure that it would have worked. Now we know that it does then others can copy us."

He shook his head, "It worked but they will be ready next time. What I intend is to have boats brought here. That will take some time, but we will prepare the ground as you have done. I will send to the Duke of Burgundy for some of his men and when we are ready then we clear the walls with archers and cross the Marne with boats. We shall finally take Meaux!"

It took almost a month until we were ready for the King was having problems sleeping and was ill again. I felt guilty for he had perhaps been too ill to organise this attack and yet he would not have had it any other way. My company and those on our flanks had enjoyed the easier month for we had our causeway and pavise in position already. Harry the Fletcher had not wasted the time and we now had another thousand arrows we could use. The weaponsmiths the King had brought made us the arrowheads so that as we waited on that April morning to begin our attack my archers knew that they could keep the French walls clear and ensure that our knights and men at arms who crossed the Marne would do so safely.

The horns sounded the attack and as the archers sent flight after flight, we boarded the boats and were rowed to the far bank. When last we had crossed to raid the tower it had been a muddy field. Now it was drier and firmer. The guns which had been brought close to us had pounded the town walls and the ladders we had brought would easily take us to their tops. This time I was not the first across the wall. This was not because my men prevented me, my body did. My wounded knee had healed enough for me to ride but clambering up a rock-filled ditch was not easy. When I had climbed the rope, I had been able to go at my own pace now I was with younger warriors who were eager and keen to get at the defenders. I saw Michael, closely followed by Jack and Sir Stephen as they fended off the swashing blows from pikes and used their own poleaxes to spear the defenders' legs and groins. The French, Scottish and Irish had endured as hard a winter as had we, but we had supplies brought to us regularly and they had not. Our archers added to the slaughter as they picked off any Frenchman who sought to

The Battle for France

bring a crossbow to bear or any Scottish archer who wished to kill one of the old enemy.

By the time I reached the top of the fighting platform, with Rufus leading the way, we had a firm hold and one of the towers, albeit a severely damaged one, was ours. The Scottish and French defenders drove at us for of all the attackers we were the only ones to have a foothold on the walls of Meaux. Our raid had yielded results and we had benefitted.

I had a shield and my sword. I had not relished climbing a crumbling wall with a weapon in two hands. Jack also had a shield as did Sir Michael. Now on the fighting platform I took command and shouted, "Shields!" The fighting platform was wide enough for four men but three of us could lock shields and hold off those who would attack us. With three shielded and Rufus and three others behind us wielding spears and poleaxes, we could hold off an onslaught. Our aim was not to take the town alone but to hold this portion and, perhaps, draw off men from the other walls.

It was a mixture of Frenchmen and Scottish warriors who ran at us and they came without order. I knew that Jack would be terrified for this was his first real fight and I said, "Jack, hold firm. You are on the left and they will swing their weapons at your shield. You are strong and your father made you a good shield. Trust to that and your arm!"

They hit us with spears, glaives, and pole weapons. Because they came in a mob, they got in each other's way but, even so, the war hammer which the Scottish man at arms brought down to smash into my helmet would have killed me instantly had it hit. My shield was above my head and he did not see my sword as I rammed it into his screaming mouth. The tip was stopped not by the bone of his skull but the back of his helmet. The war hammer fell from his lifeless hands and slid down my shield. The four behind us jabbed and poked their weapons at the faces of the enemy. I had time to glance to my left and see the axe which swung at Jack's shield. I was pleased to see that the squire kept his head. He sawed his sword across the wrist of the Scot and when the tendons were severed the weapon fell from his hand. Jack had the wherewithal to punch with his shield and the man fell on to the roof of the building below. Sir Michael was also holding his own for he had the crenulations to his right and his French attacker could not get past his shield.

The problem we had was that no matter how many we hurt there were more to take their place. When arrows began to fly from our right, I knew that Christopher had seen our plight and was using bodkins to smash into helmets. No matter how well made, a helmet can be pierced by a bodkin, especially at a range of fewer than thirty feet. As soon as I saw the arrows fly, I shouted, "Hold!" We stopped and braced. The French and Scots who were close to the wall were hit first and as they fell, or dropped, those next to them were also hit. It was relentless and no matter how many joined the attack they had to endure the gauntlet of missiles. One effect was to allow the Earl of Salisbury's men to take the other tower we had damaged. However, if we thought we had taken the town we were wrong. We were attacked in the rear by men sent from the far side of the town. Luckily, Sir Stephen and Sir Oliver were there and held them off. As dusk fell, we had a stalemate. We held part of the town walls but not enough to guarantee that we could take the town.

King Henry sent his brother, Gloucester, to relieve us. They had not attacked and so, while our two sets of archers kept down the heads of the enemy we withdrew, recrossed the river and returned, warily, to our camp. Despite wanting to, I had forbidden Rafe and James from joining us. Thus it was that we had hot food waiting for us and, by what miracle I knew not, a barrel of ale and a jug of good wine. We feasted like kings. As was usual after such a fight each blow was relived by those who had both fought and watched. Rufus, in particular, was animated. He had not killed an enemy but one of his spear thrusts had sliced the nose of a Scottish spearman.

"I shall know him when next I see him, and I will finish off the job."

Jack shook his head, "You will not for I saw Harry Fletcher's arrow end his life. Perhaps he was distracted by the loss of his nose." Jack was the son of an archer and had been trained as an archer. He knew the fletch and markings of each of my archers. Often, they would have to use the arrows provided by the King but when they could they used their own.

I just listened for this filled me with joy. There was both banter and humour in their comments but also sentiment for the older warriors, archers, and men at arms alike, would speak of those who were dead. They told of their fights and their successes. I saw Rufus and Jack take it all in. To Rufus this was new, but Jack had known many of the archers.

"Will we attack again, tomorrow, Sir William?"

I turned and looked at Sir Michael, "There will be fighting tomorrow and for the foreseeable future. We have ended the siege of Meaux but now we have the battle for Meaux and that will not be easy." I was aware that the newer and younger warriors had stopped their own conversations to listen to ours. This was a good opportunity to give them the facts of life. I had been in many fights inside towns and it was never easy. "The advantage is with the defender and always will be.

The Battle for France

They know the town in which they live and work. If we have to winkle them from buildings, then they have the advantage. Our archers are less effective in the narrow streets of towns. Remember these people are our enemies but they are fighting for their homes and their families. Even if they think they will lose they often fight without hope."

"Weeks rather than days, then?"

"Possibly, but I hope that within a week we have the town. The castle…that is another matter!"

In the end, we had the walls taken in two days and then the Earl of Warwick led the attack on the main gate and with that in our hands, we descended into the town. I kept my own men with me, but I was also given another twenty men at arms from the King's contingent. He was unwell again. The battle was as bloody as I had expected, and I ordered my men to use shields. The narrow streets were no place for pole weapons. Only half of my archers were armed with bows for they were less effective, and all my archers could fight with swords. I had a method behind my formation. I changed the front four men each time we had taken twenty paces of the street. I am not sure I could have done it with any but my retinue and familia. The first four changes used just those soldiers I had brought but then I used the King's men. It says much of my men that the first man we lost was one of the King's men. It took half a day to reach the town square, the cathedral, and the castle. Once there we suffered a barrage of bolts from the castle walls and we halted until the other elements which were converging arrived. We consolidated our position by clearing the houses. We found few women and children. Perhaps they were in the castle, I knew not. The men we found died and it soon became apparent that they had moved their treasure for most of the secret places we found were empty. I guessed it had been taken either into the cathedral or the castle.

Two days later King Henry entered the town for we had taken it and just the castle remained. The King, looking thin and grey, went with one of the French bishops we had with us to demand the surrender of the castle. The Scots and French nobles had all retreated into the castle and they were in defiant mood. Even as they rejected our offer a French trumpeter mocked King Henry. I confess that the men were all as angry as I was, and the act did nothing to soften our mood. The King seemed oblivious to the insult. He merely turned to Nicholas Merbury, "Have our guns brought forward. Let us see how they enjoy being battered by them." As his Master of Ordinance left, he turned to me, "Strongstaff I grow weary. You are almost twice as old as I am, you carry wounds and yet you have not missed a day of this battle. I have been forced to take to my bed. How do you do it?"

The Battle for France

I smiled and shrugged, "I know not for this is all that I have known. I rise, say my prayers, don my armour and strap on my sword. I am not sure that I could stop even if I wanted to."

He said, quietly, "I believe that God wishes me to stop. Perhaps Baron Fanhope was right. Had we stopped at Normandy then think how many men would still be alive. My brother, Clarence, for one."

"Do not think that way, my lord. This is almost over and then you can go home and see your son. English doctors can heal you and, who knows, by the time you return then we might have France!"

He beamed, "You have put heart into this warrior, Strongstaff, as you always do."

The guns were brought up by late afternoon. I recognised the master gunner, Jacob, who gave me a cheerful wave. Then they began to pound and to send their stones at the walls. Many of them were the stones the French had fired at us and were now rounder and smoother. I discovered that made them fly truer. The guns kept going all afternoon and all night. The air was filled with the stink of sulphur and saltpetre. Few men could sleep for the noise of both the crash of the guns and the shattering of stones on the walls. This time the stones we fired could not be reused. The night hid the true scale of the damage from us but as dawn broke, we saw the holes in the walls. By the mid-morning, the same trumpeter who had mocked King Henry sounded for a parley.

King Henry was in no mood for negotiation, "Bastard of Vaurus, you either surrender without terms or we destroy the castle. There is no other choice for you to make."

"Then, King Henry, we surrender."

It was May and the siege had lasted seven months. Those months had taken their toll on King Henry, but it was over. The King was without mercy. The Bastard and three other leaders, as well as the mocking trumpeter, were hanged. The Scottish and French nobles who surrendered were sent to castles in England and Wales until their ransoms were paid. We found a great treasure in the castle and we were all made richer by the siege for the King shared the treasure out amongst all of us. Jack could not believe the purse of coins he was given. There was also the loot taken from the captured soldiers. I took none for I needed none, but plate, mail and swords were taken by my men. There were, sadly, no horses. They had all been eaten!

Chapter 12

Two weeks after the castle had fallen Queen Katherine came from England to see her husband. She did not bring young Prince Henry and I found that sad. She was brought by the King's brother John, the Duke of Bedford. The Duke of Gloucester would be returning to England to rule our home in the King's absence. The King and his Queen spent Whitsun in Paris before the court moved to Senlis when a smallpox epidemic broke out in Paris. We all hoped that the summer weather would improve the health of the King.

The King sent for me and I wondered if it was to return to England. He had hinted as much when I had attacked the tower for him. I was wrong. He looked thin, emaciated and frail. This was not the warrior king who seemed immune to all ills. He saw my look and said, "Aye, Strongstaff, I am laid low, but my doctors have prescribed medicines and I am hopeful."

"My men and I will pray for you, my lord."

"All England, it seems, prays for me. We shall see. I need you and your men, Strongstaff. The Earl of Warwick is to take the best of the army from Meaux to Picardy to retake the castles and ports taken by the Dauphin. I will use diplomacy to bring former allies like the Duke of Brittany to our side." I later learned that King Henry's diplomacy involved threatening to have prisoners killed if his requests were not met. He had become ruthless.

"Of course, my lord. And what of your son? When will you see him?"

He shrugged, "At the moment he is a mewling infant. According to the Queen, he would not even know me. Better that I secure France for him and get to know him as he grows."

I had thought I had known the King. I did not or perhaps he was hiding things from me. Did he have a premonition that he had to act swiftly or had the birth of an heir motivated him?

I was happy to be serving alongside the Earl of Warwick. There had been a time I had thought him reckless, but I now knew he was not. He honoured me by allowing me to ride at his side when we headed for

The Battle for France

Picardy. I had seen little of him at Meaux and he wished to speak of our task as we rode.

"The Duke of Burgundy tried to take the castles of Picardy there but failed. We will not. First, however, we must take Compiègne. The Duke of Bedford is advancing towards it and we shall support him."

I looked behind us at the metal snake which followed us, "My lord, we have less than three thousand men. Some are still suffering from the effects of the Marne."

"I know but the loss of Meaux has hurt the enemy." He laughed, "They should have relieved it. The ransom from the prisoners will make the coin taken after Poitiers seem as nothing." He became serious, "You know, Sir William, that I do not expect you to fight. It is your sage advice and your superb men that I need."

I shook my head, "If my men fight then so do I. I know that I need not but that is my way and always has been."

"You are stubborn!"

I laughed, "And that too, has always been my way. It is why I stood by King Richard when all, it seemed, deserted him."

"No one can doubt your loyalty, least of all the King who values you more than any!"

A rider from the Duke of Bedford found us some miles before we reached the walls of Compiègne, "My lords, Compiègne has surrendered before we could loose an arrow."

The Earl turned to me, "And that is the effect of the fall of Meaux. The Dauphin will regret his failure to go to the aid of his supporters and now that we have Compiègne then our lines are secure."

I began to have hope that, against the odds, and with so few men as we had that we might succeed. We continued to the coast of Picardy which the French had held throughout the war. They were using Le Crotoy and St Valery to supply their forces and if we could take the Picardy castles then we might stop them.

That night I camped with my men while the Earl was camped with his nobles. Sir Stephen and Sir Oliver had seen this sort of campaign before but their squires had not. Along with Sir Michael, we watched the squires as they showed each other the treasures they had taken from Meaux. I smiled at Michael, "It does not seem long since you were like they are."

He nodded, "Aye, but they are luckier in some ways for they have other young squires. I felt like a boy when we travelled for vengeance."

"And yet that is just six short years since."

He looked into the fire and said, quietly, "That means it is six years since Lady Eleanor died."

His words stunned me, "Six years? I thought it was yesterday and yet I know that you are right. Where do the years go?"

"She was kind to me when you brought me to Weedon. I barely knew my mother and while I knew Lady Eleanor for no more than a month or so I can remember her face and voice. I still recall her affection. She was a great lady."

"And none know it more than I." His words brought back the lady with whom I had shared most of my life and yet I had been absent from her side more than I had been with her. Was the King doomed to be the same?

Rufus came over to us. He had a rondel dagger in a fine scabbard. "John thinks this is valuable, Sir William, is it?"

I took the long blade from the scabbard, "It is good steel and that makes it a good weapon. Do you mean it has value or valuable?"

He looked puzzled as I handed it back to him, "Is there a difference?"

"Of course, for if something is valuable then it is worth keeping. Value suggests that you are considering selling it. Do you need the money?"

He laughed, "Of course not. Like the others, I was given a good purse by the King."

"Then why think of selling it? A man cannot have too many weapons." I patted my own rondel dagger which was in my belt. My sword hung in my tent. I slipped my hand down to my boot and took out the bodkin dagger I kept there. "And I have a third weapon on my shield."

"Why do you need three, my lord?"

"Because I may meet a warrior better than I am and I might need to use the boot dagger, or the shield dagger, to win."

He frowned, "That is not honourable!"

Michael shook his head, "If you are fighting for your life then forget honour. Honour is for the king when he fought Sire de Barbazon in the mines. Then they could part for honour was satisfied. Had that been me either he or I would be dead!"

Jack, of course, had no such preconceptions about honour. He was the son of a soldier and he understood that war was a way to earn a living and was a case of kill or be killed.

When we reached Vimeu it was something of an anti-climax for the garrison surrendered immediately. When we entered, we saw the reason. There were less than one hundred men in the castle and the townsfolk were not committed to the cause of the Dauphin. They were close enough to Calais and the land we controlled to be pragmatic about

The Battle for France

the problem. Gamaches did not even close its gates. As we approached the walls the garrison mounted their horses and fled for Le Crotoy. They had held out against the Burgundians, but the sight of seasoned English soldiers was too much for them.

Poor Rufus was most disappointed. The siege of Meaux had resulted in riches for him and while he had wounded someone, he had not yet faced an enemy in battle. He wanted, I think, to prove himself. He had his opportunity at Saint-Valéry. This lay across the river from Le Crotoy and that was a strong castle. The Earl sent for ships to blockade the port while we positioned guns. The Master of Ordinance was no longer with us but with Jacob as the Master Gunner, I was confident.

We had learned at Meaux the dangers of a French sortie and so we were assigned to guard two of the smaller guns, called fowlers and two huge bombards. Jacob was happy for us to be with him. For us, it meant the chance for action, but we would be close to the stink that they produced. I did not know how the gunners could stand this day after day. We began the bombardment at the start of June. I was surprised at how long it took to fire them. They had to be carefully loaded and aimed. After they had fired, the insides had to be doused with water and then the whole thing repeated.

With so few men and guns, we knew that it was vital to protect what we had. I arranged a system of watches so that during the night there would be a knight, two archers and a man at arms on watch to ensure no mischief was done to the two guns we guarded. It was the second night, and I was on watch when we were called into action. I had given myself the worst watch. Michael had woken me at midnight, and I would watch until an hour after terces. I did not mind really for I knew I would want to make water. Age had brought not only aches and pains in old joints and wounds but also a bladder which appeared to have shrunk while my belly had grown! Rufus was there to fetch us drink and to maintain the fire. Kit Warhammer and Harry the Fletcher along with one of the new archers, Edward son of Edgar were also on watch.

This was our first night watch and as we sat under oiled cloaks I whispered to Rufus and Edward, "No talking. Hand signals only. If you see or hear anything then attract my attention!" Rufus' mouth began to open, and I put my finger across his lips. He smiled and nodded.

I sat between the two bombards with my sword across my knees. The gunners had given them names: Megs and Betty. I could not understand it. Unlike a sword, it was an ugly weapon. Essentially it was a metal tube ringed by more metal and resting on a crude frame. I stared across the ground to the walls of Saint-Valéry. The town had a ditch and, as with most French towns, a good wall and gatehouse. Our two

The Battle for France

guns had been tasked with reducing the gatehouse. Already the stones had destroyed some of the embrasures and damaged the walls, but we knew from Meaux that it was a slow process. The advantage we had here was no river to protect the town and no swamp to kill men insidiously through disease. The walls were just within bow range and the gunners had constructed a crude protective wooden wall with a hinged shutter to shield them from crossbow bolts. We had the two open so that we could keep a good watch. The whole town, on the land side, was ringed with the fires of our attackers. We, too, had a fire but it was hidden by the crude palisade. We knew better than to stare into the fire which would destroy our night vision and I had fixed my gaze, not on the gate but a place to the right where a tower provided shadows. There was no reason for my choice but just experience.

At the end of the first hour, Rufus fetched us some fish he had cooked on the fire. The arrogant youth I had met at Dauentre had changed. One advantage of being close to the sea was that we could find food and nets were used to gather fish each day. With a beaker of ale, the juicy fish covered in crispy skin went down well. I was just licking my fingers when a movement spied through the open gun port attracted my attention. I stared at the tower for that was where I had seen movement. At first, I saw nothing and then some shadows began to move. I could not identify them as men but that was all that they could be for animals had more sense than to be anywhere near siege lines. Without averting my gaze, I reached over to tap Kit on the shoulder and point, through the open shutters at the tower. He stared, too, and then nodded. While he attracted the attention of the others I stood, my knee complaining as I did so, and, with crouched gait headed for the fires which marked where our men slept.

I knelt next to Stephen and Oliver and shook them both, "Rouse the men but do so silently. Men are coming to cause mischief to the guns." I turned and left then to raise the watch. As I passed the spare weapons, I picked up a hatchet. If this was a raid, then it would be close quarter fighting and there would be little mercy shown. The rest of my men could guard the flanks of the bombards, but the night watch would protect Megs and Betty. I saw that Kit had given Rufus a pike and positioned him next to Betty where he would be protected by the wooden palisade. The two archers had their bows strung but, in their hands, they too held pole weapons. Kit had a war axe and was next to Megs. I sat where I had watched with my sword and hatchet.

There was little point in alerting the rest of our men for they were too far from us and the moving shadows suggested they were getting closer to us. It was now clear that they were coming for the guns.

Stephen and Oliver would have alerted the camps next to ours and they would be armed and waiting. Whoever came to do damage would be the best that the defenders had. If we could kill or capture them then that would dishearten those within the town. There was a risk that they might succeed and damage the precious bombards and fowlers, but I had confidence in my men. I could now see the shadows which were clearly men. They were attempting that which my men had done at Meaux. It meant they would have a gunner with them, and his death or capture would mean their guns would be less effective. When I began to smell them then I knew they were close. One becomes familiar with the smell of men with whom you spend every waking and sleeping moment. These men who came had a different stench. Following the smell came the noise. The Frenchmen were crossing unfamiliar ground and in the dark. The noise was not loud, but it marked the progress of the raiders. I looked at Edward and Rufus. This would be hard for them as they had never done this. Waiting was always hard; waiting to kill or be killed was harder.

Hands appeared simultaneously on the top of the palisade and the bottom of the open shutter. It was Kit who struck the first blow and he swung his axe through Megs' shutter, blindly. He hit something for there was a scream which rent the night, and, at the same moment, Rufus killed his first man as he rammed his pike into the face of the Frenchman attempting to climb over the palisade. The night erupted in shouts and screams. We had a battle in our gun emplacement. The five of us were alone although I knew that the rest of my men would be supporting us. A half dozen Frenchmen shouting French curses poured through the gun ports and over the palisade.

I stood and rammed my sword up at the Frenchman who leapt down at me with an axe in his hand. The sword impaled him and I turned to the side so that his falling body slid from my sword. I had little time to think as a man at arms threw himself through the embrasure, the open shutter. I reacted instinctively and smashed the hatchet against the side of his helmet. It deflected him sufficiently to allow Rufus to thrust the pike into the man's back. Enough of the Frenchmen had managed to get in to the guns, despite our early success, to make this a desperate fight. I confess that I went to Rufus to protect my young squire. That he had courage was clear, but I did not want him to die in such a mean place. I had had to tell Ralph of the death of his son and I would not repeat that! I threw myself at the two Frenchmen who were attempting to hurt Rufus. He was now using the wrong weapon for a pike was of little use in such a confined space, but he was making the best of it. He used it like a staff swinging the spearhead at one while also using the butt.

Betty was between us, but my sword was sharp and I hacked over the top of Betty towards the two backs. As one of the Frenchman arched his back I hacked into the side of his skull with my hatchet. The other partly turned his head and that allowed Rufus to drop the pike and use his rondel dagger. He slashed it across the throat of the Frenchman.

"My lord!" Those were Edward's last words as a huge Frenchman sliced his axe into the side of his head. I threw my hatchet at him and while it did not strike him it made him move away and that caused him to bang into his companion with whom Edward had been fighting.

"Rufus, draw sword and cover my back."

I spun around as the axeman recovered his balance and swung his axe at me. He missed, and the edge clanged off Megs' barrel. I swung my sword in an arc as I ducked beneath the sword from his companion. As I did, I dragged my bodkin from my boot and rammed it under the chin of the axeman. I sensed the French sword coming for my unprotected back but it did not connect for Rufus had used his sword well and the last Frenchman lay dying in a growing pool of blood. Only the dead remained. Megs and Betty were covered in blood and gore. We had lost our first man. Edward lay dead.

I left the bombards and, as dawn began to break saw the last survivors from the attack racing back to the walls. My archers ensured that none of them made it. As the Earl arrived with his knights to come to our aid, we saw that the attack had cost the French eighty men. In total, we had lost six but that was a small number. The two French gunners we had killed was a more significant number.

For us, however, it was a sad morning as we buried our first casualty. We had been lucky at Meaux. Was our luck running out?

The town surrendered two days later when Megs and Betty managed to bring down a section of the wall close to the gatehouse. While we invested the town the Earl held a Council of War. We had lost few men and almost achieved all our aims but Le Crotoy was a different prospect for it was a fortress and would not fall as easily as Saint-Valéry. Jacques d'Harcourt was the Governor of the fortress of Le Crotoy and it was a formidable fortress. The Earl thought that he might, now that he was isolated, be amenable to discuss surrender. In an attempt to persuade the Dauphinists to surrender, the Earl sent an English herald, the Master of the Royal Archers, and two French bishops, one of whom was the fiercely anglophile Bishop of Beauvais and the other Harcourt's brother, Jean Bishop of Amiens, to speak with the castellan. They were away for two days and when they returned it was with the news that while Jacques d'Harcourt was tempted he felt honour bound to defend his fortress. It would have to be besieged.

The Battle for France

We had barely placed all the guns in position when a rider reached us from the King. Our old nemesis, Tanneguy du Châtel was in the Loire and he had captured La Charité and the garrison at the vital river crossing of Cosne was threatened. The new Duke of Burgundy was already on his way to face him and the King was leaving his sickbed to head to Melun. He wanted the Earl and me to take our men and join him and the Duke of Bedford. The men who remained, under the command of Ralph Butler, would have to prosecute the siege.

It was a daunting journey of three hundred miles. Melun would be the halfway point and the Earl hoped that, as we were all mounted and King Henry would, perforce, have to take both guns and men on foot, we might be able to meet him at Melun. Both of us feared that the King was too unwell to participate in a battle. He was as brave as a lion but sometimes caution was preferable. In the middle of July, we found the King at Corbeil. He had been carried from Senlis by litter but it was obvious to both the Earl and myself, not to mention his brother who was already there, that King Henry could go no further. The four of us were in the abbey's hospital. He seemed lucid but I did not recognise him. Since Meaux, he had deteriorated so rapidly that I wondered at the wisdom of even attempting to make the journey to Cosne.

The Earl was the one who persuaded the King, "Your Majesty, return to Vincennes where the doctors can tend to you. Do you not trust us?"

He smiled, "You three are my most trusted of advisers and none are dearer to me. Of course, I trust you, but this is my land and its king should defend it."

I decided to be blunt, "King Henry, speed is of the essence. We must remedy this situation. Tanneguy du Châtel is a dangerous opponent. If we move swiftly then we have a chance but if you are with us, we will progress too slowly."

I wondered if I had gone too far but he nodded, "Ever the voice of reason and sense, Strongstaff. Very well proceed without me but I want regular messages to tell me how the campaign progresses."

Relieved, the Duke of Bedford said, "We shall send a rider each day!"

"I would speak with Strongstaff." The two nodded and left. He held my hand in his, "I wish a promise from you, William."

"Anything!"

"If anything untoward happens to me and God decides that I should be punished for my sins, I want you to be the bodyguard of my son."

I shook my head, "I will swear such a promise, but I am old. I am more likely to die than are you."

"You cannot for England needs you. The crown I wear is only there because of you. I do not want my son to lose the crown before he has a chance to grow."

I nodded, "Then while I live, I shall guard the Prince with my life."

"And after…?"

"Then I shall choose a worthy successor to me."

He lay back and, closing his eyes, smiled, "And you were ever a good judge of men. I am content."

Chapter 13

I was silent as we headed south. Was King Henry dying? God seemed determined to punish England. King Richard had been childless and King Henry unpopular. Now we had a King who was both a warrior and victorious, more than that he was popular and to be taken away after such a short reign seemed cruel. The first night we stayed in a monastery and I went to the chapel where I knelt. I had Rufus guard the door for I wished to be alone.

"Dear Lord, I have not asked much from you. I have lost my wife and many dear friends, and I have borne all stoically. I beg you to spare the life of Henry Monmouth. He is a good King and England needs him. He has a son who needs him. Take my old and battered body instead. Give him life and take mine. I will be content."

The chapel was silent. The candles flickered with the slight breeze from the door, but no heavenly voice spoke. No glorious light filled my head, and I did not know if I had been heard. I would await a sign.

"Amen."

To save my mind from the torment of losing the finest king I had yet served I put my thoughts to the campaign. I did not know the area and so I questioned the Duke of Bedford as our army snaked south. "La Charité, is it important?"

The Duke nodded, "It guards a crossing of the Loire and so long as they hold it, we have lost the west."

"And Cosne?"

"Equally important. While you were speaking with the King a rider came from the Duke of Burgundy. The garrison at Cosne has said that unless help comes by August the twelfth then they will surrender. We will meet with the Duke at Auxerre and he has sent a rider to the Dauphinists to settle this matter by a battle at Cosne!"

Such arranged battles were rare these days. If the enemy did choose to fight us, then that could only help us. Despite Baugé, I knew that we had the beating of the Franco-Scottish army. The two Dukes, Bedford and Exeter were confident that the French would honour the agreement. The Earl of Warwick and I were more cynical. Tanneguy du Châtel was, as the Duke of Burgundy had discovered to his cost, a

The Battle for France

dishonourable man. I was too lowly a knight to influence the uncle and brother of the King. When we met with the Duke of Burgundy it gave us a great army and all twelve thousand strong of us marched south. Despite the King's condition and his departure for Vincennes, the entire army was in high spirits. Even my retinue believed that a victory at Cosne which would end this war and deliver the whole of France to King Henry would be a sign that God was on our side and that it would heal our ailing King. I was still awaiting a sign from my prayer.

We reached Cosne on the tenth of August and the besiegers had gone. They had fled back over the Loire. They had dishonoured the agreement and it showed their fear at meeting us in open battle. It was at the Council of war we held at Cosne that I saw my true position. I was alone in urging the dukes to cross the river at any cost and to bring the French to battle. I now knew we had the beating of them. The last two occasions when they could have fought us, they had fled. They were afraid of us. The disaster at Baugé was now a distant and unpleasant memory. All that remained of it was the huge number of Scots who had come to France in the hope of defeating the English on foreign soil, something they rarely did on their own.

When we did move it was too little and too late. Worse was to come. Even as the Earl of Salisbury led men to the Loire a messenger arrived from Vincennes where King Henry resided. The Duke of Bedford and the Earl of Warwick along with me had been summoned to be at his bedside. Unlike the Duke and the Earl, I took my retinue and familia with me. They would not hold us up and I felt that they might be needed. Indeed, the servants of the other two proved to be more of a problem as they rode sumpters and even the new archers who followed me had palfreys. It was a journey of more than one hundred and eighty miles. We pushed hard and made just four stops along the way. They alerted our enemies that we were abroad. I think the three of us must have been feared by our enemies more than any other English leader save King Henry. The Duke of Gloucester had returned to England and his brother had proved to be a more than able replacement. The Earl was well respected by everyone for he had yet to be on the losing side. I think they saw me as an annoying irritant but one whose tenacity and resolve could win battles against the odds. I knew that my vengeance raid at Agincourt had created something of a legend.

It was north of the crossing of the Loire, as the road from Briare passed through the heavily forested area used by the Counts of Blois to go hunting, that we were attacked. The forty men who charged from the forests to the east were obviously Dauphinists but, as I later discovered, they came almost entirely from the ranks of Tanneguy du Châtel's retinue. My archer scouts detected them as they attacked from the east. Had we not had the Duke and Earl's servants we might have outrun them, but I doubt it. The warrior in me knew it was always better to fight than run for you never knew into what you were fleeing.

My archers were good scouts, and their warning did several things. It told us the direction of the attack and gave us enough warning to don helmets and draw swords but, most importantly, it allowed my archers to dismount, string their bows and be ready for the enemy. I had been ambushed before, but I think that it was a new experience for the Duke and the Earl. They almost froze until I shouted out orders, "Servants to the rear. Rafe and James take the archer's horses. The rest of you form up on me!"

My men obeyed instantly. I grabbed my shield and held it close to me before a bolt came flying from the forest. Numbers were hard to assess but I guessed that they would outnumber us. We had not been riding for battle and so our horses were vulnerable; they had neither shaffron nor peytrals. Luckily for our animals the crossbowmen aimed at men and not animals. Two bolts hit my shield, one of them penetrating through the layers of wood. Then my archers began to pick off the crossbowmen. The men at arms were led by a single knight and they began to pour from the trees once they realised that the ambush had been sprung and their crossbowmen were dying. In the time it took for them to realise that my men at arms had joined us, we had a long line ready to take on the enemy which disgorged from the trees. Thanks to my archers we had a solid line and the Duke, Earl and myself were in the centre. Michael was to my left and our squires were behind. The knight who led them made for the Duke of Bedford and his familia followed. They had killed one brother of King Henry and now they sought a second. They would hit us in the centre. The light horsemen with the men from Armagnac had the daunting task of taking on my ten men at arms. It was in the centre that they were pinning their hopes.

I watched the lance as it came directly for my chest. The man at arms was good for the tip never wavered and, ironically, it was that which saved me. Had it bobbed up and down I might have moved my shield the wrong way and been skewered but he was so keen to hit me square on my breastplate and knock me from the saddle that the tip was like an arrow. It was, therefore, relatively easy to deflect the lancehead down the side of my shield. He had punched at the last moment and that helped me shift the lance. He was also travelling at speed, but his horse had nowhere to go for Michael was so close to me that our stirrups were touching. As his horse's head came between ours, I swung my sword at the warrior's gorget. It was well made but I had more than fifty years of practice and my sword was not only well made but heavy. His head snapped forward as the steel rang against the plate protecting his neck and as his horse stopped, I had the chance to raise my sword and smash it down across the back of his neck. Some knights have a gorget which covers the rear too. This man at arms did not and it was a mail aventail which gave his neck some protection. My sword sliced through the mail and bit into the back of his neck. I felt it jar against the spine and the body slid from the saddle.

Michael had also slain his opponent, but the Duke of Bedford was exchanging blows with the knight who wished the glory of killing or capturing a duke. I contemplated interfering but I knew that the Duke, like his brother the King, had a chivalrous heart and would not thank me. Instead, I spurred Hercules who leapt forward, to take on the second line of men at arms and light horsemen. As I did so I was aware, through my peripheral vision that my archers and men at arms had already whittled down the light horsemen and like the horns of a bull were encircling the men at arms and the knight. Michael and Sir Stephen followed me, and Rufus and Jack filled the gap we had vacated. The next man at arms I faced was not one of the knight's familia, he had a different livery. Nor was he as good and the lancehead wavered so much that he could have hit my boot or my helmet. With a visor on his helmet, he also had restricted vision. Unconstrained by a horse to my right I jerked the reins of Hercules to my right and the man at arms went between Michael and me. His lance struck fresh air and my sword slammed across and into his back. Jerking forward he must have lost grip on his lance and Rufus had his first successful mounted combat for he rammed his sword under the man at arms' faulds. Even though he was visored I heard the screams as my squire's sword skewered him in the groin.

As I looked for my next opponent, I saw that we had won, and they were fleeing. Only the knight and the squire were fighting on. I shouted, "Yield! For you are lost!"

The knight raised his visor and saw that the two of them were alone. He shouted defiantly, "Never!" and he and his squire wheeled their horses to flee.

I had no intention of allowing them to escape, "Christopher White Arrow!"

"Loose!"

Nine arrows flew. They were all bodkins and backplates are never as strong as breastplates. It only took one to pierce the metal plate and the squire was hit by two while the knight by four. The two fell from the saddle.

I shouted, "Collect the horses and the plate. Thank you, Rufus, you did well."

Rather than being pleased the Duke of Bedford was angry, "That was not well done, Strongstaff. He was my opponent! You had no right to use archers to kill him!"

"My lord, he would not yield, and he was running away. I do not fight your way, my lord and that is why unlike your brother, the Duke of Clarence, I am still alive."

"You grow impertinent. I wonder that the King suffers you!"

I laughed for I cared not, "I have served three kings, my lord, including your father. All three valued my service and to speak the truth I am too old to change. When we reach the King, you may tell him of your displeasure, I will take his censure but not yours!" I saw that my men had gathered all that there was to be gathered. The Duke would not know but I knew that they would have slit the throats of the wounded. It was the kindest way and if a man took to ambush then this was the price he might have to pay. "Come, we are wasting daylight and time. The ambush has delayed us enough." I put spurs to Hercules and my men formed up protectively along my flanks. I did not even turn to see if the Duke and the Earl followed. I glanced at Rufus who was wide-eyed with shock.

Sir Stephen laughed, "Oh how the high and the mighty like to behave. You, my lord, are the only knight, except for the King that I see behaving like a warrior and not an overdressed popinjay trying to live up to ridiculous ideas of chivalry."

I nodded, "None the less my friends, it would not do to copy me. I get away with it because I am a belligerent old man."

The rest of the journey was uneventful, and we reached the palace of Vincennes after dark. I left Sir Stephen to see to my men and went directly with the Duke and the Earl to the King. The Duke had not said a word to me since the ambush.

The Earl had said, as we watered our horses, "It does not do to upset the Duke. If anything happens to the King, then he will be a powerful man."

I turned to look directly into the Earl's eyes. I liked him but he clearly did not know me, "I care not, my lord. If anything happens to the King, then I withdraw from court and this life. I came to France because the King asked for me and he needed me. If he is no longer here, then there is no reason for my presence. I have seen enough backstabbing and men struggling to seize the crown. The institution means nothing. It is the man who wears it that is important to me!"

The Battle for France

We almost ran down the corridor, however, when we reached the bedchamber the King was not in bed but was on a couch and his wife, Queen Katherine was reading to him. He smiled when he saw us and then his smile changed to a frown as he saw the blood on my jupon.

"What has happened?"

The Duke said, "We were ambushed on the way here by men from the Dukedom of Armagnac." He pointed angrily at me, "Strongstaff here ordered his archers to kill a knight and his squire who were fleeing from us."

The King said, reasonably, "Is this true?"

"Of course, my lord, the Duke of Bedford does not lie. Of course, he is a little loose with the truth. The knight refused to yield, and I would not let him escape for his perfidy."

"Ah! Brother, you must realise that men like Sir William here do not adhere to our code. I applaud his action for it ensured that you all arrived here, and I am glad that you are here for I fear that I am dying."

Silence filled the chamber. His brother ended it, saying, "You look well enough, brother. I shall send for different doctors."

"I have been seen by all the doctors in Paris and London. I am resigned to my death. Some days I am better than others. This is one of those days. Know that I have made my will and there is a codicil I have added. While you are all here know that I would have my brothers guard both England and France until my son is of an age to be given the reins of power." I saw the Duke of Bedford nod and look relieved. "Know too, brother, that I have appointed Sir William Strongstaff and his chosen man as a bodyguard for Henry!"

I saw the Earl of Warwick smile, but the Duke almost exploded like a bombard, "But, brother, he is old! What happens when he dies?"

"That was one of the reasons for the codicil. Sir William himself is aware of his own mortality. He will appoint one of his knights to be the guardian of Henry and whichever knight that is shall be honoured by both the regents!" He was thin and he was dying but his eyes flashed with anger, "And I will brook no arguments." He sat back and closed his eyes.

The Queen said, "He is overtired now. I pray you to leave us and return in the morning." The anger in her eyes was directed not at me but her brother-in-law.

When the door was closed the Duke of Bedford turned to me, "You have bewitched my brother and I will have this overturned!"

The Earl of Warwick put his hand on the Duke's arm, "My lord if you challenge the will think of your own position."

The Battle for France

I saw then that the Duke, no doubt like his brother, the Duke of Gloucester sought to rule the country through young Henry. He could not afford a challenge to the will. He turned to me, "You will guard the Prince and that is all!"

I held his gaze until he looked down, "As I have done since I was first charged to do so by the Black Prince. Do not presume to tell me my job, Duke John, I know how to protect a king," I paused, "from all enemies, both foreign and domestic!"

A servant waited for each of us as we left the chamber, and the door was closed. One said to me, "If you will follow me, my lord, I will take you to your chamber. Your knights will be housed in the rooms next to yours."

"And my men?"

He looked at me in surprise as though lords were not normally bothered by such trivialities. "There is a warrior hall attached to the palace. After I have shown you your room, I will take them there."

The room where my knights were quartered was close enough to the King's that I could be summoned quickly. After I had worked out a route to get to the King's side, we joined my men. The servant was wise enough to stay far enough away so that I could speak without being overheard.

"We will be staying here for some time. I do not plan on leaving until the King is recovered."

Sir Michael said, "The guards say that the priests hear his confession each morning and again each evening."

"We stay!"

Sir Stephen put his arm around the young knight, "Sir William knows his business. Come let us divide the treasure for we did well from the men of Armagnac!"

Rafe rubbed his hands together, "They may be treacherous dogs, but they make good brandy and each of the men had a bottle!"

Sir Oliver grinned, for he was fond of the fiery spirit, "You were ever resourceful, Rafe!"

Gesturing to the liveried servant I said to my men, "This servant will wait to show you to your sleeping quarters." I looked at him and he nodded. I put my arm around Rufus. "Rufus, come with me." Intrigued my squire followed me, "I have a task for you. I know not this palace. I need you to wander its corridors and find your way around. You are young and have an engaging face. If you are stopped then say that you are lost and speak in English."

"But Sir William, my French is good!"

I smiled, "Then pretend it is not. The evening meal will be served in an hour. See what you can discover by then."

He grinned, "Aye, lord."

I returned to my chamber and took off the soiled jupon. Rafe would fetch my baggage soon enough. I saw that there was water and I cleaned myself. The King was dying. I would have outlived three kings, four if you counted Edward. I would not outlive a fifth. Time was now an issue and I had to decide who would guard the King once I was gone. I did not plan on dying any time soon and from the look of the King he was fighting death as hard as he had fought his enemies, but it could not be put off and I was giving someone not only a great responsibility but also putting them in great danger. My body was a testament to that. I knew that I would now be viewing my knights and men at arms with new eyes. I lay naked on the bed and looked at the ceiling. We had done well already. Vincennes was an ancient French Palace and yet now the King of England and France, not to mention his lords, knights, men at arms and archers stayed here. We had come far, and it was galling for the King to come so close and yet still to fail. I sat up on the bed. I would not fail. I would see that his son, whom I had never seen and had yet to see one year would claim his father's inheritance.

Rafe entered and smiled, "My lord, it is good that I know you! Thank God Queen Katherine did not come in!"

"Queen Katherine?"

"Aye, she said she wished to speak with you."

"Then help me dress, you buffoon."

He smiled, "Why, lord, for she would be amused by this!"

"Why do I tolerate you?"

His face became serious, "For, my lord, we have seen behind the mask that you put on for the great and the good. We know you."

He was right and my anger evaporated like a morning mist!

I ensured that I was dressed in my best houppelande. It was too late to have my hair cut and so I had Rafe comb it as best he could. Thankfully, my thinning thatch was less unruly than when I had been younger.

"She said that she would be in the chapel, lord, and asked you to wait without." He added, "I have found my way around the palace, lord, and found a couple of ways for us to escape if we need to."

"Well done, you are learning!"

I went to the chapel and wondered at this meeting. Already folk were heading for the hall where they would dine. To arrive late would be seen as rude. I did not mind but I wondered at the young queen who might be sensitive about such things. I heard the noise from the hall as people arrived. The Queen and I would be late. She came out of the chapel with two ladies in waiting. She waved them away and then gestured for me to follow her. She was young and seemed almost mouselike to me. When she spoke, it was in hushed tones and I had to bend to enable my old ears to hear her.

"Sir William, I am pleased that the King has asked you to guard our son. I fear for his life." She looked around as though someone might hear although the only people were her ladies in waiting and they were twenty paces behind us. "I know the treachery of court and while England does not seem as dangerous as France, I will be glad if you are there to watch both my son and me."

I nodded, "And know that I will be there but, as I told the King, I am an old man."

She smiled, "My sister, Isabelle, met you once when she was betrothed to King Richard. She said you were old then." She hurried on and I saw that we were heading for the King's bedchamber.

"You will not dine with the court?"

She shook her head, "I know courts, Sir William. Men smiled at my father but there was no joy behind the smiles. They were plotting and planning what they could get. Until I know who my enemies are then I shall keep to myself. You are the only one I trust. The King has made it clear to me that you are the most trustworthy man in his realm. I needed to speak with you privately so that you know this. If you ever need to speak with me then know that I have given orders that you are to be admitted to my presence immediately." She took a deep breath, "My husband is dying, and we have not been married long. I wish to spend every moment with him." She saw my querulous look and nodded, "His doctors have told him that he has, at most, a month. Come and see him whenever you wish for he cares deeply about you. He believes that you alone can help his army secure France for our son."

"Thank you for the faith you have in me." We had reached the royal chamber and I stopped. "Until we have France then I will be needed here to help wrest the crown from your brother for the Dauphin desires it and will do anything to stop your husband wearing it."

"I know but you will send someone to watch over us, will you not? My husband trusts your judgement. He said you would find someone who was a good warrior and who was clever."

I nodded, "I have such a man in mind." Taking her proffered hand, I kissed the back of it. "I pray the King will recover and that this will not be necessary."

She was young but her eyes looked suddenly old as she said, "As do I but I fear King Henry has the smell of death about him!"

As I made my way to the hall, I had made my decision and I knew who I would appoint as Prince Henry's guard. I would delay telling him until I had to, if and when the King died. The Battle of Baugé had shown me that the King's brothers had fatal flaws in them. I could not leave France until it was secure. I owed that to all the dead. Deep down I knew that until we had France then Prince Henry would be safe from assassination or abduction. It was when France and England were his that he would become a pawn.

Distracted by my own thoughts I entered the hall and the hubbub stopped as every eye went to me. That some regarded me as a threat was nothing new, but I hoped that the majority of those who stared at me harboured good thoughts for if not then it meant treachery was close to the King. Michael stood and waved so that I could see where a place had been reserved for me. It was not at the table with the King's brother and the other senior lords; I was not surprised. I had upset the Duke of Bedford and this would be seen as a punishment. It was not for I preferred the company of my three knights.

The conversations began again as I sat. Rufus fetched me food and poured me some wine. I did not eat as much as I once had but I needed the wine. There were expectant looks on the faces of my knights and I smiled, "The Queen wished to speak with me." They looked at me as though I would elaborate but I merely nodded at their platters and said, "What is worth eating?" I smiled when I saw that I had infuriated them.

The news of the King's worsening illness brought out the worst in his nobles. Already men were seeking alliances for the news of the dual regency had been leaked and with the Duke of Gloucester in England, men were seeking to ingratiate themselves with the Duke of Bedford. The King's uncle, the Duke of Exeter was also the subject of much attention for he would have an influence on the two young dukes. My men and I, despite the fact that everyone knew I was to be the bodyguard, were the only ones who seemed immune from the disease of gossip and plots.

My knights were more concerned with the health of the King. They had heard rumours but as most of the nobles had written off the King as dead already, they had only heard talk of the succession.

I gave them what little good news I could, "He seems better than he was, and his mind is as sharp as ever but his body is wasted. If this is the dysentery from Meaux then it has lasted a long time. The Earl of Suffolk died much more quickly at Honfleur. My hope is that he will recover and return to lead our armies."

Michael wiped his hands on the cloth over his left shoulder, "You said hope, lord, but that is not what you believe."

The Battle for France

I shook my head. I would keep the Queen's confidence to myself. Stephen asked, "And we wait here until…"

I nodded, "We will go to war again, but the King summoned me to his side. Keep the men sharp and watchful. These waters in which we swim are murky, to say the least."

The three of them nodded. I did not need to spell it out.

While our mood was sombre and reflective Rufus, when we went to our chamber was bright-eyed and excited. I do not think he meant any disrespect, but he and Jack knew the King less well than the rest of us. He was a distant and lofty figure. Stephen and Oliver had helped to train him and had fought with him at Agincourt.

As he helped me off with my houppelande he chattered like a magpie telling me of what he had seen, "I have never seen so many great lords and the Duke of Bedford's squire said that his lord will rule England with his brother!"

"Do not listen to gossip. If and I emphasise if, the King dies then his brothers will be regents along with the Queen. They are answerable to Parliament and there are lords like the Earl of Warwick and the Duke of Exeter who will ensure that young Henry manages to grow into the crown and to make wise decisions."

He seemed deflated, "Then they will not lead the armies here in France?"

"They may but they have a duty to the King. The war is not yet over here in France."

"And the Duke of Bedford does not like you." I flashed him an angry look. He shrugged, "You had words on the road. All heard and the other squires think that you could lose your head."

I laughed, "And that proves my point about gossip, Rufus. If I lose my head it will be in battle! Now, I wish to rise early. I have much to do. Do not sleep across the door for I would hate to trample on you!"

I rose before terces for I needed to make water and, once I was awake, I could not sleep. My knee ached when I slept and I had found that movement helped. I went to the now-empty Great Hall. As I had expected there were jugs of ale and wine left there. I had some ale and then ascended to the King's quarters. The guards there had been informed of my unique position and one said, "The King was awake, lord, but the doctors gave him a sleeping draught an hour since."

"And the Queen?"

The sentry was a mature soldier with the first flecks of grey in his hair. I remembered him as a young man. He smiled, "The poor lady collapsed with exhaustion. When the King is awake then so is she and when he sleeps she watches him as much as possible."

The Battle for France

"I will return later."

I went upstairs again as dawn broke. I heard voices from within and the sentry said, "The King has awoken, and his doctor was summoned."

I entered the chamber and saw three doctors fussing around him. His wife was not there, and I guessed she had gone to their private garderobe. The King's eyes were closed but the pained expression on his face told me that he was awake and in pain. "Begone, leeches. If you cannot make me well then do not irritate me with your poking and prodding." The doctors saw me, and they left. They reminded me of the men who had caused the King so much pain after the Battle of Shrewsbury as they tried to remove the arrow. His eyes lighted on me and he smiled, "I cannot abide doctors. You know, William, when I am well again, and we have France secure I have a mind to go to Jerusalem. With the might of England, France, and Brittany behind me I believe we could reclaim it for God. What say you?"

"I would like to see the Holy City before I die. Aye, my lord, I shall be with you."

His wife returned and the two of us chatted about the past. He was still ill, but his mind missed nothing, and he recalled men and events from when he was a boy in Ireland as a guest of King Richard.

"I tire but speaking with you, Strongstaff, has been better than any medicine they might have given me!"

"Thank you, Sir William, you are good for my husband. Why he has better colour already!"

All three of us knew the truth but talking as though there was hope for a future was better than doom and gloom.

It was later that day that I was summoned to the King's bedside along with his brother and the Earl of Warwick. When I entered and saw Queen Katherine weeping and the King's eyes closed I feared he was dead already. The Bishop of Beauvais and a group of priests were around his bed. I saw that the doctors stood against one wall. They had left a gap in their circle for the three of us. The Bishop said, "Let us sing psalms for the soul of this great king."

We sang for more than half an hour, I saw the candle burn down, and then, suddenly, the King opened his eyes and cried out, "Thou liest! Thou liest! My portion is with the lord!" The Queen took a crucifix and handed it to the King whose eyes, whilst open, appeared to be unseeing. He held the crucifix and his wife's hands. He said, "Into thy hands, Lord..." And then spoke no more. There was the sigh of death I had heard many times before and King Henry, the victor of Shrewsbury and Agincourt died and with it the hope of England.

I said, almost silently, "Farewell, my friend. I had thought you would have outlived me but that was not meant to be. I shall now finish the task you appointed to me and retake France and then, God willing, I will watch over your son."

Chapter 14

As soon as I left, I headed for my men. They were doing as I had asked and practising. I gathered them around me, "The King is dead!"

My men at arms and archers were hard men. They all knew that death could be around the next hedgerow but when they heard my news some of them openly wept and all of them were distraught. I know not how long they stood there in silent thought. I could not measure such time. Rufus was the one who broke the silence. "And what of us, lord?"

His words made my men come back from the reverie of memories, the battles they had fought with the King and their lives with him and all looked at me. I took a deep breath, "I have a task to finish. The Dauphin still claims the throne and until it is secure for the new King, I cannot leave France. But none of you, save one, is under any obligation. Now is not the moment for you to give me an answer but if any wishes to return home, or even to accompany the King's body then I shall happily pay for their passage to England." They nodded, "Sir Michael, I need to speak with you, privately. Come and walk with me."

Michael was as intrigued as any by my words. Rufus, I could see, was desperate to follow us. I pointed to the others, "Rufus, wait here!"

I headed for the river which lay a mile away from the great castle. I said nothing for the first half mile for there were others close by and I was selecting each word that I would say to Michael. When I did speak, I did not look at Michael but stared, through the trees of the hunting park, towards the river. It was the Marne and it had been Meaux on the Marne which had killed my king. "The King entrusted me with the guarding of his son. I did it for him, his father, Henry Bolingbroke, and poor King Richard. He also asked me to finish the task of retaking France for his son."

"How can you do both?"

"I cannot. That is why I ask you to guard the young Henry while I finish my appointed task. When France is safe then I will relieve you of your obligations." He was silent. I saw a young deer, startled by our appearance, race off down a game trail. "I know what it is that I ask. Know this, Michael, that I do not command. I ask. You can say no, and I shall not think the worse of you."

He shook his head, "It is an honour, my lord, but I do not think I am worthy! I thank you for the trust and faith you have in me but I do not believe that I am the man to do this."

I laughed, "And when Prince Edward asked me the same then my thoughts were like yours. You will have to learn how to do the job and, when he is old enough, you will need to train him as a warrior, but I believe that you can do it."

He stopped and looked at me, "But when he is old enough to need training then you will have returned. You will be the one to make him a great warrior like his father."

"Perhaps, but you have a natural ability. Sir Stephen and my men at arms know that." We had reached the river and there was a fallen log. The walk through the wood had both tired me and cause my knee to hurt. I sat, "So, what do you say, Michael? You will need to guard the Queen too, that goes without saying."

"Of course, and I am happy to be given the honour although I shall miss the others."

I nodded. "As I missed the Blue Company. You will never forget them, nor will they forget you and should you ever need them then they will be at your side in a heartbeat."

"Good for they are like brothers to me."

"There is one thing more. The death of the King has made me feel my mortality and I have no will. When we return to the castle, I shall see the lawyer who wrote the codicil to the King's will. I intend to write my own. The first thing I will do is something my wife urged me to do on her deathbed. I will adopt you and you shall become my son."

He beamed and I cursed myself for not having done it before. It was such a simple act and yet it meant more to him than the knighthood which had been bestowed upon him. Perhaps Eleanor always knew that!

"And you should know that I intend to leave Weedon to you. Neither my sons nor my daughter need it. It is the place where Eleanor and I were our happiest and whilst it is a small manor, I am sure that you will be happy there."

He nodded, "I shall but you have done so much for me already. You need not make such a grand gesture."

"It is not a gesture for it makes me happy and I know that I do not need to. I want to. I will write to my sons and when you return to England then you can deliver the letters."

We stood and I embraced him. Despite the death of the King, I felt an inner peace I had not felt in a long time. My wife's spirit could finally rest. I let Michael tell the others his news. Over the next days, each of them came to tell me that they were all happy to continue to serve with me in France. None of them begrudged what I did for Michael in fact they were all full of joy at what I had done. I hoped my sons and daughter would not either. I wrote the three of them each a long letter expressing not only my wishes but also the thoughts behind those wishes. I paid for copies of the new will. The whole business was expensive, but I knew that when I hired the lawyer. I sent a copy to each of my children and gave one to Michael. King Henry had shown me how to prepare for death.

    I never saw the King buried. That was to happen many months hence, after his father-in-law, King Charles of France died. The King died on the last day of August and was not buried until the end of the first week in November. I was very much an outsider for the Duke of Bedford took charge. He had King Henry's body embalmed and placed in a lead-lined coffin. On the top of the coffin was placed a lifelike effigy of the King. The funeral cortege then wound its way first to Rouen and thence past Abbeville and Agincourt before a fleet of ships took the coffin and the royal party up the Thames. At each nightly halt, the streets were lined with mourners for the man the French called Henry the Conqueror. The guarded coffin spent each night in a church. It was a statement by the Duke of Bedford. The King was dead, but his power still remained. The Earl of Warwick, as well as the Duke of Bedford, accompanied the coffin.

    As soon as the King's coffin left Vincennes my men and I went with the Earl of Salisbury to return to the unfinished task of defeating the Dauphinists. The death of King Henry had dismayed those loyal to Queen Isabeau and even King Charles, but they put new heart into the Dauphinists and when the Duke of Brittany threw his weight behind the rebels then we had to begin again. It was as though all the work we had done was for nothing. The Duke of Burgundy was still our ally and so the Earl and I rode to Nevers to meet with him and plan our strategy. It was in October as we were assessing how many men we had to face the French that we heard that King Charles, latterly called the Mad, had died and the Dauphin, also called Charles, declared himself King of France. More men flocked to his banner. While the old King Charles had been alive then many had remained loyal. Now with King Henry dead and the Dauphin waving the Oriflamme we had not just a civil war but a real war.

    I could tell that the Duke was having second thoughts about being our ally. This was despite the fact that the Duke of Bedford was engaged to the Duke's sister Anne. The Earl did his best to persuade him to take the field against an ever-increasing number of rebels and Scots.

He was a gentle man and not the whirlwind that had been his father. "It is almost winter, my dear Earl, and I cannot afford to keep my army in the field. Perhaps next year, eh?" To me that sounded like a man procrastinating in the hope that we might simply go away, and he would not have to do anything.

If we did nothing, then I knew the war would stall and we might lose all that we had gained. The King had not stopped when we had taken Caen. It was time for me to take the reins. King Henry would have wished it. I suggested a sort of compromise, "My lord, if you could provide provisions then we can take the war to the French and their allies. We will provide the warriors, but they must be fed."

I saw the debate on his face. It was a small price to pay and he could move closer to the fence he wished to squat upon. "Very well then. I shall instruct the castellan here that you will be using Nevers as your base. I will return to Dijon." It reminded me of the Bible story where Pilate washes his hands of the issue. He would hide in Dijon.

The Earl and I were left then with a tiny portion of the army we needed. He was very much downhearted by the refusal of the Duke to join us. I was more philosophical, "This is easier, my lord. We have enough men to watch the French. We have the recently arrived Sir Thomas Rempston and his retinue who are fresh and eager. First, we find the Dauphin and then move the army to block his moves. Hopefully, the Duke will see the wisdom of continuing the fight and when the King is buried more men will, I hope, come from England."

My words put heart into the Earl, but I knew that the onus was on me to find the Dauphin. I led my men, in late November towards Bourges. This was not the season for war but that meant nothing to my hardened company. As we headed through rain-filled skies, we used our normal formation. Two archers at the fore and the rest at the rear with the baggage. I rode between Sir Oliver and Sir Stephen with Rufus just behind me. We all missed Michael for he had the most pleasant of manners and a sense of humour which would brighten just such a miserable day as we rode towards Bourges. We would have to get used to this for he was still with the Queen and the coffin, heading for London. Once we crossed the Loire ford close by Givry we were in the disputed land. We had tents with us for we could not guarantee to find places to stay. The first night we found a deserted farm in which to stay so we had hot food as we could light a fire in what had been the kitchen.

As yet another rainstorm struck us Sir Oliver said, "This is when I miss Michael the most. He would have thought of something amusing to make us smile."

Sir Stephen nodded, "And yet would you change places with him, Oliver? I would not. How Sir William put up with the conniving courtiers I know not."

Rufus chirped up, "But he is with the greatest nobles in the land, surely his life will be full!"

I shook my head, "I fear that he and Jack will have their work cut out. I did not do my young knight any favours. Here we can be ourselves, but Michael and Jack have to play a part and present a face which will be acceptable to men they may well not like." I was thinking of the Earl of Oxford who duped poor King Richard!

The next day we resumed our ride and, once more, it was a murky, grey day. We rode along a quiet and seemingly empty road. Farmers had no work for their fields were fallow and only fools ventured forth in the rain. Not long before what would have been noon although we could not see the sun, we stopped to rest the horses and eat stale fare. The rain had ceased but all was a shadowy and cloud filled day. We changed the two scouts so that we had fresh eyes and headed along the quiet road.

"Are there any Frenchmen in this land, lord?"

I smiled at Rufus. He had much to learn. War was largely dull and consisted of monotonous duties punctuated by violence. Just then Harry Fletcher, our lead scout that day, whipped his horse's head around and rode back with another archer, Paul Broad Back, close behind. Immediately we drew swords and my archers strung bows. There was danger ahead. The rain helped us to hide although it would make the bowstrings less effective, and I waved my men into the fields which lined the road. There were enough trees and bushes so that when we dismounted, we were as good as invisible. We heard the hooves of the dozen or so riders who passed us, oblivious to our presence, heading towards the river. I waited until they had passed before waving over Harry.

"I take it they didn't see you?"

He snorted as though I had insulted him, "No, lord. Their heads were down, and they were hooded."

"Then we wait here until they return and follow them." I turned to Matthew the Millerson, "You and Harry stay close to them when they return but make sure that you are not seen. Either they come from a castle or they have a camp. I would know both which and where."

As we waited Rufus asked, "Why did we not ambush them, lord? They had no idea we were here."

"Simple Rufus, we need to know where the enemy army is to be found. If they are just a rogue patrol and come from a castle that tells us much. It means that the Dauphinists may not be abroad. We are a patrol to find information and not to collect treasure."

I think that if Michael and Jack had been with us then they would have been questioned by my curious squire even more thoroughly than the couple of cursory questions to me. He had learned to limit his questions to the irascible old knight. The rain stopped briefly and then began again. An hour after they had passed us the Frenchmen returned. As Harry had said they were hooded and could see little beyond the road they rode. Harry and Matthew mounted and followed and then the rest of my company headed down the road. The shorter days made dusk seem longer and I was wondering where they were heading when we caught the lights and fires of a small town ahead. Harry and Matthew appeared from the side of the road to halt us. "They entered the town ahead, lord. There is no wall around it."

"Let us see if we can find out more." I dismounted and said, "Sir Stephen, take command." I went to the sumpters led by Rafe and James, "Unload two of these." While they did so I took off my spurs and my helmet and coif. I handed my sword to Rufus. "Keep this for me until we return. Rafe, mount the horse." Apart from Rufus, Rafe had the best French of any of my men. "I intend to scout out the town. Wait here for me."

James said as Rafe and I mounted, "And what about a camp, lord?"

"Owen the Welshman, take a couple of archers and see if you can find somewhere to camp."

We rode until we could see the town and the brazier of the night watch. The light from the fire diminished their night vision and we dismounted as yet unseen. Leading our horses would make us seem less of a threat and I exaggerated the limp from my knee. No one expects a lame man to be a danger. This was not a large town, but I saw, in the gloom, a castle in the distance. It looked to be an old-fashioned motte and bailey castle but with stone walls. It lay just beyond the town on a higher piece of ground. I could now work out that the patrol had come from the castle but if we turned around then we might arouse suspicion.

One of the town watch stood and advanced towards us, "Are you lost, friend?"

I nodded and laughed, "Aye, we are from the north, around Bretuil and this is all strange land to us. What is this town?"

"It is Nérondes, the manor of Giscard de Nérondes. Have you not heard of him in the north? He was at the Battle of Baugé and slew a great English lord."

I turned to Rafe, "See, I told you we should have turned off after the river."

The Battle for France

Rafe played the fool, "Sorry, master, you are right."

I began to turn Hercules around, hoping that the man would not notice what a fine horse he was. "If you ask the lord, he may let you stay in the castle. There will be room for the Scottish lords who were staying with him have headed to Bourges at the muster. The Dauphin gathers his army."

I shook my head, "I am dull company, and I must reach the home of my wife's uncle."

We mounted and started to head back down the road, "Where does he live?"

I pulled the hood of my cloak up and feigned deafness.

When we reached my men I said, "Mount. Has Owen returned?"

"Aye, lord, he has found a suitable wood just two miles away."

"Then let us ride."

We had a cold, fireless camp but one sheltered by trees and we ate our rations. I told the others what we had learned. "The Dauphin is at Bourges. That, I believe, is thirty miles to the west of us. It is a large place and from what I could deduce he is gathering his forces there."

"Do you think, my lord, that he plans to attack soon?"

"A good question, Sir Stephen, and if we were talking about King Henry then I would say aye, but the Dauphin seems nervous about facing an enemy unless he outnumbers him. From the Earl of Salisbury, I learned that when the Duke of Clarence was slain at Baugé he was heavily outnumbered. I think that is why we saw the French patrol out. It helps us."

"How, my lord?"

"Simple, Rufus, we ambush his patrols. We now know that they head for the river. Perhaps the inclement weather prevented them venturing across the river but if we can keep them in the dark then the Dauphin and his Scottish allies may well be reluctant to attack. We need the Duke of Burgundy and his men if we are to defeat our foe. All we do now is thwart his attempts and keep him blind."

I was weary and aching when we reached Nevers. The Earl of Salisbury and Sir Thomas had quartered the rest of the men either in the castle or in houses in the town. The Duke of Burgundy was not a fool. The presence of our men made Nevers a town which could be well defended. As I had realised, heading towards it, this was now the border and if the Dauphin came then he would have to fight to take it. Leaving Sir Oliver to see to the men and Rufus my horse I went, with Sir Stephen, into the Great Hall whose roaring fire made me smile as I entered and took off my cloak, handing it to a servant. The Earl and Sir Thomas had already begun to demolish a jug of wine.

The Battle for France

"From your smile, Sir William, you have had a good patrol."

"It is the fire which heartens me, my lord but you are right, we have learned much." A servant handed me a goblet of wine from the Rhone, rich and heady I did not drink it all down. I savoured it and let it warm me as it slipped down. "The Dauphin is at Bourges."

The Earl of Salisbury waved over his squire, "Fetch me my map!" He smiled at me, "I like maps. I am surprised more fellows do not use them."

I nodded for I agreed with him, "It is forty-odd miles from here and they are using the garrisons from their castles to probe."

The Earl of Salisbury said, "And did they detect you?"

Sir Stephen was with me and he laughed, "This must be the first time you have served with Sir William Strongstaff, my lord. He is only seen when he wishes to be."

I nodded at the compliment and the squire brought in the map which was laid on the table. "We let the patrol pass unharmed and I discovered that the Dauphin has a mixed army of Scots and Frenchmen at Bourges. My guess is that they are patrolling as far as the Loire," I jabbed my finger at the blue line on the map."

The Earl of Salisbury said, "Just five miles from here."

"I propose that instead of venturing forth into the land controlled by the French we send a daily patrol of mounted archers just beyond the river to the hamlet of Givry. There is a wood close by. It is not a bridge but a ford the French will use."

The Earl of Salisbury did like maps and that was obvious as his finger traced the line of the river north. "Your plan is a good one but what if they choose not this road but one further north. Auxerre is a Burgundian stronghold."

The four of us studied the map and I nodded, "You could be right but, until we have more men, my lord, we must cut our cloth to fit."

He nodded and stroked his beard. He was a decisive man. "Then I shall take my retinue and head north to Auxerre. From what Strongstaff says the patrols here will only require forty men at most. They will be able to prevent the probing by the French and I would sleep happier knowing that all the rat holes are barred."

The Earl of Salisbury was the senior lord and in command; we agreed, "Aye, Sir Thomas that makes sense and I will write to the Duke of Bedford and ask for more men."

We were now so far from the ports in the north that a message sent to England might take a fortnight or more even if sent by a fast rider. Since the death of King Henry most English troops were in castles. Until the spring then help from home would not be forthcoming.

The Battle for France

It was December before we had to draw a bow. I went out twice a week with my archers and four men at arms. Sir Stephen and Sir Oliver each did two and the knight, Sir Thomas, who was but recently arrived in France, took the seventh. My only worry was that some French sympathiser in Givry might send word to Bourges of our patrols but as the days passed and we came to know those who lived in the hamlet we realised that they were Burgundians, and they were happy to help. We had seen no sign of the French and Rufus was becoming restless.

On that December morning, as we left while it was still dark and rode along a road which had a rare frost he grumbled, "This is not the work of a knight, lord. Kit Warhammer could lead this patrol!"

Kit was behind us and said, cheerfully, "Why, thank you, Master Rufus, for that compliment and we all thought that you could do it alone!"

I smiled as my squire flushed, "You asked for that, Rufus. You should know by now that my men at arms are the equal of any knight. I am needed here for these are my men and it is a poor leader who asks others to do his job for them. King Henry never shirked when he was a young squire. He rode abroad with me happily hunting brigands or fighting his father's enemies. This is preparation for the day you will become a knight." I paused, "Although I fear that day is still some time off." He looked shocked. "You have improved but there is still some way to go. All of this will teach you skills. The Duke of Clarence thought he had all the skills he needed but obviously, patience was not one of them and it got him killed at Baugé. This is dull and it is boring, but it is training your mind." He was silent as he reflected on my words.

We had done this enough times now to know what we did and where to wait. The road passed through a wood, but the leafless trees afforded little cover and we wished to remain hidden. The ivy-covered and long-deserted house half a mile from the hamlet was a better place to wait. There we could tether our horses and while two archers hid in the woods, just four hundred paces from us, the rest of us were able to shelter behind the crumbling walls of the house. Two more archers waited across the road behind the tangle of weeds and spiky shrubs. The men gambled with dice and I would sit and let my mind wander back over my life and to speculate on the future lives of Michael and the young King. I knew I would never see King Henry become a man. I would soon be seventy and I felt my age. I knew no other soldier who was as old as me in fact except for a few churchmen who did not have to ride to war I knew none as old as me. One day I would ride to war and my luck would desert me. I had outlived so many that I wondered if I had been chosen to tread this path. Was I the hope for others that a man could be a knight and fight in many battles and yet live? Four kings had died in my lifetime and that was a wonder. I looked up as the sun came from behind a cloud. It was bright although the air was chill. The breeze came from the east and there lay mountains. The people of Givry had told us that they did not suffer snow here, but I wondered if this year could be the exception.

The whistle from Owen the Welshman made us all alert. I stood and donned my coif and helmet. I took off my cloak and drew my sword. I nodded to Rufus who went for the horses. We had yet to see any enemies and I had wondered if they would wait until spring to reconnoitre aggressively. The ten archers we had with us each nocked a bodkin arrow. The men at arms and Rufus had spears. We heard nothing at first, but I knew that Owen, who was the scout four hundred paces from us, would not warn us unnecessarily. Men were coming down the road. I had just sixteen men. If this was a large number, then we would have to send a shower of arrows and then race for the ford. The level of the Loire was relatively low. The rains when we had first begun this watch had meant we had to swim part of the river but now the water only came to our buskins. The men of Givry told us that when the spring rains came then the ford would be impassable for a month or more.

Even Rufus had learned to curb his natural enthusiasm and remain as still as possible. I was the one who now found it hard to remain without moving as my knee stiffened and ached when I did not move it. I heard the hooves and, through the ivy and scrubby shrubs, I saw horses and metal. The riders would be cloaked for it was cold. Having discarded our own cloaks, we felt the chill. The French cloaks would impair them albeit briefly. A distraction for a heartbeat was sometimes the difference between life and death. It was Much the Archer who was the last man in the line. He would let them pass unless he heard me give the command to loose. I could hear their voices at they chatted: they were not expecting trouble. I heard the end of a joke which insulted Englishmen and two Frenchmen laughed. As they passed me, I saw that there was a knight and his squire while the others were men at arms. I began to count as they passed. Twelve had passed when I heard the whistle from Owen. The last had passed him. One of the Frenchmen turned and shouted to the knight that he had heard something. As the knight ordered them to halt then I had but one decision to take.

"Attack!"

Ten arrows flew and my four men at arms raced to the road to slay those that they could. My days of racing were gone but I hurried as quickly as I could. I saw five men who, although they had plate and mail, lay on the ground bleeding their lives away. My men at arms and Rufus had taken advantage of the confusion and as I reached the road saw another five men at arms tumble from their saddles. Even though the surviving French had managed to draw weapons another ten arrows had headed their way. Two found shields but five more hit flesh and two struck horses. The knight had two arrows, sent by Much sticking from his plate but they had obviously not penetrated deeply enough into flesh. I hurried towards him, holding my sword two handed. He spied me and spurred his horse. A rider who charges down a man on foot normally has the advantage. My many years of experience came to the fore and as he pulled his arm back to strike at me, I stepped to my right and swung my sword at his leg. He had mail chausse and metal greaves, but my blow hacked into his calf and then the flank of his horse. My sword sliced through flesh and the leather strap holding his stirrup. It grated along the bone and a combination of the loss of his stirrup and his horse attempting to veer away meant he fell to the ground. I was aware of movement behind me and was just in time to see the knight's squire rear his horse to clatter into my skull. Had I been a young man I could have shifted out of the way, but my injured knee meant that I was fixed to the spot and I held up my sword as my only defence. I was doomed. It was Rufus who saved me. He ran from my side and rammed his spear into the unprotected groin of the squire who had stood in his stirrups to make his horse rear. He toppled backwards and was followed by the horse which, falling on him, crushed his body.

The eight Frenchmen who had survived turned and ran. Three had arrows already in their armour and limbs and another three were hit before they were out of range. I saw no Frenchmen who were left alive near me and I sheathed my sword, "Thank you, Rufus, I owe you a life!"

He grinned, "You are my lord and besides he has a fine sword and scabbard."

Much shouted, "Sir William, the knight lives but he is close to death!"

My strike had severed the lower part of the knight's leg. If there had been a fire, we might have saved his life, but the pool of blood told me he was doomed. "My son?"

"He was your squire?" He nodded, "Then he is in heaven now!" I hoped that the youth had been shriven or else he would not be.

The knight opened his mouth, no doubt to curse me, but his head flopped to one side and he died.

"We will bury them here. Collect the horses, plate and weapons."

That evening Sir Thomas wondered what effect our ambush would have. I rubbed my knee, the fight had made it complain all the way back. "I think it tells the French that we are here. If they intend revenge or to shift us then Sir Stephen or Sir Oliver leading the next patrols will know."

"I will go with both of them and we will double the men just in case. You have done enough, Sir William."

I smiled, "Enough… it is not a word I have used very often!"

Chapter 15

That was the last fight of the winter. By January when the ground was cold and hard and no more patrols had headed our way, it became obvious that we had deterred the French. A messenger came from the Earl of Salisbury to tell us that they had been forced to discourage the French who were probing towards Auxerre. Although we had been few in number our efforts had made the French fear us. We had bought the Duke of Bedford time.

The end of December was enlivened by a letter from Michael. He had been taught to read and write and was justly proud of the skill. It had been Eleanor who had taught me, and I had been older than Michael when I had learned. My scrawl was like that of a spider who falls into wine and then into the ink to wander across the parchment.

Windsor, November,

Lord, we have just come from the funeral of King Henry. The whole journey from Vincennes to London was awe-inspiring. The people of Normandy all grieved for the King and the route from the Thames was lined with the great and the poor alike all of whom bowed their heads and wept. The coffin lay in St Paul's cathedral and there was a service. The next day the coffin was mounted and covered with banners and devices representing the Trinity, the Virgin, St George, St Edmund, and St Edward. The Queen and I followed it, both of us draped in black to Westminster. Behind us walked great lords, archbishops, and bishops. The coffin was laid before the Great Altar close to the tombs of Edward the Confessor and King Richard.

I remembered that it had been Henry himself who had overseen the burial of King Richard.

The next day the funeral took place and I sat behind the Queen. Something happened then which the Earl of Warwick told me was usual when a King was buried but I had never seen it. A knight I did not recognise who was mounted on a warhorse and with full armour

whilst wearing a crown rode up to the high altar and the coffin. Then the household knights stripped him of the crown, weapons, and armour. I was told, later, that this was done because as an anointed king, King Henry had been a knight of Christ. Now that he was dead, he had to go to heaven devoid of all trappings of knighthood and royalty.
I confess, Sir William, that I was moved to tears by the ceremony. When I apologised to the Queen, she said it marked me as a gentleman more than any force of arms. Now the task you appointed to me begins. The Queen is both kind and thoughtful. Is it dishonourable to say that I love to be in her presence? The child needs his wet nurse more than he needs me, but each night Jack and I sleep behind the door of his chamber. Having seen the funeral of his father then I am even more aware of the responsibility you have given to me. Know that I will discharge my duty as well as I am able, but I look forward to your return so that it may be done properly.
Your servant and adopted son,
Michael of Weedon

 I read the letter many times over the next months. It was a comfort to me, and it also made me realise the weight I had placed on the shoulders of young Michael. We maintained our daily patrols, but they always ended the same way, we returned to Nevers not having seen a Frenchman. I became restless. I was not winning France for the young King and I wondered if I should return to England, to do that which I promised King Henry. In the end, it was the French who made my decision for me. The Dauphin and his army besieged the French town of Cravant. It was a small town but an important one as it controlled two rivers. The populace sent to the Dowager Duchess of Burgundy for succour and she appealed to the Earl of Salisbury. Every English soldier on the Burgundian border was summoned and we left Nevers happily. We were to rendezvous at Auxerre. When we reached there in the middle of July, I was eager to fight.
 It was the Earl who counselled caution. He and his son in law William Willoughby commanded the army and the Earl knew our shortcomings and weaknesses better than any. "Sir William, much as I would like to face the Scots and these rebels we do not have enough men. I have done as you did at Nevers and scouted out the enemy. Darnley, the Earl of Douglas, the Scot who leads the army, has eight thousand men at the siege. We have, at the moment, less than fifteen hundred English soldiers. I hope for another five hundred who are

marching south. We have two thousand Burgundians, but the artillery is provided by the citizens of Auxerre!"

I had faced worse odds than two to one, "And how many archers do we take?"

"We hope to have fifteen hundred when all arrive."

"Then we shall prevail." I was confident enough in our longbows to be able to make the prediction.

By the twenty-eighth, the army was gathered and all four thousand of us marched south. Rufus had lost all of his edges now and looked like the rest of my retinue, a veteran. His beard had filled out and unlike many of the English warriors, he did not bother shaving. His hair was tied, like most of my men, behind his head. The sun had bronzed his skin and he rode with the swagger of one who knows his own ability. This had not happened overnight but my men at arms, archers and knights had gradually chipped at the façade he presented until he was one of them. They had not had to do this with Michael for he had come to us like me, a camp follower, a worldly-wise young man who would not be taken advantage of. The first night we had arrived in Auxerre the squire of a recently arrived knight from England thought to mock Rufus' appearance. The new squire was twice Rufus' size and well-muscled. My squire did not rise to the bait but smiled and the squire took that for weakness. It was a mistake. Later that night, as the squires went to check on the horses Rufus was waiting and when the other squire did not apologise Rufus gave him a beating. John, Sir Stephen's squire witnessed it and told Sir Stephen. The next morning there was barely a mark on Rufus, but the other squire looked as though he had been set upon by a band of brigands. No one dared to mock Rufus again and, to his credit, he never mentioned the incident. That was a mark of his growth.

We went at the speed of the cannons from Auxerre and it was slow going. We reached a position two or three miles from the town and saw the French and Scottish lines on the evening of the thirtieth. We camped and held a council of war. The Earl heeded my advice to fight, as we had at Agincourt, a dismounted battle. The bridge over the River Yonne made that decision for us and it suited our archers. The horses were led to the rear with the baggage and they were guarded by the Auxerre gunners and pioneers who embedded stakes before the camp in case the enemy tried a cavalry charge. The Earl and I went to assess the French position. They had prepared well and any attack by us would have resulted in disaster. I pointed south. "There is a bridge here my lord. If we left the baggage and guns here, we could face them across the river.

The Battle for France

Let us invite a charge from them. They outnumber us and our archers could win the day for us."

I saw the Earl weighing up the advantages and disadvantages of such a move. "It is a risk Strongstaff."

"Do we want to relieve the siege, my lord? If we do then we either conjure another two thousand men to fight them or make them attack us."

He nodded and said, "You are right, but I am not happy about this."

"Trust in our archers and men at arms, my lord."

We moved after dark heading north back up the river until we found a ford and then we marched south to be close to the bridge. When the French awoke, they saw that we were now across the river from the town. They had to shift their entire position and this time they had no opportunity to make it hard for us. There was a bridge, but we could see that it was guarded. We arrayed for battle and the Scots and the French quickly redeployed their men. The river was just fifty paces wide and both sides were well within the range of the other, but I knew the superiority of our archers. For three hours we faced each other. The enemy had the numbers to attack whilst we did not, but they lacked the courage. The French crossbowmen and the Scottish archers reluctantly began the battle when we started to advance. The Earl gave the command and our archers sent two thousand arrows in reply. Some of the Scottish arrows found flesh but more of ours plunged and tore into the Scottish archers and French crossbowmen. As the enemy missiles decreased then our archers began to target the French men at arms.

I stood with the Earl beyond the range of the enemy arrows which, in truth, would not have harmed us. They were war arrows. I saw the French begin to waver. It was the experience of a lifetime which led me to make a suggestion, "Earl, we could charge across the river. It does not look deep. Our archers can protect us until we make the other bank."

He looked dubious but Lord Willoughby, his son in law, said, "Give me fifty men at arms and I will force the bridge at the same time. If Sir William can attract their attention, then we can outflank them."

The Earl looked at me for I would be leading the men who would take all the risks. I nodded, "We can win, my lord. It is the Scots who will be full of piss and vinegar! The French will flee and if we cannot handle Scotsmen we should retire to our castles."

"Then let us do it!" He cupped his hands. "For God, King Henry and St. George!"

That raised a cheer and, drawing my sword and rondel dagger, I hurried as fast as my lame leg would allow, to the river. I knew I looked

The Battle for France

foolish for I was the old man and the shock of descending into the water might be enough to kill me, but I had lived long enough. I wanted to bury no more knights or friends. I also counted on the fact that every English man at arms knew the story of Strongstaff. As I leapt into the water, I heard a roar from behind me and then splashes as first Rufus, then Sir Stephen and Sir Oliver followed me with the rest of my men at arms in close attendance.

I heard Matthew Millerson shout, "Archers, if any Frenchman or Scottish brigand comes close to hurting Sir William Strongstaff then they will answer to me! God defend the defender of kings!"

I had been at Agincourt but crossing that fifty paces of water I cannot recall as many arrows flying above us. It was like a goose feathered wind which swept the enemy away from the other bank and kept us safe. A couple of arrows clanked off my helmet and my plate, but none came close to hurting me. I struggled to get out of the river and Rufus and Edward had to push me up. As soon as my feet touched the ground a pain shot up from my knee. I was in agony, but I put the pain from my head and lumbered rather than ran towards the French and Scots. We had shocked them but now they came at us. I used my sword two handed for it was longer than most other swords and although the pole weapons and spears the enemy used could hold me at bay, I had fought in enough battles to know how to outwit an enemy. The first Frenchman obviously expected me to fear his poleaxe. For his part, he was not sure which part to use and when he made his decision his swing was slow. I whipped the sword up and under the head. I smashed into the langet, the metal which protected the shaft. I knocked the head into the air and the blade of the axe scraped along the armour covering my arm. His weapon was now useless, and I bundled into him. As he fell over, I rammed my sword into his throat.

Rufus was next to me and along with Sir Stephen the three of us, with Sir Oliver behind me were the tip of a wedge which drove into the heart of the French and the Scots. Sir Stephen knew how to use a poleaxe and he hacked into the helmet and head of the first Frenchman he met. Rufus was young and agile. He twisted and turned as he jabbed and poked with his broad headed spear. He mesmerized the Frenchman with the speed of his hands, and he found a gap between the amour of the faulds. He had been taught to twist the head and it enlarged the hole and drove into the man's gut. The French man at arms I faced had a war hammer and I saw by his grey flecked beard that this one was not a novice. His problem was that once he swung at me, he would not be able to halt the swing. I had never had time for honour and so I feigned an injury. I stopped and pretended to cough. He saw his chance and swung. He brought the war hammer from my left towards my right intending to smash into my side. I spun to my right on my good leg and as the head missed my breastplate by the width of a finger my sword came around his back to hit him where his faulds met the backplate. It was a weak part of the protection and I was lucky. The edge slid between the two pieces of armour, into the gambeson and then into his side and back. I tore the sword out and saw blood and entrails upon the end. It was a mistake, however, as my knee complained and almost screamed with pain.

Our archers had crossed the river and were now using flat trajectories to send arrows at such close range that even the best armour was not enough. The French fell. The Dauphinists had taken enough and they ran. Even as they fled, they were slain by our deadly archers but the Scots, no doubt buoyed by Baugé, fought on. The Scots were the poor relations of the French and their armour was less well-made. Some still fought in mail. I saw their leader, the Earl of Buchan. He had the oathsworn members of his clan near him and I knew that he would die hard. I stopped to allow my two knights to join me.

"Rufus, guard my back!"

Sir Thomas and the Earl had also joined us. From the blood on their jupons, they had been in the thick of the fighting, but it was about to become bloodier. Some of the Scots still used the small buckler and they also carried a shorter sword. I could feel the blood coursing through my body. This was what I had been made for. I was a warrior honed by the battles of the last fifty years. Before now I had kept one eye on the King I guarded. Now I fought because I wanted my men to win and I did not care what happened to me. It made a difference. I felt invincible. I swung my sword in an arc, and it struck the Scottish buckler which faced me square on. The man reeled and I knew that I had hurt his arm, but he still managed to swing his sword at me. It hit my breast place and did no damage. I cared not if my armour ended the battle needing the weaponsmith. We would avenge the Duke of Clarence at Baugé! I raised my sword above my head and the Scot thought he saw his chance. He lunged with his sword at my face. Most men would have turned away, but I knew that my sword would strike at the same time as his and I gambled. His sword pricked and gouged into my cheek, the opposite side from the scar I bore and I saw the look of joy on his face. It lasted just long enough for my sword to smash into his helmet. The helmet was old, and it crumpled. My sword carried on and as the man was not wearing an arming cap it hit his skull. I think he lived barely a moment or two after he drew blood.

The men before me were brave but not brave enough to face the bloody greybeard who seemed to fight like a Viking berserker. Suddenly a Scot rose from the ground where he had feigned injury and swung a mace at my head. I just reacted and slashed with my left hand. The mace fell from his lifeless hand as my dagger ripped across his throat. I sheathed my dagger and bent to pick up the mace. It took a few moments but helped me to recover my breath. The respite helped me to gather my wits and to see how my men fared. Sir Stephen's poleaxe had broken in two and he wielded it one handed whilst using a rondel dagger in his left. Sir Oliver had a war axe and a hatchet. Rufus had the broken spear in one hand and his sword in the other. The three were whole. I then watched as Sir William Willoughby, having taken the bridge, led his men to attack the rear of the Scots. With our archers raining death upon them it was a slaughter. We did not offer quarter and they did not seek it. It was always that way when we fought.

It fell to Sir Stephen to end the slaughter. He fought The Earl of Buchan and while the Scottish lord was an accomplished knight, Sir Stephen had been fighting since a boy and it could only end one way. Knocking aside the Scot's sword Sir Stephen lunged with his broken poleaxe. The Earl of Buchan used his shield to deflect it, but he merely succeeded in sending the spike into his own eye. As he fell to the ground Rufus skewered the standard-bearer and as the flag fell to the ground the few Scottish nobles who were still alive surrendered. These were Scottish soldiers we were fighting, and it did not pay to relax until it was certain that they had surrendered. John, the squire, had taken the sword from the Earl of Buchan and was tending to his wound. Edward had the standard in his hand and he still had a sword drawn. Rufus, my men at arms and archers were ensuring that any wounded who were close to death were relieved of their pain and removing weapons from the other wounded and the handful who had surrendered. That done I took off my helmet and scanned the field. Peter Poleaxe lay dead as did Much the Archer. I saw most of the others, but a full count would have to wait.

As I dropped the coif from my head, I felt the blood begin to flow from the wound in my cheek. I tore a piece of cloth from the jupon of a dead French knight and held it to the wound to staunch the bleeding until it could be tended to. As was usual when we fought the Scots it had been a bitter fight and while we had emerged victorious the majority of the Scottish soldiers had fought until the end and many men were wounded. The healers would be busy. The gates of the town opened, and the people flooded out. I was confident that my men, at least, would know the dangers. Some of the townsfolk would be bent on vengeance and wish to hurt the besiegers. Others would seek to benefit from the dead. My men at arms and archers were now collecting what they could from the dead. They began with the knights, squires, and men at arms. I doubted that they would get around to the others. Rufus returned with a good sword taken from a French knight and a purse. He was grinning but when he saw my bloody face his expression changed.

"My lord, you are hurt! Healer!"

"Peace, Rufus. King Henry fought all day with an arrow in his cheek. All that will result is an ugly scar and I am long past worrying about my looks. I am just glad that I am alive. Have our dead cared for."

Sir Stephen and Sir Oliver, looking like butchers from an abattoir in their bloodied jupons, came over. "Sir William, you are a greybeard and a leader. You do not lead the fight! You let us through!" Stephen pointed to the wound, "And that is the result!"

"It is my way, Stephen, as well you know, and the King would have been the first across had he been spared!"

He waved an arm at some of the English dead; they came from the retinue of Sir Thomas, "They died because they did not know the Scots. It is like fighting a pack of wolves. You keep fighting them until all life leaves their body. It is good that we come from the border and know such things." He pointed to the knight he had taken, the Earl of Buchan. "Remember him, lord? He sent those men to ambush you. He must regard you as his nemesis."

I nodded. "And Douglas is over here too although I did not see him today. You will make much money from the ransom of the Earl for his father is the Regent of France!"

Stephen shrugged, "My wife will soon spend it, lord!"

The Earl of Salisbury had been in the thick of it too and, with his helmet under his arm, he wandered over to us. "Bravely done Sir William. The King would have been proud." I nodded. "Your men did well too. I have my son in law pursuing the French who fled. I believe they will return to Bourges and Cravant and Auxerre will be safe. I will go to the town. We need food and accommodation at the very least."

"Aye, and what then? Do we return to the south or are there other plans?"

"That depends upon the Duke of Bedford. Before you arrived from the south, we had a message that he was on his way back to Normandy and he was bringing reinforcements."

I was relieved. I had feared that the two brothers might be too concerned with trying to exert their influence on the Queen and therefore her son. There was no way that Michael could protect the two

The Battle for France

from the King's brothers. If they wished to use them to take power, then they could. As we headed into the town, I reflected that the struggle to control the crown would come later. My wound was healed by a priest who tut-tutted as he first cleaned and then sewed it. He had been forced to shave my beard for the wound was long and deep. I tasted blood for the next month.

That night as we ate, the scale of our victory became apparent. We had captured not only the Scottish leader, the Earl of Buchan but also Louis, Count of Vendôme. He was a prince of France. In addition, we had taken two thousand prisoners while fifteen hundred lay dead. The majority of the dead were Scottish. That suited all of us as the French were richer and the ransoms we received would be huge.

After we had eaten and while the others celebrated our victory in drink, I went to the castle's chapel. I needed to pray. I had thought I would die that day and yet God had spared me. I wondered why. When I had been younger, I had rarely felt the need to pray. Like every soldier I had confessed before battle for I wished to go to heaven if I died but that had been the extent of my religion. Since the death of Eleanor, I had pondered on the afterlife. I wanted to spend eternity with my lady and so I took to my knees in every church. I prayed for an hour. I also prayed for the souls of my two men who had fallen. I did not know them well, but they had chosen to follow me, and I would include them in my nightly prayers. Others might forget them but not I.

When I emerged, I discovered Rufus; he was seeking me, "My lord, we wondered what was amiss! The Earl of Salisbury feared your wound was worse than we had thought. He sent me to look for you."

I smiled, Rufus was young enough to be my grandson and I felt old. "I went to pray, that is all. The days of carousing and celebrating victory are passed." In truth, I had rarely become drunk. I remembered how drink had ensnared my father. Red Ralph had always cautioned me against becoming a slave of the serpent, drink. "Come I will share a goblet with you and my familia and then we shall retire. This victory is just one step on a longer journey. King Henry would have been delighted but he would have been planning his next step."

We spent a week in Cravant. The Earl sent out mounted patrols as far as Bourges and discovered that the French had retreated towards the Breton-Norman border. We had hurt the French. We took our prisoners to Auxerre for Cravant was too small to support our army. As the harvests were collected in, we realised that we would not have to fight again this year, at least not in a major battle for the enemy had been hurt and were regrouping. It was November when the ransoms from Scotland were paid. The Earl of Buchan's eye had healed but it gave him a terrible aspect and did nothing to make him mellow. He would not speak to us and left hurling curses at us. We heard after he had rejoined the Dauphin, that he was made Constable of France. He became the effective commander of the French army. As we headed back to Paris, where the Duke of Bedford awaited us, we discussed the move.

"It is a mistake, my lord, not for us but for the French. They think that because the Scots were at Baugé they are able to defeat us. It is not true."

I nodded, "I know Sir Stephen. That was an error by the Duke of Clarence, and you are right. I just wonder why the Dauphin does not use Tanneguy du Châtel. Have they fallen out?"

Rufus shook his head, "Would you trust a murderer, lord? I think that the Dauphin must have realised the dangers of keeping a viper close to your bosom!"

Chapter 16

We spent Christmas close to Paris at Vincennes. It was a poignant place for it was where the King had died. It was like a royal court once more as the Duke of Bedford had assembled the warriors who had recently arrived from England. The Earl of Salisbury was feted as the victor of Cravant. Sir Stephen was sought out too as the man who had captured the Scottish earl. I did not mind that I was ignored. It was a world I enjoyed. I asked the steward where we were to be quartered and I was pleasantly surprised by the chamber allocated to Rufus and to me.

When we were in the room and as Rufus unpacked our baggage he asked, "Lord, why did you not stay below? You would have been accorded great honour."

I smiled and sat on the bed so that he could take off the boots I used when riding. I had some old soft buskins which I preferred indoors. Others wore handmade shoes made by the most expensive cordwainers, but I was an old soldier and knew what was comfortable. "Rufus, I have been feted and given honours aplenty and after a while, you realise it means nothing. I was at the Bridge of Lussac where Sir John Chandos, a hero of Crécy fell. The whole of England mourned his loss, but you do not even know who he is, do you?"

Shamefaced he shook his head.

"It is not your fault. England soon forgets its heroes and once you know that whatever deeds you do will last less time than a loaf of bread it becomes easier to have clear vision."

"Clear vision, Sir William?"

"Aye, you do what you do for your country and King, of course, but more important are the men with whom you fight. The two who died at Cravant will soon be forgotten by others, but their shield brothers will remember them as will I. Walter, who died at Agincourt and who was avenged at the cost of my knee, is always in my thoughts. He was taken before he had time to sow any crops. His life was short and who knows what he might have achieved. We might have hoped for a crop of fine oats, but he did not even get weeds. His life will always be filled with what if. His father and his mother still remember him as do I."

The Battle for France

The boots were now off and before I took off my mail and donned my houppelande I rubbed my feet. It gave me pleasure. These days I enjoyed the simple things,

I smiled at Rufus for I could see that I had worried him. "Do not fret, Rufus, you see an old man and once I would have enjoyed the honours which the Earl and Stephen enjoy. You will be honoured one day but, if you are as lucky as I am to have lived so long you will see that those honours mean naught. It is how your fellow warriors view you which is important." I shrugged, "At least that is what I think."

A reflective Rufus helped me to dress and I left him to do the same while I wandered the grounds of the magnificent castle. It was cold and I needed a cloak, but the leafless trees and a slight frost gave the hunting park a magical quality. As dusk descended, I headed back inside, and an equerry was waiting for me.

His Grace the Duke would like a word, my lord."

I nodded, "Of course, lead on."

I was taken to a private chamber close to the Duke's quarters. He was using it as a study and there was a clerk at the desk and a scrivener. Their inky fingers told me what they were tasked with. The Duke said, "Leave us. You may continue to write when Sir William has departed."

"Yes, my lord."

"Sit and have some wine."

I poured myself a goblet and there was an awkward silence which I did not feel obliged to fill. I had not asked for this meeting, he had.

Eventually, he relented and began to speak, "When last we met, we parted on if not ill terms then not the way two brothers in arms should."

The Duke, having made a sort of apology and mindful of what King Henry might have wished, I nodded and said, "Duke John, I have known you since you were a boy. You know that I am a irritable old curmudgeon who speaks his mind. I always have done. Indeed, I fell out with your father on more than one occasion." I saw him smile, "However, I never failed in my duty to the crown and to England. Do not expect me to change overnight. This year I celebrate three score years and ten. That is all that the good book allows us. If you do not wish me to speak the truth and tell you if I believe you have made a mistake, then send me home to Weedon. I can bear the disgrace. If, however, you wish me by your side to let these few grey hairs give you the experience they have bought then know I am as loyal a knight who ever drew sword."

He beamed, "And I know that. You must forgive my outburst when my brother told me his wishes. I was not thinking and to be honest, my thoughts were more that we might lose France! You and the Earl of

Salisbury have shown me that my fears are groundless and the two of you shall be the rocks upon which we build our hopes." He leaned forward, "I have plans." I waited and sipped the most excellent claret which had been poured for me. "I am not my brother Henry, nor am I Thomas. I am a different sort of fighter. When I was growing up my mother had some wooden blocks made for me. They were colourfully painted and, apart from my wooden sword they were my favourite plaything. I loved building them slowly and methodically so that I could build a wall higher than my brothers. I always took longer than they did, but I always succeeded. That is my plan for Normandy. We take each Dauphinist stronghold, garrison it, build up our forces and move on. We will not be reckless. My brother showed us the way at Agincourt and you, along with the Earl, repeated the feat at Cravant. We use the bow and stakes along with the strong hearts of English men at arms and we will defeat them."

I nodded and downed the goblet, "And I will do all, in the time left to me, to achieve that aim."

He looked suddenly concerned, "You are not ill, are you? If so, I will send for the finest doctors!"

I laughed, "The leeches did your brother little good. No, I am not unwell." I pointed first to my face and then to my knee, "These recent wounds have told me that I am not invincible. The Scot who did this last one was no great warrior, but he was lucky or perhaps I was, I am not certain but in battle, as your brother discovered at Shrewsbury, fate can send danger at any time. Had it not been for John Bradbury then your brother Thomas might have been king." I saw him take that in. Had the Duke of Clarence led us at Agincourt then we might have had a totally different outcome.

"Thank you and I am glad that you are well. You will outlive us all. You have seen four kings buried already!

"And I do not wish to see a fifth!"

He made the sign of the cross and said, "Quite so." He stood, a sure sign that this was over. "Nothing will happen until summer, but I would rather you stayed close to hand. Your men may go home but as I will need your advice, I wish you here at all times."

"And you shall have it!"

That was good news for my men and, that evening, as my knights and I sat in the Great Hall for a feast of celebration I told them that they could return home.

"And leave you here, my lord?"

I laughed, "You think I will get into trouble? Fear not, I will not venture forth and Rufus is better now is he not? When this is over, I will

The Battle for France

speak to the men at arms and archers. Christmas in England with your families will be a good thing." I could see that they were torn and as we ate, I persuaded them that this was for the best. I had lost two men and wanted to lose no more. I sent Rufus to ask my men to wait for me to speak with them before they retired. I knew, of course, that they would not retire. There were games of chance and copious amounts of drink to be consumed. I was merely asking them to stay a little sober until I had spoken to them.

Having had to persuade my two knights I knew the words to use and it was easier. They accepted my advice. "We will all return when we are summoned, lord."

I nodded, "Of course, Kit!" I had no intention of summoning them. When they were home they would stay there.

I turned to leave with Rufus. We had barely closed the door when Rafe and James appeared, "Lord, you know that we will not be leaving."

"But there is no need to stay!"

"Lord, neither James nor I have a family. Weedon without you and Lady Eleanor would be a graveyard filled with ghosts. We do not mind this life and we will return to England with you and not before. Our minds are made up."

I heard the determination in their voices and nodded, "Very well, and thank you!"

Our men left us three days later. I had their pay from the campaign and with the armour and weapons they had sold they went home rich men. Each of them had at least one spare horse and I knew that they would have a good Christmas. The night before they left, we all gathered in the warrior hall they were using and feasted. None of us became drunk. If anything, we were maudlin and sentimental as we spoke of dead friends and past campaigns. Most of the evening was spent reflecting on the relatively short life of the best king any of us had known. It gave us the opportunity to talk of Shrewsbury, to the squires and the young warriors who had not been there. As I was the one with the information, I was questioned about the wound to King Henry and the long operation to remove it. I thought that poor Rufus was going to be sick when I recounted the operation, but he bore it.

They intended to leave early the next day and to try to get to Le Havre in less than three days. It would be a longer sea voyage but that would still be shorter than the ride. Now that Rouen was ours it was a safe route. I did not keep them carousing until late but, before I left, I spoke with each of them. I spoke with my longest-serving veterans for a

The Battle for France

long time and my farewell was tinged with sadness. I had spent the better part of the last six years with them in France.

"You will come to see us, lord, when you return? You will wish to visit with Sir Ralph and Sir Will I know."

"Aye, Stephen. In fact, if events turn out well, I may take a ship to Hartness and show Rufus the country which makes the best warriors. The ones who have cowed the Scots."

Oliver looked at Rufus, "Aye, lord, for he has only fought them here in France. Scotland, Rufus, is their natural country and they are sly fighters. When you and Sir William come, we shall take you to hunt them!"

I shook my head and laughed, "We are at peace with them! King James is an ally!"

Sir Stephen shrugged, "You would not know it from the way they tried to kill us at Cravant!"

"Aye, well, they failed."

"Take care, lord!"

I smiled, "I will but I was not meant to die in bed nor would I wish to be as Red Ralph and leak my life away drop by drop."

They rose and left before I had the chance to rise and see them off. There were now just four of us left and we were busy from dawn until dusk. The Duke had meant what he said, and we pored over maps each day. He had sent scouts out and received reports each week from the castellans of the castles we now controlled. After a month we left Vincennes and headed for Rouen. This was the capital of Normandy and as the Governor of Normandy, the Duke had to manage the peace as well as winning the war. It soon became clear once we reached Rouen that the Dauphinists had regrouped. The Earl of Buchan had been ransomed but instead of returning to Scotland he had joined the Dauphin at Tours and more Scots were flocking from Scotland to have the chance to avenge the dead and to fight the old enemy.

I was impressed by the Duke's approach. He looked at every castle in Normandy and assessed the threat to them if they were ours and how we might take them if they were held by the Dauphin. The enemy we would have to contend with was Charles d'Albret, Count of Dreux. Married to Anne of Armagnac he was a supporter of the Dauphin. We had killed his father at Agincourt but despite that, he had yet to wage war on us.

"That, Strongstaff, is our first objective. Thanks to the French king we have Évreux and that gives us a good base to control the land south of the Seine. We take the Count's home of Dreux and garrison it. The castle at Ivry is the most powerful in the area and the French hold it.

The Battle for France

The donjon, it is said, was the model for the Tower of London. When that is ours then we can move towards Chartres and the Dauphinist stronghold of Orléans. If we hold that then we have the three richest cities in France and we will have won the war."

I must have misjudged the Duke for the plan was as sound as any of King Henry's. It was built on solid foundations and moved progressively towards Orléans. He would win the war not by force of arms but pure economics. He would starve the French of money.

He gave me my task and that was to ride the land so that I would be as familiar with it as any Frenchman. It was during that time that I came to know the Earl of Salisbury, his son in law and Sir Thomas Rempston. Along with the Earl of Warwick, now returned to France, we became the council of war which planned the spring campaign. We had to gather our ordinance. We no longer had Nicholas Merbury, but Jacob was still in France and I recommended him to the Duke who heeded my advice and appointed him to command the ordnance. Ivry was forty miles away from Rouen and the Duke ensured that the approaches to the city were securely held by our troops.

Rufus was part of the council of war just by the fact that he and the other squires were used to fetch and carry. Each night as we prepared for bed he was animated as he went over all that he had seen and heard. It was as fine an education as any warrior could wish. "And will you be fighting, lord?"

I knew why he asked; he hoped that he would have the chance to use his weapons.

I shook my head, "Not in a siege. That is a young man's work. I will advise and I will watch. I fear, Rufus, that the next time you fight it will be when the Dauphin finally decides to meet us in open battle. Cravant will have put doubts in his head."

"We can still practise for war, can we not, Sir William?"

"You can and I am certain that Rafe and James will happily hone your skills. It was they made Michael the warrior he is."

"I wonder how he is doing."

"Do not envy him for if anything his life will be duller than yours. Every moment of every day will be the same. He and Jack will have to be where the young King and his mother go. He will have to be on watch and on his guard every waking moment. He will have to sleep behind the door of the baby's chamber and there will be no prospect of action." I paused to let that sink in and then added, "And if he does have action then he cannot make a single mistake. If he does then the King might die! Do not envy him for I know that I gave him a poisoned chalice."

"Yet you gave it to him. Why, my lord?"

"I will not live forever. At the moment the child is safe, and this quiet time will allow Michael to get to know the court and to learn how to react to any threat. He will grow into the job. Hopefully, if the Duke's plan works, then I shall be able to return home and relieve him of the ennui!"

We took Dreux with a bloodless victory. We simply rode into the town and garrisoned it. Not as defensible as Ivry, the French decided not to waste men. It was June when we were ready to march south and begin the siege of Ivry. The reports had told us that the Franco-Scottish army was in Bourges and ready to move. Not long after our victory at Cravant the French had enjoyed a rare victory over an Anglo-Burgundian army at La Brossinière. It had not been a large battle, but the French had defeated English longbowmen for the first time. Our reports warned of enthusiasm in the French and Scottish camps. The Scottish elements were led by the Earl of Buchan and the Earl of Douglas. They had two and a half thousand men at arms and four thousand Scottish archers. They had even hired two thousand Milanese cavalry. There were horsemen and horses which were completely encased in tempered steel. They were a formidable enemy. Altogether we discovered that the French, Scots, and Italians could field sixteen thousand men. We could manage, at best, nine thousand. The Duke's strategy was clearly the best one. He had the Earl of Salisbury maintain a line of mounted men to the south of Ivry. They would give us warning of any attempt to relieve the siege.

This was my first siege since Meaux, but the conditions were not the same. There was a river, the Eure but it was far enough away from the castle not to be a defensive obstacle and the castle itself rose above the town, river and city affording us the chance to mine. Here we would not have the pestilence which had cost us so many men at Meaux. The bombards and fowlers pounded at the walls while miners dug shafts to undermine the walls. The Duke knew that the French would have countermines and so, at the end of the first fortnight, men at arms were sent with the miners. Once the mines joined there might be battles beneath the castle and we would be ready. The Duke planned well. We had plenty of archers as well as crossbowmen. I still preferred archers, but I had to admit that in sieges crossbows could be effective. Their slow rate of release was not an issue and they kept up a steady shower of bolts at their gunners.

Rufus could not believe the difference between this siege and the one we had endured at Meaux and I explained why to him, "It is summer, Rufus. King Henry had little choice but to fight in winter as

The Battle for France

the siege went on so long. Hopefully, this one will be shorter but even if it is as long this is a healthier battlefield."

Although I had said we would not be fighting the old soldier in me ensured that we were camped close to the guns and the front line. We both became used to the stink of the guns as well as the noise. When the Duke did not need me, I would watch the bombards as they hurled their stones at the walls. It was slow but relentless work. The walls were nine feet thick in places and the inaccuracy of the bombards meant it was almost impossible to send two stones at exactly the same spot on the wall. The infill between the dressed stones on the two sides of all the walls meant that when we did have a breach it was filled by smaller stones falling from above. I was there when we saw one large stone fall from the wall and there was a small avalanche of cobbles, pebbles, and shattered masonry which followed it making a glacis. Jacob told me, as he readjusted Betty, he had brought the same guns with him, that he would try to hit the stones above the hole. I watched as he did his best but all he succeeded in doing was hitting around the damaged section without adding to it.

He was in a philosophical mood as the guns were cleaned out at the end of the day. "We did well to make the hole, my lord. We now have a target and tomorrow is another day."

Rufus said, "So tomorrow, Master Gunner, we will have a breach we can attack?"

Jacob laughed, "If miracles happen then aye, Master Rufus, but if we hit above the hole twice in the next few days then I will be happy." It was all part of the squire's education.

I realised the effect of Cravant when we heard the French and their allies, including the Count of Narbonne, were heading north and west and that they were not heading to Ivry. Although the guns continued to fire the men at arms were taken from the mines so that we could be ready to fight a battle if the French deviated from their route and tried to relieve the siege.

The Duke sent for me and asked me to find the French. I was given Sir John Page and his men. He had four men at arms and ten mounted archers. I was happy for this task suited me. Rufus was excited as it meant action. I chose a southwestern route and as we headed for Nonancourt Sir John asked why.

"It is always easier to see where an army has been than where it is. Once we find where they have passed then we follow that road. As soon as we see their baggage we shall know where they are but more than that by determining the plan of march we can work out where they are

The Battle for France

going." I saw the scales fall from his eyes. My experience of fifty years was benefitting another young knight.

We did not reach Nonancourt for we found their detritus at Illiers-l'Évêque. The Normans there were quite happy to tell us that the huge army had headed west and appeared to be going towards Verneuil, an important town. Sir John wondered if we should return to tell the Duke. I shook my head, "We have a little information but that can be a dangerous thing. We ride closer and see if they have it besieged."

It was dark by the time we reached the French and Scottish camps, and to my dismay, they held the town. Had it capitulated without a fight? If so that was dangerous for the Duke. Others could follow suit. I had not had to do anything dangerous since my men had left but now I did. I turned to the knight, "We need a prisoner, a Scottish one. Sir John, I want your two best cutthroats."

He looked at me blankly, "Cutthroats?"

I smiled, "Which of your archers scare you the most? They are the ones I will take." I dismounted and handed my reins to Sir John's squire. "Come, Rufus, I think that you are ready for this."

The two archers he brought to me both had the gnarled and nobbled faces of brawlers and that suited me. "You can leave your bows you will need hammers, hatchets and daggers. It is murder we are about!"

Their grins told me they were happy about the turn of events. They knuckled their foreheads and the huge archer with the broken nose said, "I am Big John and this is Harry the Fist, my lord. It is an honour to serve with you!"

I nodded, "You won't need your horses. We want a couple of Scottish prisoners. Once we have two then the rest can die." I took the mace from Hercules' saddle. It was the one I had taken at Cravant. "Rufus and I will see to the prisoners, you two watch our backs."

Darkness had fallen completely, and I could see fires from the ordinary soldiers, the wild Scotsmen and the French spearmen. I guessed that they would camp with their own kind. We headed over the darkening fields through a field of some growing cereal. We moved half crouched but I was confident that the enemy would not be expecting us to reconnoitre so quickly. Despite my age, I could still move silently as could the archers. It was Rufus who was the noisiest.

I stopped for I heard a noise ahead of me. It was the sound of someone making water. I moved forward again. The man must have drunk a great deal for he sounded like a horse. I crept up and realised his head was down as he pulled up his breeks. I acted quickly and I brought the mace down on the back of his head; he fell face down in his own piss. I was about to ask Big John to pick him up when a Scottish

The Battle for France

voice shouted, from some yards away, "Hey Angus, what are ye doing." The voice laughed, "You havna found a sheep, have you?" There was silence and I waved the other three to take cover while I waited for the Scot to approach closer. "Come on, Angus! We can make money from these Frenchmen!"

I was lucky; he approached looking down for he was a little drunk and unsure of his footing. He saw his friend's body and his natural reaction was to hurry forward.

"Are you ...?"

He got no further for my mace hit him on the back of the head. I waved over the two archers who hoisted the bodies effortlessly on to their shoulders. I waved them and Rufus away and then made my way back. I did so slowly so that the others could bind and secure the two unconscious Scotsmen.

By the time I reached Sir John the two were trussed up and over the saddles of the two archers. Big John grinned, "I have never seen a lord like you, Sir William! Why, you could be an archer!"

I knew he could pay me no greater compliment and I bowed, "I thank you, Big John. Feel free to take their purses and their weapons."

Harry the Fist looked a little shamefaced, "We already have, my lord!"

We headed back for the long ride through the night to the siege lines at Ivry.

The Battle of Verneuil 1424

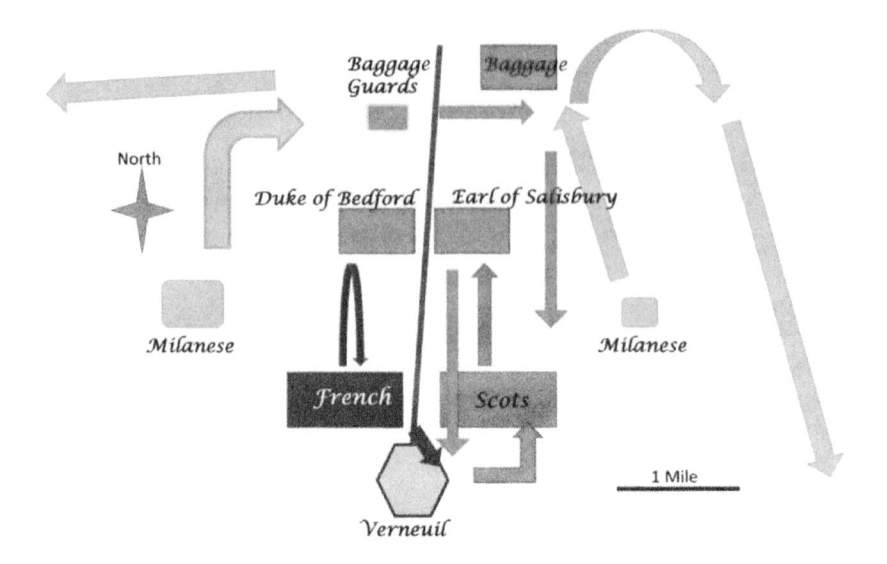

Chapter 17

We were all weary, especially me, when we rode up to the Duke's tent. My knee had ached for the last four hours. The Scots had awoken a few miles from the camp and threatened all sorts of violence on those who had taken them. Big John and Harry the Fist soon silenced them. It was still night-time for we had ridden all night. The sound of our hooves awoke the Duke and the earls who were tented nearby. They emerged wrapped in cloaks.

I dismounted and as my foot touched the ground my knee complained. Rufus was well aware of my injury and he stood close by so that I could rest my arm on him. I nodded my gratitude. The Duke and the earls did not notice the wince and the gesture from Rufus.

"Well, Strongstaff?"

I gestured to the two men who were being pulled from the backs of the horses, "They have taken Verneuil and we saw no evidence of a fight. I took two Scottish prisoners so that we might question them and discover how they did this." The Duke and the others had the puzzled looks of men awoken who did not understand a word of what was being spoken. I had thought of this all night as we had ridden back. "It could be that Verneuil simply opened their gates to allow the enemy in or the French and Scots could have used a trick. It might be that the castellan collaborated with the enemy. I thought two prisoners would give us the answer."

The Duke nodded and strode towards the one called Angus, "I am the Duke of Bedford. Scotland is a vassal to the English crown and France is ruled by my nephew. I demand that you speak the truth. How did your army take Verneuil?"

The man called Angus, the congealed blood still on the side of his head pulled his head back and spat at the Duke. The Duke, fortunately, was far enough away for the spittle to miss but Big John's fist connected so hard with the Scotsman's stomach that all breath was driven from him.

"Harry the Fist, have you your rondel blade?"

"Aye, my lord." He whipped it out.

I nodded towards the groin of the other one and Harry, grinning, had the point there in an instant. I knew that he was applying pressure for the Scot began to stand on his toes.

"Try now, my lord. This one may be more amenable."

"Well?"

His words tumbled out like stones from a breached wall, "It was a trick, my lord, the Earl of Buchan had some of our men pretend to be English and we told the castellan that we were men from your army and had defeated the French. As soon as they opened the gates we were inside." Despite the dagger, he was proud of what they had done, and he grinned, "We lost nary a man!"

The Duke nodded, "Thank you. Sir John, take these two traitors away and hang them!"

"Bastard!"

That was all that the Scot managed for a fist in the ribs, which cracked some of them, from Big John made further cursing impossible. They were dragged away.

The Duke suddenly seemed to notice Rufus still supporting me, "Rufus take your lord to the healers and have them look at his knee. Thank you, Sir William, we will dress and when you return, we shall eat and plan our next move. This Earl of Buchan is cunning!"

The noise of our return had roused the camp early and the healers were awake. The doctor took down my hose and shook his head at the scarred knee. He was an older doctor and he had little hair and what there was reflected white in the firelight. "You know that this wound, whilst healed, should have prevented you from going to war." I nodded. "Then you wish me to allow you to continue to ride and to fight?"

"If you can."

"I can but all that I will be doing is bringing closer the day when you cannot use the leg at all. Do you still wish that?"

"A wise warrior never looks beyond the next battle. Let us say, doctor, that this will be my last battle and I shall retire at the end. Will that ease your Hippocratic conscience?"

He smiled, "You have not changed, Sir William. I was at Shrewsbury and saw you then. Squire, watch what I do. This bandage will need to be removed each night and rebound each morning. I have some salve which will ease the pain but it will not heal."

Rufus and I both nodded. He smeared the fragrant salve on the wound and then bound the bandage around. He did it so tightly that I saw I could not bend the knee at all. I could live with that. I would have to mount Hercules using the other leg, but the relief was immediate, and I wondered why my stiff neck had stopped me seeking help before.

The Battle for France

When he was done, I said, "Thank you, Doctor."

He shrugged, "I have done little. You should go home, Sir William. You have served your country long enough."

"Can a man ever do that? I owe the crown and my country all. Many of my friends have died for it, surely I can bear a little pain."

We returned to the Duke's tent where a table had been laid and squires and servants waited to serve us food. It was awkward to sit but, with the help of Rufus I did so, and as we were the first there, I had my stiff leg stuck out to the side. Rufus went to help serve the food, but I shook my head, "You need not serve me. See to the horses and then yourself. If you can grab some sleep then do so." He looked as though he was going to argue but I shook my head, "This is a command."

"Aye, lord. You are stubborn, my lord!"

I smiled, "I know!"

The others joined me within moments of Rufus' departure. The Duke saw my leg and said, "Whatever we decide, Sir William, you will not be needed to fight."

"That is my decision, lord, for I fear we will need every man we have."

"How so?"

"They outnumber us two to one. Our plan, your plan, was a good one. Even your brother could not have devised a better strategy. Taking the enemy castles one by one and then defending them was the right thing to do but now we must ride forth and meet them in the field. Even one man missing might make a difference. I shall fight at your side."

He nodded. The squires and servants had laid out the food and the Duke started to eat, the sign that we could too. I was starving. One of the first things we had done when we had camped was to build some bread ovens and the bread I took was still warm, almost hot. The smell was almost enough to satisfy me but as I smeared some local butter on the hot bread, and it began to melt, I realised I had not eaten since the previous day. I ate as though this was my last meal.

As he ate the Duke spoke his thoughts aloud. "Sir Thomas, you have scouted the land what is your view?"

The Earl of Salisbury wiped his mouth, "The best approach would be from the north. The river guards the south and whilst it can be crossed, I think repeating the trick of Cravant would be foolish. From what Sir William said, they have two thousand plated men and horses. The town has a moat. I can see why the French chose to use a trick to take it. We need somewhere we can face them and fight a defensive battle."

The Duke looked around. I nodded, "The Scots will be eager to fight us and avenge Cravant. It cost a great deal of coin to ransom Buchan and now he commands the French army too. That is their mistake. We lost one battle and that was because we were reckless. When my Lord Salisbury ordered us to cross the river that was a considered move."

The Earl chuckled, "Which you suggested, Strongstaff!"

I shrugged, "The Earl is right. We need a place to wait and draw them on to our men at arms while our longbows do what they do best, harvest our enemies."

The Duke ate slowly. "We will need to leave some men here to maintain the illusion that we remain and to protect the gunners. A thousand men should manage that. We will leave the day after tomorrow and march to Verneuil. Salisbury, you will be the vanguard for you know the best route and the ground." He looked at me. "You, Strongstaff, will be with me."

I had eaten well and, wiping my mouth I shook my head, "With respect, my lord, I should be with the Earl of Salisbury. It is bad luck to break up successful formations and the Scots, seeing our two banners together will be eager to avenge Cravant. Use us to draw the sting from our foe."

He nodded. "As usual, Strongstaff, there is little point in any of us arguing with you!"

I was weary and when we reached our quarters I lay down and slept the sleep of the dead. It was dark when I awoke and Rafe and James had hot food cooked. Rafe smiled when I left my tent, "Had a good nap, my lord?"

"Aye, and I hope that food tastes as good as it smells. I could eat a horse with the skin on."

Rufus said, "You should have let me change your bandage, lord."

"You can do so when I have eaten. I will be too awake to sleep but I would write some letters."

James shook his head as he handed me a mug of ale, "I never could understand all those squiggles, my lord. Why do you write now?"

"Because we have time. We do not leave for another day and I would have my sons, daughter and adopted son know what it is that we do. My wife used to enjoy reading my letters. She said it gave her great comfort as she waited at Weedon to hear news of us. The Duke will be sending letters back to Rouen and thence England so I can add mine." I looked at Rufus, "And have you written to your father?" The guilty look told me that he had not. "Your father knows better than any how dangerous war is. When news of success and failure reach England he will not know if you live or die. His grey hairs will multiply. Write a letter to him even if it is just a scribble to give him the date and to tell him you live." I knew that Sir Stephen and my other men would have told all our family and friends that we were alive. They would not have mentioned my wounded face for that would fill them, especially my daughter, with fear.

We ate and then, by the light of the campfire I wrote four letters. Each one was personal for my family were all different. I wrote to Alice in the same terms as I would have written to Eleanor, masking the pain, death, and disease. My sons and Michael would have letters which told of the campaign and how we fared. Those at Weedon would have to wait until one of those to whom I had written, visited. Michael would be with the King and the Dowager Queen. The ones at Weedon were probably the closest to me for they were my veteran warriors who had left war. When I had finished the last letter, I wrote another one, shorter this time to my steward to give him both information and instructions. That made me feel better. I allowed Rufus to take the bandage from my knee and Rafe found some brandy to mix with the heavy red wine from Chinon. Along with the salve that gave me the best night's sleep I had enjoyed in a long time and I woke refreshed.

The next day was spent in preparation for our departure. We had much to pack. Rafe and James had four sumpters they would be leading. We had been successful and acquired weapons, treasure, and booty. They would guard it.

Even though Sir John Page led our scouts I knew that we would be seen approaching Verneuil. You cannot hide eight thousand men. As I rode, just behind the scouts, the Earl of Salisbury and I discussed what the French and the Scots might do.

"Suppose, Sir William, they hide behind the walls of Verneuil? It would be as hard as Ivry to besiege."

"True but the Dauphin has made a fatal error. He has appointed the Earl of Buchan as Constable of France. The Earl of Douglas is there too. I have met both of them. Buchan tried to have me killed in England, up on the borders. They hate England. Douglas was captured after Homildon Hill and then again at Shrewsbury. We have taken the family fortune twice. The two Scots will not sit behind a wall and wait. They will attack as they will see this as the opportunity to regain their honour." I paused, "They will want to get me. King Henry is dead, and few others remain from Shrewsbury. If I am killed and the army defeated, then the dishonour is expunged."

"You know that, yet you still go to battle?"

"What else can a knight do?"

Chapter 18

That I was proved right gave me some pleasure for when we reached Piseux, just a couple of miles north of Verneuil, we saw the French and Scottish arrayed for battle. Although they were going to fight, I knew that they had not done so recklessly. They had chosen ground which suited their two thousand Lombard cavalry. The Duke waved his leaders to him. "We will do as we did at Agincourt. Dismount and leave the horses close to the baggage. Captain Young," he called over a man at arms, "take two thousand men, those without plate armour, archers and spearmen, and guard the baggage! Embed stakes into the ground."

"My lord!"

I knew that would be difficult for the summer sun had baked the ground like rock. The one thousand archers he had were his best defence against the enemy.

The Duke turned to us, "We will form one battle. I will take the west side of the road and Salisbury, you and Strongstaff will take the east. Our plan is to hold them until they weaken, and we can drive them from the field. The archers, Captain Jenkins, will form ranks behind us."

"Aye, lord."

"Today those squires who have mail or plate will have to fight as men at arms." Rufus would have to come of age very quickly or his bones might lie on this Norman plain.

We rode to the place we would defend. James came with us and he took Hercules to lead him back to the baggage. I handed him my reins. "You and Rafe stay close to the baggage. If things go awry and Rufus and I fall then take our horses and leave."

James laughed as he pulled Hercules around, "Lord, that will not happen. There are enough Scots fighting this day to guarantee that we shall win!" The Scottish banners were all moving to face our wing of the battle. It was what I had expected. Buchan and Douglas sought the Earl of Salisbury and me! I had armed for a bloody fight. I had my sword as well as the mace I had captured. It would be a handy weapon when we were in close combat. I also had a poleaxe which, when he returned from taking our horses to the rear, Rufus brought. He would be behind me with a spear. He was much stronger than when he had joined

The Battle for France

me but Rafe and James had not had time to teach him how to use one properly. I saw that, alarmingly, the Milanese heavy horses were lined up in two groups on the flanks of the French and Scottish troops ahead of us. They were the most dangerous element of the enemy's army. We waited.

The Bishop and Beauvais along with other priests and bishops came and we knelt before holy relics and we were all absolved of sin. Symbolically the Duke received the blood and body of Christ. We sang the Te Deum and rose while the priests and the relics returned to the baggage. We waited, again,

At noon the Duke came over to me. He had his herald with him leading a spare horse, "Strongstaff, the Scottish know you. Go with my herald and ask what terms they seek."

I cocked a questioning eye at him, "My lord, if you wish to precipitate a battle then this is the best way."

He smiled, "Had I wanted a peaceful end to this day then I might have sent another, more moderate man. I want this ended and if they appear reluctant to fight then that gives me hope."

After handing my poleaxe to Rufus I mounted, "Take care, my lord."

"I do not fear this meeting, Rufus, I go with a herald and with both armies watching, there will be no treachery."

"Remember John the Fearless, my lord!"

I nodded, "That was du Châtel and the meeting was shielded from the eyes of others. There are more than twenty-five thousand pairs of eyes upon us now. I will be safe... for a while, at least."

As the Earl of Buchan was the commander in chief of the French army, I approached him. As I neared them, however, it was the Earl of Douglas who mounted a horse and rode to me with the Earl trotting along behind with the Count of Aumale, the French leader. He halted ten paces from me, "So, gutter rat, you are here to surrender?"

I smiled, "No, my lord, I am here to give you the chance to do so. Half of your army are subject to an oath of fealty to the King of England. This is an act of treason."

Earl Douglas became angry, "We swore no oath! We fight not in our homeland but here on this foreign soil! Why are you here?"

"To ask what terms you wish."

He laughed, "Then these are the terms, we will neither seek nor give quarter!"

I nodded, "I can understand that from you, my lord, for it cost your family a fortune after Homildon Hill and Shrewsbury not to mention your incarceration. But you, Lord Buchan, you have only been captured once. Do you really wish to die this day?"

The Battle for France

I had angered him, and his face reddened, "Your luck will run out this day, Strongstaff!"

I looked pointedly over my shoulder, "Why, my lord, do you have more assassins coming to try to kill me!" His head dropped and I smiled, "It matters not for I have dealt with such killers my whole life. But you, Count, do you wish the same treatment for the French? You are not the rabid Scottish dogs we are used to slaughtering. Do you wish no quarter?"

He did not look convinced, but he nodded, "The Earl of Buchan is our Constable, and we stand by him." He hesitated, "You are outnumbered more than two to one, Sir William! You cannot win."

I nodded, "As we were at Agincourt and that turned out well for us, did it not, Count?" I let the words hang in the air and then turning my horse, said, "It is hot. I shall return to my Duke and give him your terms. Buchan, Douglas, you know where I shall be. I pray that you will reach me before I blunt my sword. I would rather give you each a quick death than beat you to death with an iron bar!"

As we headed back the herald shook his head, "You have made yourself a target, my lord!"

I smiled, "I was born a target and even had the Duke sent another my fate was sealed. The Scots will come for me and Sir Thomas."

The Duke was pleased with the outcome. He had feared that the enemy would melt away as they had done for his brother. As the afternoon wore on so the enemy showed no signs of advancing. That they were the ones who would have to begin the battle was obvious for their Milanese mercenaries were waiting ominously on the flanks. Only fools would march towards a mounted enemy.

Servants brought us drink to refresh us and the Earl of Salisbury shook his head, "This cannot end well, Strongstaff. They can come whenever they wish."

I smiled and drank the lukewarm ale, "The longer this goes on the more chance we have to win, lord." I used the cup to point, "His horsemen and their mounts are encased in armour. At least our plate has some ventilation to give us some cooling air." The Milanese mercenaries had dismounted at noon. "Their horses are mighty warhorses but see, they wear a scale crinet around their necks and a full plated shaffron around their heads. With the thick hide caparison, they are well protected and almost impervious to weapons, but the heat will make them tire so quickly that they might only be capable of just one charge. Then look at the Scots. They are champing at the bit. They see that they outnumber us and wonder why they do not charge." Since the meeting, the Count of Aumale and the French leaders had been in full debate. The Earl of Buchan and the Earl of Douglas had crossed to them many times. "The Scots are urging the French to attack but they remember Agincourt. Do they wish the same result? They will attack, my lord, but the longer they take the better it is for us." I smiled, "Our biggest problem will be making water with all this armour."

He laughed, "You are a soldier through and through, Strongstaff. This must seem as nothing to you for you have been fighting since before I was born."

"Would that it was so, Earl, but each time I fight, since the day I defended the body of Sir John Chandos at Lussac Bridge, I have been willing to die and give my life for my country and my fellow warriors. Today is no different."

I wondered as the afternoon dragged on if there would be a battle. Rufus was anxious next to me, "Sir William, if we camp here is there not a chance that they might try a night attack?"

"That would not happen for they fear us more than we fear them. If they do not attack, then we have won for they will have to withdraw. They must assume that we are being reinforced and that tomorrow we will have even greater numbers."

"But we do not!"

"They do not know that and as we are outnumbered and yet have not advanced to meet us then they must wonder if there is another army heading here to join with us."

It was at about four in the afternoon, from the position of the sun, when they showed signs of movement. First, their Milanese mercenaries mounted and then their Scottish archers and crossbowmen advanced before them. The Duke first ordered our archers forward and then shouted, "The army will advance and engage these traitors!"

The Earl shouted, "Present weapons and prepare to defend yourselves. "Bedford and St George!"

The men all took up the shout, cheered and those with shields banged the pommels of their swords upon them. It made an intimidating sound. We began to march slowly towards the enemy. I suppose my lame leg and the unwillingness of any of our front rank to overtake us helped to keep a steady pace. The archers reached their allotted position and began to loose their arrows. The Scottish replied in kind. Their duel meant that we suffered few casualties and, I guessed, the enemy the same. Then the horns sounded, and the enemy began their advance. The Milanese horsemen headed north towards us. It took just a few moments to realise that they were not charging our main battles but heading along our flanks. They were heading for the baggage! While that could not be construed as a good thing, I thought it a waste. Had they charged our flanks then they might have caused enough damage to break our lines. The archers on the right were dispersed. They took shelter behind us. The battle of the baggage was behind us and as our archers fell back before the Scottish men at arms all of our attention was on the wall of screaming Scotsmen heading towards us. We had no idea about the fate of Captain Young and his men. Our archers had managed to send bodkins at the Scots so that their front rank was not the one with which they started their march. That proved crucial as some of the arrows had hit warriors who might have hurt us. We were becoming disordered by the archers permeating our ranks and so the Duke ordered a halt.

It says much about our discipline that we were able to do so and when the last archer had passed us then we reformed ranks. The Duke of Narbonne led his men to charge towards the Duke of Bedford and that initiated a general attack by the French. It was a messy charge and the Duke of Bedford held us all in a solid mass to withstand the onslaught. Surprisingly, the Scots maintained their steady advance. The thought passed through my mind that they had remembered Homildon Hill and Shrewsbury when reckless attacks had hurt them.

As the Duke of Narbonne's men crashed into the Duke of Bedford and his men we heard a clash of steel from behind us. The ones at the rear of our men turned and I heard the cry, "The Milanese are amongst the baggage." I prayed that Rafe and James my two rocks were safe and the memory of the attack on the squires at Agincourt sprang to mind. This time there were two and a half thousand men defending it. The Lombards would not have such an easy time of it. Like the rest of the men awaiting the clash of arms with the Scots, I put those thoughts from my head. The Scots were still steadily advancing although our archers now had the range and both the Scottish front rank and the men of Narbonne began to suffer casualties. Then the Milanese cavalry to our left side charged us and the longbowmen behind us had to switch targets. It allowed the Scots to advance again and so the Duke of Bedford gave the order for us to advance.

I had Rufus, carrying my standard, behind me and the Earl of Salisbury next to me on one side and Sir John Page on the other. We marched in step and that helped us. I saw, ahead, that the Scottish men at arms we would face were plated as were we. This would be a test of the weaponsmiths we used as well as men at arms. I was confident about mine. I held my poleaxe above my head. Without a shield, it was hard to defend against a downward strike. The men chanted and cheered as they took each step.

The Battle for France

To my right, it was, 'Bedford! Bedford!' Most of those around me chanted, 'Montague! Montague!' I heard behind me some men chanting, 'Strongstaff!' It surprised me for I only had Rufus with me. It was just a noise, but it heartened each of us.

When we were less than twenty paces apart a Scottish voice ordered the charge, and they ran at us. Rufus would plant the standard into the ground when we hit each other. It would be a marker and if I saw it then I would know that the Scots were winning. I had faced so many charges in my life, some on foot and many mounted, that I was probably uniquely experienced on that field. I knew which man at arms I would face. He was a stocky knight with a large mace. It was so big that it took two hands to hold it. I knew that if he struck me, I was a dead man. Fortunately, unlike me, he was not sure which knight he would strike. It would become apparent when he was two paces from me but as my poleaxe outranged his weapon those few moments of indecision might help me strike the first blow.

I timed the strike perfectly and I put every ounce of my strength into the blow and, as he had an open sallet helmet I saw the realisation that he had delayed a heartbeat too long. His mighty mace was heading for the side of my helmet when the poleaxe struck his helmet and first cracked and then burst asunder the metal. It gouged and ripped through the mail coif and arming cap before it split the skull in two. Such was the power of the blow that those on either side were covered in bone, brain, and blood. Both the Earl of Salisbury and Sir John Page took advantage and killed the distracted Scots that they faced. Above us, I saw that the archers had managed to reform, and the sky above was blackened by the missiles they showered upon the enemy.

I lifted the poleaxe again as more Scots approached. Their heads were lowered to avoid an arrow in the face. Henry Monmouth had survived such a wound, but he was rare. I spied the man at arms in the kettle helm who approached. He had a spear which was longer than my poleaxe. I was already swinging when the spear rammed into my chest. Rufus must have been watching for a moment before it struck, I felt his body push into the back of mine. My breastplate was the second strongest defence I had; my helmet was the best. The breastplate held and like the man at arms I had first killed that day my poleaxe split helmet and head. Standing in the hot sun for most of the day had weakened me but I took heart from the fact that all those who advanced towards me looked equally drained.

There were no longer lines of Scots who were advancing. There were groups of warriors, probably in their family or clan groups, but most were still marching towards our standards, stuck in the ground and drawing men like moths to a flame. We had only moved a step or two beyond the first point of contact but already the dried brown swathe upon which we fought had become a bloody lake. It was slick and slippery; I do not think I had ever seen so much blood before. Three men were coming towards me and so I changed my swing to a horizontal one. I had less chance of making a killing blow, but my fifty years of fighting told me that it was the right decision. I hit the man on the left of the three Scots in the side of the head. I do not know if I killed him, but he fell and, in his falling, knocked another to the side. The axe head hit his falling body on the back of his helmet, and I saw Sir John Page's pointed sabaton drive up into his face. The third man was unlucky. The axe head hacked into the wrist and he dropped his weapon. I had found the space between his gauntlet and the plate protecting his forearm. The hand hung by muscle and tendons. Sir John's squire skewered him with a spear.

It was then I saw the Duke of Narbonne lead his men from the field. They had suffered enough of the butchery and the relentless arrows which fell like rain from the sky. They fled towards Verneuil and that set the whole left wing of the French fleeing for safety. The Duke of Bedford led the charge to chase them to the very walls, ditches, and moat of Verneuil. For us we had no such luxury for the Scots looked determined to stay and to slaughter us. They seemed not to care that they were being hewn down in their hundreds. They still outnumbered us many times but, thus far ,we seemed to have the upper hand for we were more skilled. As far as I could tell we had lost few men compared with the Scots.

I watched the Earl of Douglas rally his men for I saw that his retinue had suffered heavily. Seeing my standard still flying he raised his war hammer and pointed it at me. Those who were left from his retinue screamed and ran towards our part of the line. I saw that Douglas himself hung back a little. I had fought him before and he had lost to me. I was an older warrior, but he would want my weapons blunted and me wounded before he risked another humiliating defeat. The archers behind us kept sending arrows and now that they had the range, for we had not moved forward like the Duke of Bedford, their arrows plunged down and some of those trying to get at me fell before they could reach me. I twisted the poleaxe in my hands so that it was using the hammer head. I scythed the weapon in an arc. The slippery, body covered and bloody ground before me was treacherous and running was dangerous. The first Scottish knight fell just four feet shy of me. The hammer head connected with the knee of the next man and despite his poleyn, I shattered the kneecap and he fell. The man who had slipped tried to rise and that was not an easy thing to do for a man covered in plate. He had to use his hands to do so and as he rose, I saw a gap in the plate. There was just mail close to his neck and I drove the spike into the gap. He screamed and I twisted. The blood spurted and that told me I had hit some vital artery. I had to pull the spike out quickly for more of Douglas' men and the Earl himself were just a few feet away.

Sir John and Sir Thomas, on either side of me, had slain men too. In many ways, they were helped by the fact that the Douglas men regarded me as the main enemy and their weapons came for me. I was weary and my stiff leg complained and ached. I had stood for almost eight hours and that was too long for a man of seventy. Two of those who came at me held the long wooden spears they had used at Flodden. They outranged all our weapons. The wooden heads both came for my face at the same time. Swinging the poleaxe up I deflected them but a third Scottish warrior with a sword was quick enough to dart in and use the tip of his sword to slip between the plates on my fauld. The sword did not penetrate deeply but I felt the blade penetrate the flesh in my lower side. The Scot had no opportunity to either push further or enjoy his victory for Rufus rammed his broad-headed and bloody spear into the Scot's face. I used the butt of my poleaxe to swing it at the head of the next man as the two lone spears were pulled back for a second attempt. An arrow was sent horizontally from behind me to smash into the face of one of them and the axe head of my poleaxe bit deeply into the haft of the long spear rendering it almost useless.

When the arrow came horizontally past my shoulder then I knew that the masses of men at arms who had begun the battle behind me were now spread out and that archers were closer. That told me the bloody nature of the battle. My battle was limited to what I could see and that was the men of Douglas coming for me. The Earl of Douglas was now just twenty feet from me and flanked by two men at arms, he advanced. Rufus was now just behind me. His body guarded the standard and I feared for my squire. If he survived this battle, he would be a better warrior, but his survival was in doubt for this was as bloody a battle as Agincourt or Shrewsbury and both had hung in the balance for the longest time. This time there was no Henry to make the difference!

Douglas had a war hammer and he held it above and behind his head. He would swing it down at my head knowing that if he missed the head, he had a good chance of striking my shoulder. Either blow would either incapacitate me or kill me. Our men at arms were now bold enough to step from the line and use the points of spears or the spikes on poleaxes to jab at the faces of the advancing Scots. The bodies of their dead were an obstacle for the Scots and the spearpoints and spikes whilst not being fatal, hurt and deterred the Scots.

Suddenly, Douglas was within range and I swung my poleaxe a moment before he started to swing his war hammer. He was using the beak of the hammer for, aimed at a helmet, it usually caused a mortal wound. I swung at the wooden shaft of the hammer. The war hammer did not have a metal langet to protect it and a weakened hammer was of no use. The two weapons collided in the space between us. The axe head bit deeply into the hammer's haft. They held above our heads. We were close and had I not had the weak knee I would have risked kicking my sabaton between his legs. As it was, I could only stand.

"Today you die, Strongstaff!" He spat the words at me and spittle flew through the air. He was red in the face and it was not through exertion for he was angry beyond words and that was never the best way to fight.

"Perhaps, Douglas, but not at your hands. You were always a piss poor opponent and you have not improved since Shrewsbury!" I pulled hard on my poleaxe and, in the pulling, weakened the haft of the war hammer. As Douglas jerked his own weapon there was a crack and the head began to fall away from the haft. I brought up the haft of my poleaxe to strike the Earl in the side. He reeled and I quickly pointed the spike of the poleaxe and rammed it under his left armpit. His besagew had fallen in the fight and there was no protection. He screamed as blood flowed. He drew his sword and advanced. He was fighting an old man and his pride was badly dented. He came on at me almost recklessly and that was no way to fight. I was cool still and calm. I could not move and was fixed to the battlefield like a stake at Agincourt. Had he been cooler he would have used his own mobility to defeat me. Instead, he came directly at me, swinging his sword in a wide arc. I brought the hammer head down to drive his sword towards the blood-soaked ground. I then brought up the axe head to smash into his gorget. There was not as much power in the blow as I would have liked but I cracked his gorget. He raised his sword to bring it down on my head and holding the wooden part of the poleaxe with my left hand and the metal head with my right I held the poleaxe above my head. The sword struck the langet and although it did its job and protected the wood the dent and the bend made the poleaxe less effective than it had been. Of course, the Earl had the problem that he was bleeding heavily from the wound under his left arm and each time he raised his sword his movements were more laboured.

I saw that the Earl of Buchan's standard was now closer. He had been on our right when Douglas had begun his charge and was now heading for the Earl of Salisbury. I wondered if the battle was coming to its decisive moment. As with all battles, I knew not what was going on elsewhere. Were Rafe and James dead or fled? The latter was unlikely. Had the Duke succeeded against the French? Were the Milanese mercenaries preparing for another charge, this time into our flank? To an old soldier such as I, those questions filled my head but the instincts I had developed meant that my body still fought as though controlled by another.

I held the poleaxe closer to the head and this limited how I could swing the weapon. I punched the axe head at the right side of Douglas' gorget. I had weakened the left side already. When I pulled back the weapon, I saw that there was a dent. Douglas raised his sword again to hit down at me and, once more, I held up my poleaxe. This time his blow struck close to my left hand and broke the haft in two. I had left what was, in effect, an unwieldy axe and a shaft of wood.

"Now you die!"

Douglas pulled his sword back to drive it into my face. As I pulled back the broken poleaxe, I rammed the broken shaft at the Scottish lord. The jagged end found his good eye and as he screamed, I pushed all the harder and then retracted it. The blood and gore at the end of the broken haft had the remnants of Douglas' eye upon it too. I was becoming weary beyond words and as Douglas put two hands to his sword and struck blindly at me, I threw the broken shaft at him and used the poleaxe two handed. His sword hit the top of my helmet as the axe head hit the damaged gorget and sliced into it as though it was parchment. His blow stunned me, and I saw stars. The blade bit into his neck. My arms kept moving as though through their own volition and his head was half severed before I could stop the swing. The now eyeless skull hung down.

The men around me cheered but to me, the sound seemed distant. The last few Douglas men ran to avenge their leader, it was the Scottish way. Rufus, seeing that I was disorientated stepped forward to spear the standard-bearer and throw the Douglas standard to the ground. The others were slaughtered where they stood and they died around the standard and unlucky earl.

Sometimes in battles, there is a moment of peace and this was it. The death of Douglas had an impact. It put heart into our men and dismayed the enemy.

"Are you alright, Sir William. Your helmet is badly dented."

I smiled at Rufus, "I am well and the battle hangs in the balance. The Earl of Buchan lives still. It was one of my men who blinded him, and I insulted him at the start of this battle. We have to defeat him."

The Battle for France

The Earl of Salisbury said, "There is no dishonour in going to the rear, Sir William."

I tossed the unwieldy poleaxe to the ground and took my mace. "I have a weapon here which will crush and crack Scottish heads."

Just then there was a wail and I saw, above the advancing Scots, the banner of the Duke of Bedford leading his men to attack the Scots in the rear. Although my hearing was not what it should have been, I heard, 'Clarence! Clarence!' as they advanced.

"This is the moment we win, my lord. Let us take heart and end this Scottish threat once and for all!" My voice was filled with the hope that this would be my last battle and I would be able to go home.

The Scots who advanced were now, in the main, wielding swords and axes. The longer pole weapons had been damaged or destroyed in the bloody mêlée that was the battle of Verneuil. They advanced with determination and, I suppose now that they were surrounded knew that they would lose but Earl Douglas had set the terms. There would be no quarter sought nor given and they either won or they would die. I knew then that although I could leave the field with honour, I had to see this through, if only for the memory of King Henry. The Earl of Buchan's standard came towards us. I had seen the patch on his eye when we had parleyed but now, he wore a helmet with a visor and his features were hidden. His oathsworn were before him. He was no coward, but they would die to protect him from harm.

I saw a knight detach himself from the Scots and run towards me; it was a direct challenge. He roared, "I am Alexander Buchanan and I slew Clarence! Now I will kill the man who slew my lord, Douglas!"

He had a two-handed sword and he lurched towards me swinging the weapon over his head. He was not going for my head but my left side. Sir John, next to me, chose that moment to step to his left to enable him to slay the Scotsman he was fighting and that allowed Sir Alexander's sword to strike my side. I had already committed to a two-handed stroke with the mace and I braced myself for the impact. His sword found a gap between breastplate and fauld. It grated against my mail and I heard the links as they were ripped. It tore through the gambeson and the undershirt I wore. The blade grated against my ribs and feeling the bones the knight sawed backwards. I felt the blood begin to seep from the wound. My mace, however, had connected with the side of his helmet. Unlike when we had taken prisoners, this was not a gentle tap but a blow which crushed helmet, coif, and skull. The killer of the Duke of Clarence fell dead at my feet.

"My lord you are hurt!" Rufus saw the blood and I knew that the wound was a bad one but before I could even think about moving, a

The Battle for France

difficult enough task in itself, two things happened. The Earl of Buchan roared a challenge at me, and a Scot threw the head of a broken war hammer at me. It struck the side of my helmet and, for the second time in the battle, I saw stars. I swung the mace backhanded at the Earl and connected with his left arm. His sword struck the side of my armour close to where Sir Alexander had hit me, and the blood flowed faster. My vision was becoming dizzy and I was not sure that I could keep my feet. I swung my mace again and it rang against the Earl's sword. Suddenly, everything became hazy and I could no longer hold my mace. The loss of blood had weakened me but it was my sight which caused me problems. I could no longer see, and I began to fall. I did not want to but my body would no longer obey me. The heavily bandaged knee meant it was my other leg which collapsed, and I saw the sword of the Earl of Buchan swing through the air where I had stood. If he had connected then I would be dead. As I lay on the ground, I thought how strange an end this would be. The next blow would kill me, and I would die without a weapon in my hand for I could no longer grip the heavy mace and it had fallen. The sounds of battle faded, and I entered a black world.

Then a light grew, and I heard a voice; it was Eleanor, my wife, I could see nothing but her voice was warm, comforting and loving, "Come Will and let me tend to your wounds. Now you are home."

Michael

Epilogue

It was Rufus along with Rafe, now in a cart who brought back Sir William's bones, his weapons, his armour, and the news of the great victory of Verneuil, the victory which the Duke of Bedford dedicated to its hero, Sir William Strongstaff. The letters we had received had been our last communication with him and in mine I sensed that he knew his end was nigh. We had heard of Sir William's death, weeks earlier when England both celebrated the great victory and mourned the loss of the King's protector and the Queen had given me permission to be at Weedon to greet the two who had survived the battle. Jack had improved as a squire and I knew that he could deal with any issue. I had to be there at Weedon for without Sir William I might be a corpse myself. His sons and his daughter came to Weedon too and we spent the night before the arrival of Rufus and Rafe speaking of Sir William's life. The latter part, since Agincourt had been spent with me and both Thomas and Henry, as knights were keen to know all. Sir William had always been modest about his achievements. We were all closer that night than at any time either before or since. It was as if the spirit of the greatest knight in England was with us.

    The sound of the cart told us that our lord had arrived. Peter, the ancient doorman, opened the door and I saw that the old man was close to tears. He was part of the fabric of Weedon. We were silent as the chest with the bones was taken from the cart and four of Sir William's archers carried it reverently into the Great Hall and placed it upon a table. The room was packed for every man at arms who lived close by and archer who had drawn a bow in his service was there. Those further afield, like Sir John, Sir Ralph, Sir Will of Stockton, Sir Stephen and Sir Oliver were too far away to be able to reach us for this, the saddest moment in my life. I saw hard men at arms and archers weeping as they stood around the table. Alfred and his wife Sarah had ale to hand and food, but I knew that none would eat. This would be a tale heard in silence. It was my hall now, but I gave the best chairs to the three ladies and when all had either wine or ale in their hand, I raised my own goblet and with a voice barely able to form the words for I was close to breaking, I said, "Sir William Strongstaff, the greatest warrior of this or any age. The world will never see your like."

I drank quickly so that I would not be able to unman myself. Henry and Thomas nodded approvingly.

Rafe, who had gone to war with a lame leg, had lost one eye and half of his left hand at Verneuil and looked like a shadow of the man who had trained me. He was almost unrecognisable. He poured himself another beaker of ale and drank half of it before saying, "Master Rufus asked me to speak first and tell all of you how I saw the battle for I never saw Sir William fall." His voice broke and he swallowed some ale to strengthen his resolve. "James is the lucky one he died on that day at Verneuil and he is with Sir William now."

Alice, Sir William's daughter, all draped in black put her hand on Rafe's, "My father would not wish for another to die for he was more than fond of all his men and warriors. Speak for we would know what happened that August day. Perhaps it will help us all to sleep easier and put the spectres of the night from our heads."

Nodding he emptied his beaker which I refilled, "The Italians, the Milanese horsemen, charged and the arrows, bodkins all, bounced from them. They fell upon the longbowmen who fled to we servants and priests at the baggage. Damn Captain Young, he and the men who should have defended us took to their horses and ran!"

Sir Thomas could not contain himself, "He fled and left you to your fate? Even at Agincourt that did not happen."

Rufus spoke for the first time, "That was how it happened, my lord, and their flight led to English garrisons being slaughtered but the coward paid for it. The Duke took him, tried him and had him hanged drawn and quartered."

Rafe nodded, "Yet that will not bring the dead back. I pray that he rots in hell. The Milanese fell upon us and it was almost impossible to find somewhere to strike a blow let alone cause a wound. James brought down one knight by going beneath the beast and gutting it." He shook his head, "Brave but foolish for the horse and rider, falling, crushed my friend." He looked up at Kit Warhammer, "We three began together and I could do nothing to save James. My friend was dead, and I had not said goodbye. It was too soon and too sudden. I could not say goodbye to the best friend I ever had. It made me fight on. I could do nothing to save my friend, but I leapt on the knight and drove my bodkin dagger through the eyehole of his helmet. As I stood a Lombard swept his sword down. It took my eye and half of my hand, but I did not stop. I thought that day was my last on earth and I determined to take as many of them as I could with me. We fought on and the Italians ran when our archers reformed and were able to hurt the Milanese by loosing from less than twenty paces. Many paid with their lives, but we drove them off and then we watched the battle. The Duke drove the French battle to the edge of Verneuil and although it was some way away, we saw the French die. Some fell in the moat and were drowned while others were simply butchered before the walls of the town they so treacherously captured. Good riddance I say, poxy Frenchmen! Then the Duke turned and attacked the rear of the Scots. When Sir William's standard did not fall, I thought he lived. It was as Master Rufus fetched his body to the rear that I knew my world had ended. He persuaded me to return with him here, but I know not if life is worth going on."

I put my hand on his shoulder, "Sir William wrote a long and detailed will when we were at Vincennes. I was made to read the will so that there could be no misunderstanding for we know what lawyers are like. You and James were given a pension of five hundred crowns a year each." All looked in amazement and Rafe shook his head. "Sir William, as you know was a careful man who planned well but he was also a realist. He knew that one of you might not survive and you are to be given James' share. You are a rich man."

He shook his head, "I am the poorest of men for my lord is dead as is my best friend."

Kit said, "Rafe, you still have friends, and we can keep both Sir William and James alive by speaking of them and remembering. Those memories make us all rich men."

Rafe nodded and drank the ale I had poured for him. All eyes went to Rufus. This was not the arrogant young noble who had annoyed Sir William so much when he had first arrived. Sir William had worked his magic as he had with so many squires. He had taken the raw clay and made a warrior. His only failure had been Walter and that was a failure not of his making.

Rufus stood, "First, I would like to apologise. There are two apologies. I came to you as the most unpleasant young man and had you all beaten me to within an inch of my life, I would not have blamed you." That made everyone smile. "The other reason is that I did not save his life and that was my appointed task."

Rafe stood and shook his head, "That is not true, know you all that the Earl of Salisbury himself commented on the courage of Master Rufus and offered to knight him there and then on the battlefield. You have naught with which to reproach yourself, Master Rufus."

Sir Henry said, "And when my father is laid in his tomb then I shall knight you, Rufus."

The Battle for France

He shook his head, "I am not certain if I wish to be a knight."

As Rafe subsided to his chair I said, "Rufus, you would be dishonouring Sir William's memory if you refused the dubbing. He took pride in making knights. Now on with the story for it is clear that the only one who knows it is you."

He nodded, "All the enemy came for him. I am sure that the blow which eventually killed him was struck well before the end. He was wounded three or four times and yet he laid low many Scotsmen that day. When we took off his cracked helmet, we could see the indentation where he was struck. There were two such wounds on his skull." He nodded to the box of bones. "When they are placed in the coffin you will see the marks. He must have known that he was mortally wounded and yet he continued to fight and to fight harder than any other. When he finally fell at the feet of the Earl of Buchan that vile, one-eyed Scotsman raised his visor to view the recumbent Sir William and he lifted his sword to finally kill his nemesis. I rammed my sword into his exultant face and then the Earl and Sir John Page and I had to fight for our lives as the Scots behaved like a pack of rabid dogs trying to get to us. Sir William's spirit must have been watching over me for I bore a charmed life and when the Duke and his battle joined ours we slaughtered the Scots to a man. It was a victory but there was a bitter taste in my mouth." He shook his head, "I think that the Duke and the lords who fought that day felt the same for there was little celebration. The Duke and the Earl openly wept and knelt by Sir William's body. The Duke said, 'England has lost a rock upon which many a victory was built.'" Rufus looked almost ready to break and he said, in a small voice barely discernible, "And as dear as my father is, I have lost someone even closer. My world and England will never be the same." He sat.

Rafe patted the squire's arm with his good hand, "After the Bishop of Beauvais had said a mass over our dead, we took Sir William and boiled his body so that we could bring home his bones. The Duke paid for the casket to be made and we had an escort of his household knights to escort us to Calais and thence home. The Archbishop of Canterbury came to meet us on the London road and took us to his cathedral where Sir William's bones were laid on the tomb of St Thomas Becket. The same happened at Westminster where he was laid on the tomb of his friend and lord, King Henry. No knight ever had a more honourable journey home. On the Great Road, people lined the road and bowed their heads. It moved me more than anything, my lords. And now he is at home."

We all sat or stood in silence. The rest of the evening was spent in quiet reflection. His children and Alfred, along with me had all received a letter from him but we did not compare what he had said for I knew, from my letter, that it was both intimate and private. Nor did we discuss the will. All of that was immaterial. The man of war had died and had lived a life without peace.

The archers of Weedon made the coffin in which we placed the bones and the casket. None of us wished to view the skull. When he was able Rufus had told us of the combats Sir William had fought and his sons and I deduced that the two blows to his head had been the ones which killed him. We laid him in the village church. It was too small for the mourners who wished to be there, and they spilt outside listening to the priest's words. Lady Eleanor had a carved effigy on the tomb they shared, and the stonemason worked for six months to match it with one of Sir William. I returned to my duties but Rafe, who became a caretaker for the hall told me, when I visited, that the knights who had served him all came to pay their respects and none of them was able to hear the tale of Verneuil with dry eyes. The ragged camp follower who lived longer than any warrior I had ever known cast a long shadow. I still live in that shadow and each day as I guard the young King, I am mindful that no matter how good I am I shall never equal the exploits of Sir William Strongstaff, defender of the crown and protector of kings. I know what he would have liked as an epitaph, warrior. For that is what he was.

The End

Glossary

Aketon- padded garment worn beneath the armour
Ballock dagger or knife- a blade with two swellings next to the blade
Barbican-a gatehouse which can be defended like a castle
Bastard Sword- two handed sword
Besagew- a circular metal plate to protect the armpit
Bodkin dagger- a long thin dagger like a stiletto used to penetrate mail links
Brigandine- padded jacket worn by archers, sometimes studded with metal
Chamfron- metal covering for the head and neck of a warhorse
Chevauchée- a raid by mounted men
Cordwainers- shoemakers
Cuisse- metal greave
Dauentre-Daventry
Esquire- a man of higher social rank, above a gentleman but below a knight
Familia – the bodyguard of a knight (in the case of a king these may well be knights themselves)
Fauld- hooped skirt which hung from a breastplate
Fowler-a nine-foot-long breech-loading cannon
Galoches- Clogs Gardyvyan- An archer's haversack containing all of his war-gear
Gardyvyan- archer's war bag
Glaive- a pole weapon with a curved head and short spike
Gules- a heraldic term for red
Houppelande -a lord's gown with long sleeves
Horsed archers-archers who rode to war on horses but did not fight from horseback
Hovel- a simple bivouac, used when no tents were available
Jupon- Short surcoat
Laudes- the first service of the day (normally at around 3 a.m.)
Langet- a metal collar protecting the top part of a pole weapon
Mêlée- a medieval fight between knights
Pele or peel tower-a simple refuge tower with access to the first floor via an external ladder
Poleyn- a metal plate to protect the knee
Pursuivant- the rank below a herald
Pyx-a small, well decorated and often jewelled box used to take the host to those too sick or infirm to visit a church

Rondel dagger- a narrow-bladed dagger with a disc at the end of the hilt to protect the hand
Sallet basinet- medieval helmet of the simplest type: round with a neck protector
Sennight- Seven nights (a week)
The Pale- the lands around Dublin and Calais. It belonged to the King of England.

The Battle for France

Maps

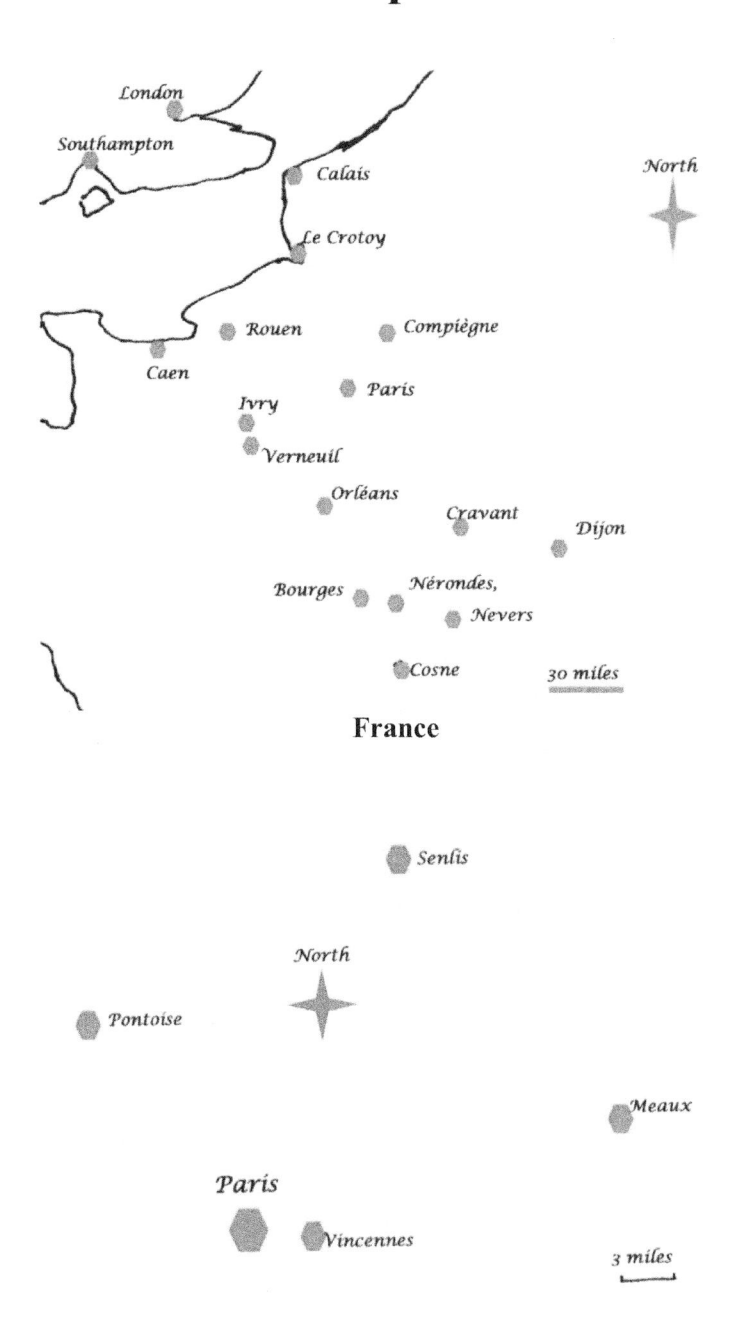

France

Paris

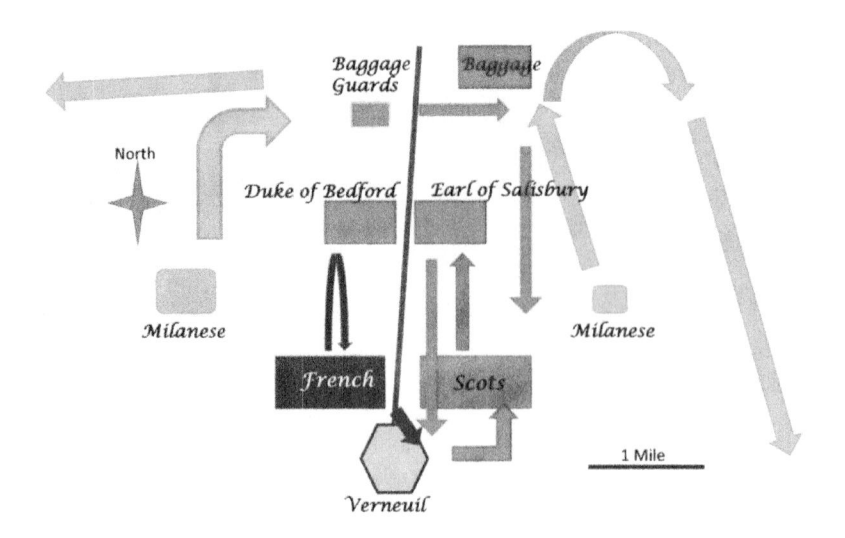

Battle of Verneuil

All maps are the author's own work

Historical Notes

For the English maps, I have used the original Ordnance Survey maps. Produced by the army in the 19th century they show England before modern developments and, in most cases, are pre-industrial revolution. Produced by Cassini they are a useful tool for a historian. I also discovered a good website http: orbis.stanford.edu. This allows a reader to plot any two places in the Roman world and if you input the mode of transport you wish to use and the time of year it will calculate how long it would take you to travel the route. I have used it for all of my books up to the eighteenth century as the transportation system was roughly the same. The Romans would have travelled more quickly!

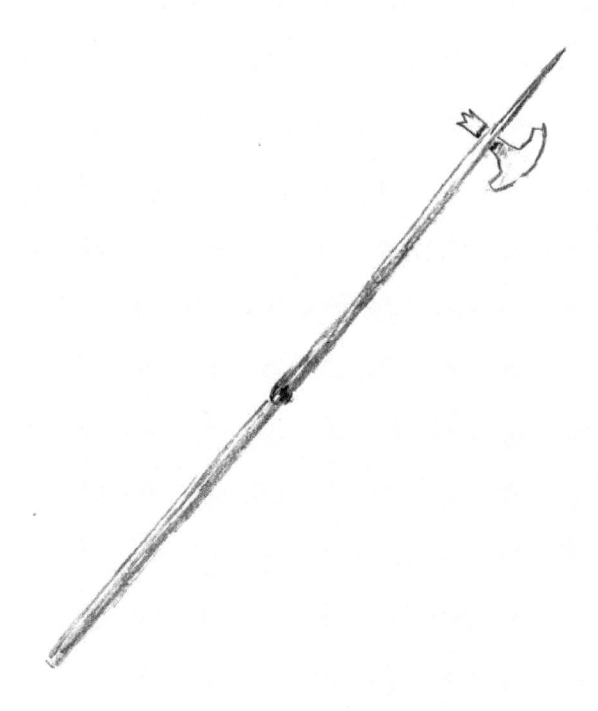

A poleaxe such as Sir William might have used. (Author's drawing)

This is a work of fiction but almost everything which happened from the time the King went to France really happened the way I wrote it. The King's death has me mystified for in all of my research dysentery either kills within a short time or there is a recovery. The King took almost a year to die. Perhaps, with the exception of John Bradbury, King Henry was unlucky with his choice of doctors.

The Duke of Burgundy's rescue of the Queen who had once hated him did happen. Queen Isabeau seems an interesting character for the young man who was tortured and hurled in the Seine was not the first lover she had taken. The events of this incident took place when she was 47 years of age!

The battles of Baugé, Cravant and Verneuil were the last hurrah of the Scots who sought to fight the English away from their homes. It is said that the French were happy to be rid of their allies for they fought in a wild and reckless way.

The Battle of Verneuil, 1424 was called a Second Agincourt. The Allied Anglo-Burgundian army was led by the Duke of Bedford and they had just 8,000 men. They were faced by a French army of more than 16.000. Led by the Earl of Buchan half were Scottish. They also had 2000 elite Milanese mercenaries who were completely encased in armour with armoured horses. The allied army left 1500 men with the baggage and formed up to face the Franco-Scottish army. They faced each other for more than six hours in the heat of an August day. Eventually the Duke of Bedford began to advance. The Milanese cavalry rode not to the main English Battle but the baggage train where they disperse the archers and men at arms guarding it. The Scots had said that they would neither give nor expect quarter.

Amazingly the English and the Duke's Burgundian allies broke the French Battle and most of their leaders were slaughtered close to the town of Verneuil. They then turned on the Scottish element which was led by the Earl of Salisbury. The Scottish were slaughtered, not a prisoner was taken. The Earl of Buchan had been made Constable of France and he died along with Earl Douglas.

Books used in the research:
- The Tower of London -Lapper and Parnell (Osprey)
- English Medieval Knight 1300-1400-Gravett
- The Castles of Edward 1 in Wales- Gravett
- Norman Stone Castles- Gravett
- The Armies of Crécy and Poitiers- Rothero
- The Armies of Agincourt- Rothero
- The Scottish and Welsh Wars 1250-1400
- Henry V and the conquest of France- Knight and Turner
- Chronicles in the Age of Chivalry-Ed. Eliz Hallam
- English Longbowman 1330-1515- Bartlett
- Northumberland at War-Derek Dodds

- Henry V -Teresa Cole
- The Longbow- Mike Loades
- Teutonic Knight 1190-1561- Nicolle and Turner
- Warkworth Castle and Hermitage- John Goodall
- Shrewsbury 1403- Dickon Whitehead
- Agincourt- Christopher Hibbert
- British Kings and Queens- Mike Ashley
- Agincourt 1415- Matthew Bennett
- Ordnance Survey Original series map #81 1864-1869

For more information on all of the books then please visit the author's web site at http://www.griffhosker.com where there is a link to contact him.

Griff Hosker
January 2021

Other books by Griff Hosker

If you enjoyed reading this book, then why not read another one by the author?

Ancient History

The Sword of Cartimandua Series
(Germania and Britannia 50 A.D. – 128 A.D.)
Ulpius Felix- Roman Warrior (prequel)
The Sword of Cartimandua
The Horse Warriors
Invasion Caledonia
Roman Retreat
Revolt of the Red Witch
Druid's Gold
Trajan's Hunters
The Last Frontier
Hero of Rome
Roman Hawk
Roman Treachery
Roman Wall
Roman Courage

The Wolf Warrior series
(Britain in the late 6th Century)
Saxon Dawn
Saxon Revenge
Saxon England
Saxon Blood
Saxon Slayer
Saxon Slaughter
Saxon Bane
Saxon Fall: Rise of the Warlord
Saxon Throne
Saxon Sword

Medieval History

The Dragon Heart Series

The Battle for France

Viking Slave
Viking Warrior
Viking Jarl
Viking Kingdom
Viking Wolf
Viking War
Viking Sword
Viking Wrath
Viking Raid
Viking Legend
Viking Vengeance
Viking Dragon
Viking Treasure
Viking Enemy
Viking Witch
Viking Blood
Viking Weregeld
Viking Storm
Viking Warband
Viking Shadow
Viking Legacy
Viking Clan
Viking Bravery

The Norman Genesis Series
Hrolf the Viking
Horseman
The Battle for a Home
Revenge of the Franks
The Land of the Northmen
Ragnvald Hrolfsson
Brothers in Blood
Lord of Rouen
Drekar in the Seine
Duke of Normandy
The Duke and the King

New World Series
Blood on the Blade
Across the Seas
The Savage Wilderness
The Bear and the Wolf

The Battle for France

The Vengeance Trail

The Reconquista Chronicles
Castilian Knight
El Campeador
The Lord of Valencia

The Aelfraed Series
(Britain and Byzantium 1050 A.D. - 1085 A.D.)
Housecarl
Outlaw
Varangian

**The Anarchy Series England
1120-1180**
English Knight
Knight of the Empress
Northern Knight
Baron of the North
Earl
King Henry's Champion
The King is Dead
Warlord of the North
Enemy at the Gate
The Fallen Crown
Warlord's War
Kingmaker
Henry II
Crusader
The Welsh Marches
Irish War
Poisonous Plots
The Princes' Revolt
Earl Marshal

**Border Knight
1182-1300**
Sword for Hire
Return of the Knight
Baron's War
Magna Carta

The Battle for France

Welsh Wars
Henry III
The Bloody Border
Baron's Crusade
Sentinel of the North
War in the West

Sir John Hawkwood Series
France and Italy 1339- 1387
Crécy: The Age of the Archer
Man At Arms : The Battle of Poitiers

Lord Edward's Archer
Lord Edward's Archer
King in Waiting
An Archer's Crusade

Struggle for a Crown
1360- 1485
Blood on the Crown
To Murder A King
The Throne
King Henry IV
The Road to Agincourt
St Crispin's Day

Tales from the Sword

Conquistador
England and America in the 16th Century
Conquistador (2021)

Modern History

The Napoleonic Horseman Series
Chasseur à Cheval
Napoleon's Guard
British Light Dragoon
Soldier Spy
1808: The Road to Coruña
Talavera

The Battle for France

The Lines of Torres Vedras
Bloody Badajoz
The Road to France

The Lucky Jack American Civil War series
Rebel Raiders
Confederate Rangers
The Road to Gettysburg

The British Ace Series
1914
1915 Fokker Scourge
1916 Angels over the Somme
1917 Eagles Fall
1918 We will remember them
From Arctic Snow to Desert Sand
Wings over Persia

**Combined Operations series
1940-1945**
Commando
Raider
Behind Enemy Lines
Dieppe
Toehold in Europe
Sword Beach
Breakout
The Battle for Antwerp
King Tiger
Beyond the Rhine
Korea
Korean Winter

Other Books
Great Granny's Ghost (Aimed at 9-14-year-old young people)

For more information on all of the books then please visit the author's web site at www.griffhosker.com where there is a link to contact him or visit his Facebook page: GriffHosker at Sword Books

Printed in Great Britain
by Amazon